OHIO

# DOMINICAN
## UNIVERSITY™

SINCE 1911

# WIND TAMER

# WIND TAMER

## P. R. MORRISON

BLOOMSBURY
CHILDREN'S
BOOKS

Published by Bloomsbury Publishing, New York, London, and Berlin
Distributed to the trade by Holtzbrinck Publishers

Library of Congress Cataloging-in-Publication Data
Morrison, P. R.
Wind tamer / P. R. Morrison.
p.    cm.
Summary: Archie learns on his tenth birthday that he is about to inherit the family
curse of cowardice unless he fights the powerful hurricane that will take his bravery.
ISBN-10: 1-58234-781-6  •  ISBN-13: 978-1-58234-781-3
[1. Courage—Fiction. 2. Uncles—Fiction. 3. Winds—Fiction. 4. Hurricanes—Fiction.
5. Knights and knighthood—Fiction.] I. Title.
PZ7.M837Win 2006        [Fic]—dc22            2005057179

First U.S. Edition 2006
Typeset by Dorchester Typesetting Group Ltd.
Printed in the U.S.A. by Quebecor World Fairfield
2   4   6   8   10   9   7   5   3   1

Bloomsbury Publishing, Children's Books, U.S.A.
175 Fifth Avenue, New York, NY 10010

All papers used by Bloomsbury Publishing are natural, recyclable products
made from wood grown in well-managed forests. The manufacturing processes
conform to the environmental regulations of the country of origin.

*For Andrew, Arthur and Ethan*

# Chapter One

Just before midnight on the eighteenth of December, the small Scottish fishing village of Westervoe was hit by a westerly wind. It rocked the boats anchored in the harbour, whistled along the deserted main street and raced up the hill among the closely built houses, slamming garden gates, blowing soot down chimneys and spinning the church weathervane. But it saved its full force for the last house near the top of the hill.

'Windy Edge' was three storeys tall with small windows peering out of a thick layer of ivy. Its red-tiled roof was just visible above the horse chestnut tree that stood out front, and because the house was more than two hundred years old, it seemed the ivy was the only thing stopping it from blowing down.

Archie Stringweed lived in this house with his parents, Jeffrey and Cecille. His room was in the attic, and his window looked out over the village rooftops towards the sea, which meant he could hear and feel the full force of the wind. Tonight it sounded particularly agitated, keeping him awake as it moaned and whistled in the eaves.

But as Archie lay in the dark with his eyes closed, listening to the tree branches knock against the windowpane, he realised something was not quite right. Not because he was afraid the gusts might blow in the windows and suck him out into the night – which was bad enough – but because he was sure the wind was talking to him. And though he couldn't understand what it was saying, he knew it was something he didn't want to hear.

There was something else too. He thought the wind was watching him. Lately it had appeared round corners and laughed in his face, and crept up on him from behind and blown him along the pavement. Sometimes it draped itself around his shoulders and screeched in his ear.

Archie was about to pull the quilt up over his head to shut out the wailing when something unexpected happened. He lay perfectly still and listened. He could hear only silence. The wind had suddenly died.

He opened one eye – which was blue. Then the other – which was green. Through a small skylight directly above his bed, he saw the sky was no longer dark and cloudy, but bright and clear with the sheen of highly polished glass. A shooting star crossed it, trailing a silvery-green tail, and he jumped out of bed and rushed to the other window, pulling back the curtain just in time to see it reappear over the roof, travelling so fast it kept disappearing then reappearing from behind the branches of the tree. He closed his eyes and made a wish.

'Please, please, please . . .'

When Archie reopened his eyes, the star was gone.

He rested his hand against the windowpane and it felt like ice, making him shiver all the way down to his toes. He spread his warm breath across the glass to make a fine mist and wrote his name, 'Archie'. He breathed another fine mist on the windowpane and began to trace the outline of his face: a perfect oval. He added his ears (bigger than he would have liked), a nose (neither too small nor too big) and a smiley mouth (top lip similar in width to the bottom). Then he drew two almond-shaped eyes. He was outlining the unruly tufts of his sandy-coloured hair when a sudden movement in the reflection distracted him. He turned to see a small flickering ball of green light hovering by his bed.

Archie stood absolutely still. His first instinct was to call out to his mother and father, but even as that thought crossed his mind he discovered it wasn't fear he felt but curiosity. He couldn't take his eyes away from the flickering, shimmering light and he felt perfectly calm as a small voice inside his head told him not to be afraid.

Archie tiptoed across the room and the green light floated upwards, sending the knights dangling from the mobile above his bed into a gentle spin.

'What do you want?' he whispered.

The light drifted up and over the top of his head towards the door.

'We have to be quiet,' he told it. 'My mum's a light sleeper.'

He opened the door and the sound of his father's snoring drifted up from the floor below. The light hovered above his shoulder, creating a green path on the stairs, inviting him to follow. Archie tiptoed down, hesitating on the first-floor landing to look towards his parents' partially open bedroom door. With the coast clear, he crept down the next flight, which was much wider with a thick wooden banister and a creaky stair, third from the bottom. To avoid standing on it, he clung to the large wooden ball on the stairpost and swung himself to the floor, landing beside the grandfather clock just as it chimed midnight. Archie gave a startled yelp. Seconds later his mother's voice was calling to him.

'Archie?' Her voice was a mixture of nervousness and sleepiness, which made her sound like someone else, a stranger who had crept into the house while he'd been listening to the wind. 'Is that you down there?' she asked, her worried voice moving closer.

The light, which had been hovering in front of the clock face, shrunk to the size of a marble and disappeared inside the umbrella stand, leaving Archie in the dark hall with only the faint glow from the streetlamps to break up the black.

His mother's silhouette appeared at the top of the stairs.

'What are you doing?' she asked softly.

'I . . . I was just getting a drink of water.'

'Go back to bed,' she whispered. 'Don't wake your father.'

His father was snoring so loudly Archie didn't think that was a possibility, but he climbed back up the stairs anyway.

'Night, Mum,' he said as he passed her on the landing. She stretched out a hand and stroked the top of his head.

'Archie?'

'Yes?'

He heard her take a deep breath, as if preparing to say something important, but instead she wrapped her arms around him and held him so tightly he could hear the beat of her heart through her tartan pyjamas. She gave a tired sigh and a lock of long dark hair fell forward and tickled the end of his nose. He felt a sneeze coming on.

'Did you get chilled?' she asked, unaware that the

unbearable tickle on his nose was making him shake.

'I'm fine,' Archie managed to say and then the sneeze erupted.

'Go to bed. Keep warm. You know how you wheeze when you get chilled.'

He began climbing the stairs to the attic, but he knew she would wait there until he was safely in his room. He turned to look back down at her. Her hands were clasped together beneath her chin, as if praying, but Archie knew this was something she did when she was worried. His mother worried a lot.

'Goodnight,' he said as he climbed the attic stairs.

'Sleep tight,' she whispered as he closed the door.

But sleep was the last thing on his mind. Archie sat on the edge of his bed wide awake. He was tempted to go back down and look for the strange flickering ball of light, but the chances were his mother was awake, particularly since the grandfather clock was still chiming. He waited until it struck the final chime before opening his door just far enough to look out.

The house was as silent as it could be through his father's incessant snoring, and dark too. He left the door ajar and went back to bed to wait for the ball of light's return, but as the wind began to rise again he heard someone whisper his name.

'*Aaaar-chee.*'

It didn't sound human and it didn't sound like a

ghost, but when it gave a shriek like a laugh he knew for sure whose voice it was and this time he knew what was being said.

'*He's coming. He's coming,*' the wind wailed outside his window.

Archie pulled the quilt over his head and disappeared into the warm depths of his bed. And that is where he stayed, sweating and afraid, until the wind became a distant hum and the shadows began to fade. Finally he drifted off to sleep, unaware of a small ball of green light resting on his pillow, watching over him until the first rays of morning crept back into the room.

# Chapter Two

It was 8.53 a.m. when Archie walked down the stairs in his pyjamas. He was halfway through a yawn when there came the heavy thump of the doorknocker. He opened the door and the postman smiled beneath his peaked cap.

'Morning, Archie. Got a special delivery here.' The arms of the postman's thick red and blue jacket scraped against his body as he looked at the address on the package.

'To be signed for by A. Stringweed, Windy Edge, Westervoe, Scotland, UK. Now I wonder who that might be?' he teased.

Archie swallowed an excited yawn. 'It's me! It's my birthday today.'

'Not another? Didn't you have one last year as well?' A gust of wind came racing up the garden path and tried to blow the postman's hat off.

The rush of cold air nipped at Archie's bare feet and

he shivered, reminded of something from the night before, but it would have to wait because the postman was asking him to sign the special-delivery book. He was writing the letter 'A' when the pen was plucked from his fingers. He looked up, and there, as if having appeared from out of nowhere, stood his mother, wearing her blue fleecy dressing gown and the faint scent of bacon. A warm cloud of air had trailed her from the kitchen and Archie got the smell of toast and tea too. She was looking at him as though he'd just committed a very dangerous act.

'Archie,' she sighed, and her large brown eyes blinked warily. 'You mustn't open the door without checking who is on the other side.' The wind rattled the letter box as she added, 'You never know who might be lurking out there.'

The postman wasn't at all happy to be considered a 'lurker' and to prove his point he gave a small cough of disapproval.

'Morning, Cecille,' he said stiffly.

Cecille didn't seem to notice. She was more concerned with the brown paper package the postman held out towards her. She accepted it as though she couldn't quite bring herself to touch it. A look of disappointment settled on her face as she examined the handwriting.

'This can go with all the others,' she mumbled.

'It's a present from Uncle Rufus. Isn't it?' said Archie. 'It's got foreign stamps and postmark.' He looked up at her. 'Do I get to keep it this year? I'm *ten*, after all.'

But Cecille's lips remained tightly shut while she signed the delivery book, parting just long enough to allow her to thank the postman. Archie was about to say something himself when the door was firmly closed. Seconds later an assortment of coloured envelopes was pushed through the letter box, followed by the post-man's voice saying, 'Happy birthday, Archie.'

But Archie was already following his mother down the hall, watching the belt from her dressing gown dragging along behind her, picking up dust from the carpet. He was trying to think of a way to claim Uncle Rufus's parcel, which she was carrying in her out-stretched hands as though it were something to be kept at a safe distance. Then her elbows suddenly jutted out either side of her body and she began to power walk.

'The bacon!' She took a sharp right turn into the kitchen.

Just inside the door was a large wooden kitchen table buried beneath old newspapers, loose change, a screw-driver, pens and pencils and a tube of hand cream. This was in addition to the usual breakfast dishes. Archie watched his mother set the parcel on top of the news-papers and hurry over to the stove where she picked up a sizzling frying pan.

Archie's father, Jeffrey Stringweed, was seated at the kitchen table, one hand holding his head, the other a mug of tea. He gave a lopsided sleepy smile and, raising his head out of his hand, said, 'Happy birthday, Archie!'

He was wearing crumpled blue and white striped pyjamas and misshapen sheepskin moccasins. His brown hair was a dishevelled clump of knots and his eyes were edged in half-moon shadows that rested on bags of droopy skin. He looked at the parcel sitting on the pile of old newspapers.

'Postman been already, Cecille?'

'Yes, and you were supposed to be listening out for him.' She turned from the stove and gave him a meaningful look. '*Remember?*'

Slowly the realisation dawned. 'Oh . . . yes,' and Jeffrey gave a long wide yawn. 'Can't seem to get out of sleep mode this morning. Feel like I've been drugged.'

Cecille turned back to the business of the frying pan and shook her head. Something very odd was happening to Jeffrey. It had started two weeks previously and was getting steadily worse. Each morning he would open his eyes, but it would take another hour or so for him to fully wake up. It was as if he were sleepwalking, as if he didn't really know where he was. A couple of times he had walked out the front door still wearing his slippers, and on another occasion he'd left for work but

17

had forgotten where he was going by the time he got to the front gate. As the morning progressed his memory would improve, and by the time he returned home in the evening he was his usual self. So far he had avoided any serious repercussions, but because he was the manager of the local bank it was becoming a worry. Right now he was struggling to remember what Cecille had said with regard to keeping an eye out for the postman that morning.

Archie interrupted his thoughts.

'Dad, I got a parcel from Uncle Rufus and Mum's not letting me open it.'

'Uncle Rufus? Well, well,' and Jeffrey cleared his throat before asking, 'That so, Cecille?'

Cecille appeared to be talking to the frying pan as she announced, 'Every year it's the same. Rufus sends something completely unsuitable.' She was flipping the bacon over to crisp the other side when it fell off the fork and landed wrong side up on top of an egg. 'I can't even begin to guess what goes through your brother's mind, Jeffrey. You'd think he *wanted* to maim his only nephew – his only godchild.' She stabbed the fried egg with the fork and then jumped backwards as it spat hot oil in protest. She licked the oil from the back of her hand and mumbled, 'Rufus *knows* this year is different.'

Archie saw his father shoot her a cautionary look, and it crossed his mind to ask, 'Why is this year different?', but he was preoccupied with the unopened package lying tantalisingly close to the edge of the table.

'I'm old enough to open my own presents,' he announced. 'I am *ten*.'

Jeffrey's bloodshot eyes flicked again to Cecille. 'Well, he *has* got a point there . . .'

Cecille turned to face him, looking very hot and bothered.

'All very well you saying that, Jeffrey, but who's going to pick up the pieces when he severs an artery?' And then, pointing the fork at him, she raised her voice, adding, 'Certainly not *you*, who practically faints at the sight of a cracked egg.'

Jeffrey was surprised at this uncharacteristic outburst. 'Are you feeling all right, Cecille?'

She nodded, but didn't look too sure. 'I'm sorry . . . I don't know what came over me . . .'

Archie, meantime, had felt a sudden and unexpected flood of bravery.

'You have no right to keep my present from me.' He grabbed the parcel from the table and ran out of the door. He heard what he thought was the fork fall to the floor and then Cecille was swooping out behind him, following a few paces behind as he raced up the stairs, three at a time.

'Cecille?' he heard his father call. 'Perhaps this year . . .'

Archie ran into the bathroom and slammed the door shut behind him, his heart hammering as he turned the lock.

'Open that parcel and there will be no birthday tea this afternoon,' Cecille announced, and the door shuddered as she rattled the handle.

Archie looked down at the package in his hands and tried to decide which was more important to him: tea with George and Sid, or opening the mysterious parcel. What could it contain that was so dangerous? After all, he was more or less an adult now, and it *had* been addressed to him.

He crouched down and tore away the brown paper, then removed two layers of bubble wrap, but as he removed the third layer something small and metallic fell on to the tiled floor. There was a moment or two of silence on both sides of the door, then Cecille was saying, 'I want you to open the door.'

Archie picked up the object. It was a small gold coin with strange markings on it, and as he held it in his fingers an icy current ran through his skin. He dropped the coin and it rolled across the floor. He lay down on his stomach to look at it more closely against the white tiles.

'I am going to count to five,' Cecille was now saying, 'and if you haven't . . .'

But Archie wasn't listening because he was sure he'd

seen those markings somewhere before, if only he could remember where.

Cecille began counting loudly, 'ONE . . . TWO . . . THREE.' The door shuddered. 'Archie? I'm giving you one more chance to open the door.' There was a long pause and then she announced very loudly, 'FOUR.' The door handle rattled and there was panic in her voice as she called out, 'JEFFREY! He's not opening the door.'

Soon after came the sound of Jeffrey's reluctant foot-steps on the stairs and the murmur of voices.

Archie, meanwhile, was examining the coin. Interestingly, it didn't have the cold chill to the touch he had felt moments earlier. He ran a finger over an engraving of a bird with outstretched wings, then turned the coin over. On the back he found an engraving of a dagger, with a handle of entwined snakes.

'FIVE!' Cecille said.

Seconds later Jeffrey was saying, 'All right, Archie. I'm coming in.'

Archie opened the door.

Jeffrey was standing side-on to the doorway, shoulder raised ready to charge. He didn't move and neither did Cecille. They both appeared to be studying him carefully. Certainly Archie felt braver as he returned his mother's questioning stare.

Jeffrey took a step closer for a better look, hesitated a

moment as if preparing to choose his words carefully, and then in his usual calm tone asked, 'What you got there?'

Archie opened his hand to reveal the coin in his palm.

Cecille gave the object a glance that lasted as long as it took to reassure her it presented no hidden dangers. It was to Archie that she gave another searching look.

'Was there anything else in the package?'

Archie shook his head. 'No.'

'Was there a card or letter with it?' Jeffrey was asking.

'No.' Archie looked again at Cecille's steady stare. 'It's gold,' he told her and held it up so she could see it more clearly. 'I think it's a good-luck coin.'

'Good luck?' Cecille repeated. 'It can't be . . . surely Rufus wouldn't . . .' And she turned and walked along the landing towards her bedroom, disappeared inside and closed the door.

Jeffrey was still examining the coin. 'If there was no card, then we don't know for sure it's from Uncle Rufus.'

Archie wasn't convinced. 'Well, we don't know any-one else living in a foreign country, do we?'

A faint sob came from his parents' bedroom.

'What's going on, Dad?'

'Nothing to worry about. Your mother just needs a

minute or two on her own.' Jeffrey put his hand on Archie's shoulder. 'Let's go down to the kitchen and rescue the bacon, shall we?' He gave an exaggerated lick of his lips. 'Mmmm . . . I'm hungry.'

But Archie wasn't feeling hungry at all. Why was his mother acting so strangely? And why had she not wished him happy birthday? Not only that, he didn't appear to have one other present apart from the gold coin.

He was feeling confused and for some reason a little frightened too. Partly because it wasn't the first time he'd heard her say the words, *'this year is different'*, but also because of the way she had spoken them, as though she knew something unpleasant was about to happen.

The grandfather clock was chiming nine as they reached the bottom stair, prompting a memory flash from the night before. Had it been a dream, or had he really stood there in the dark with a strange ball of flickering green light . . .

Jeffrey was wandering into the kitchen, still trying to sound enthusiastic about having overcooked bacon and eggs for breakfast, unaware that Archie was no longer following in his footsteps. Archie was, in fact, pulling umbrellas and walking sticks out of the wooden stand and peering inside, but disappointingly there was no ball of light lurking at the bottom. He was replacing everything when Jeffrey reappeared at the kitchen door wearing a puzzled expression, but then a flash of recognition crossed his face and he smiled broadly.

'I'm afraid you won't find your birthday presents in there, son.'

# Chapter Three

As far back as Archie could remember the same thing happened every year. A parcel would arrive on his birthday from Uncle Rufus only to be whisked away unopened. He had first become aware of this a few days short of his fifth birthday. Cecille had gone out to buy eggs to bake a birthday cake, and Archie was helping Jeffrey and Grandpa Stringweed make repairs to their garden shed after another night of storm-force wind. They were just about to start nailing the wood together when Archie heard the thud of the front-door knocker and he ran round the corner of the house, almost colliding with the postman coming the other way, carrying a small brown package.

Archie had first marvelled at the exotic stamps and then he had begun to slowly read the name written in black ink in large block letters: ARCHIE STRINGWEED. While Jeffrey and Grandpa had fallen into conversation with the postman about the ivy climbing up the exterior walls, he had opened his very own parcel. Inside he found an old, grey, canvas drawstring bag containing the strangest pair of swimming goggles he'd ever seen.

He held them up to his face. 'They're too big,' he said, fighting back tears of disappointment. 'The water will get in.'

Grandpa had looked on in astonishment, but it was the postman who spoke.

'They're not swimming goggles. They're flying goggles. Second World War, by the look of it. I'd be careful with them if I was you. Valuable, I'd say.'

Grandpa gently took them away while Archie explored the layers of wrapping paper. 'Look! There's a card too!'

But Grandpa wasn't listening; he was staring at the goggles with a sad, faraway look in his eyes. The same expression he had worn when his pet budgie was killed in a freak accident the year before, squashed by the living-room door as it blew shut in a sudden draught.

When Archie had asked Grandpa to read the card, he had shaken his head and said in a very quiet voice, 'Maybe later.'

But by the time Cecille returned home, the goggles and the card had disappeared. Archie hadn't been too disappointed, because she'd promised to buy him a new yellow pair, but he was conscious of a change of mood in the house. Everyone was in the kitchen, talking in hushed voices. They would stop and smile if he went in to get a drink or a biscuit, but as soon as he walked out again the voices would resume and there was no mistaking who they were talking about. The name 'Rufus' was mentioned over and over again; in a rather sad way by Grandpa, in a very matter-of-fact way by Jeffrey and with growing impatience by Cecille.

Eventually Grandpa had put on his hat and quietly left the house, as though he couldn't bear to talk about it any more.

What was it about this strange, faraway uncle that had such an effect on the family?

Only the week before his tenth birthday, for instance, the moaning wind outside his window had wakened Archie, and as he'd crept downstairs in the darkness to get a glass of water he'd heard his mother's raised voice. He'd crept towards their bedroom and stood outside the door, open just far enough so he could see her seated at the dressing table. She was wearing her big blue dressing gown and was busily brushing locks of brown hair. His father was lying in bed and all he could see of him was the top of his head reflected in the dressing-table mirror.

'What's Rufus up to?' she was saying. 'Last year he sent a pocket watch and not even a new one, but a battered old thing that had seen better days. And that sharp pin sticking out of it could have caused Archie serious damage. The year before it was a torch. Bad enough it didn't work, but the metal was worn and ragged. And as for his first birthday, do you remember? He turned up with a knife.'

'A dagger,' his father had interjected wearily.

'Nine years he's been gone. The first two years we didn't even know if he was alive or dead.'

Jeffrey groaned.

Cecille continued, 'He just upped and left, leaving you to pick up the pieces. I suppose Rufus thinks the occasional postcard to your mum and dad makes it all right, and sending those peculiar presents and weird cryptic cards to Archie lets him off the hook. Well, it doesn't, not as far as his godfather duties are concerned.' She swung round on her stool to look directly at Jeffrey. 'He's been sending them since Archie was three, but now it's time to stop. Rufus knows *this* year is different. I want you to keep an eye out for the postman. Are you listening to me, Jeffrey? If any strange birthday presents arrive, I want you to put them in a box with all the others – the cards too – and I want you to send them back to Rufus . . . wherever he is. I don't want them in the house any more.'

Archie had heard his father give a sleepy grunt and his mother finished brushing her hair.

'It's just plain weird,' she said to herself, 'all of it.'

Then she switched off the bedside lamp and got into bed.

Archie had forgotten about his drink of water and crept back upstairs to consider what he'd just overheard. He put to the back of his mind the words, 'This *year is different*', while he looked up the word 'cryptic' in his dictionary. It had taken a few attempts since he wasn't even sure how to spell cryptic, but eventually he found it: 'secret, mysterious; obscure in meaning'. Uncle Rufus had sent secret and mysterious cards. And what was that about a dagger and a torch and a watch? Archie had calculated that if Uncle Rufus had given a present each year since he was three, then a total of eight presents, including the dagger he had been given on his first birthday, were somewhere in the surrounding rooms. Not only that, he would have to find them before his father packed them into a box and returned them to Rufus. Something very odd was going on, and now that he was almost an adult, he had every intention of finding out the truth.

# Chapter Four

Archie was beginning to think his tenth birthday was going to be a thoroughly miserable day. It hadn't got off to a very good start, particularly with his mother and father in deep discussion behind their bed-room door. He sat in the kitchen on his own eating a breakfast of dried-out bacon and egg. He just didn't understand why his mother was so upset at Uncle Rufus for sending a good-luck coin. He looked at it lying on the kitchen table next to his plate. What possible harm could a small piece of gold do him?

Eventually his parents came downstairs behaving as if nothing odd had happened at all. Cecille had dressed herself in a long cardigan of various shades of brown, clipped on her favourite gold drop earrings, pulled her hair up into a high ponytail and accentuated her 'everything-is-fine' smile with red lipstick. To add to this sense of normality she and Jeffrey agreed that Archie could keep the coin but that it should be held in a place of safety.

'Just in case it's valuable,' Jeffrey advised.

Cecille suggested he put it in his money bank, but Archie'd already decided to hide it in his box of magic tricks, most probably in the pack of playing cards, just in case she changed her mind and came looking for it when he wasn't around. He realised he was going to have to be extra-vigilant, and that included keeping his eyes open for clues as to where all his past birthday presents from Uncle Rufus were hidden. As for the cryptic cards, he was sure that if he found them and read them, he would get to the bottom of the mystery. It seemed the most obvious place to start looking for everything would be his father's study, down in the basement. But he was going to need a very good reason to go through his cupboards and drawers without permission.

Archie had been pondering the problem for so long that Cecille eventually looked at him and asked, 'Are you going to open your birthday presents, Archie?'

Five parcels of varying size were set out on the sofa in the living room. Which just went to prove his parents were very good at intercepting the postman and concealing packages.

The largest present was a square box wrapped in red paper. Archie decided to leave it till last and instead opted to open the small green one. First he read the gift tag: '*Happy Birthday, Archie. Sorry we can't be with you today, but save us some birthday cake until Grandpa is feeling better. From your loving Grandma and Grandpa Stringweed'*.

His grandparents lived in Breckwall, a small town seven miles away, and every year they visited on his birthday, but this year Grandpa Stringweed was ill.

'Bad headaches,' Cecille explained. 'Dizziness too.' Which was a worry as up until a few days ago he had been in perfect health, well enough, in fact, to repair the stormproof shutters on his house windows and fit draught excluders on all external doors.

Archie picked up the small green box and shook it, trying to second-guess what might be inside, before peeling away the wrapping to reveal a transparent box. Inside was a watch that was also a stopwatch and an alarm clock, and a flashing fluorescent-blue light lit up the face when you pushed a button. Archie tried whistling with pleasure, but even though he was now ten years old, he couldn't pull a clear sharp note from his lips.

There was some Lego and a book on the crusades from his Aunt Sylvia and Uncle Will, and a chocolate-making machine from his two cousins. Then came the big red box from his parents. They were both smiling nervously as he began to unwrap it.

Archie'd been asking for Rollerblades since he was seven and each year his mother had said, 'Maybe next year, when you're a bit older. They're too dangerous for a small boy who lives at the top of a hill.'

Well, he was ten now. Surely this year he was old enough? From the shape and weight of the box he decided it couldn't possibly contain anything else. In his excitement Archie tore at the paper with both hands, already imagining himself racing around the school playground to the awe of every single pupil and teacher. He caught sight of his mother smiling nervously, her hands clasped under her chin, her ponytail hanging over one shoulder. His father was nodding, urging him to reveal the well-wrapped surprise. In the next moment Archie ripped away a large piece of red paper to reveal the words 'walkie-talkies'.

'We thought it would be fun to talk to you while you're up in your bedroom,' his mother was saying as he stared in disappointment at the box. 'Save me calling to you to come down for tea.' She leaned over and gave him a big kiss on his cheek. 'Happy birthday, Archie.' And then, before he knew it, she had wrapped her arms around him and hugged him. 'We love you very much.'

'Thanks, Mum.'

'There's more,' Jeffrey was saying. 'Look inside the box.'

Archie opened it and was happily surprised to find a computer game he'd been wanting for ages called 'Knight of the Five Tigers'.

'Great. Thanks very much.' He was admiring the knights on the cover when the telephone rang.

'I'll get it,' said Cecille, and she dashed out of the room, closing the door behind her. Seconds later she was back, saying, 'Wrong number.'

'Who were they looking for?' Jeffrey asked.

Cecille didn't appear to hear him because she clapped her hands and announced, 'Let's get this lot tidied up.'

She became very busy, picking up wrapping paper and moving Christmas cards on the mantelpiece to make room for Archie's birthday cards, but she was acting strangely again because even though she was smiling, Archie could see a single tear welling up in the corner of one eye.

'Want to try out the walkie-talkies, Archie?' his father was asking. 'The batteries are in them. Ready to go.'

'I'll take one upstairs with me. I thought I'd start building the Lego.'

Archie had walked up the first flight of stairs with his presents when the walkie-talkie crackled into life.

'Calling birthday boy, calling birthday boy. Can you read me?'

Archie could hear his father perfectly clearly, since his voice was also drifting up the stairs from the living room.

'Birthday boy reading you loud and clear,' he replied through the handset.

'Is birthday boy happy?'

'Birthday boy is very happy,' said Archie, which was true, but as he began the climb up to his attic room he couldn't help but feel that a pair of Rollerblades would have made him happier still.

# Chapter Five

If Archie was disappointed with his walkie-talkies, he was quickly cheered up by a visitor to the house soon after.

Ezekiel Arbuthnott lived in a small cottage lower down the hill, next to the church. He was a retired teacher, treasurer of the village hall fund and an experienced inshore fisherman. Ezekiel's other interest was the weather. What he didn't know about cloud formation, wind direction and the mood of the sea wasn't worth knowing. He was also Grandpa Stringweed's best friend. The two of them enjoyed telling Archie about their boyhood adventures, and because Ezekiel's memory was so good, he never forgot Archie's birthday. Sometimes he was a day or two late with his present or even a day or two early, but for Archie's tenth birthday he was knocking at the door at 10.30 a.m., holding a red and white carrier bag and looking very pleased with himself. Beneath his flat cap and waterproof jacket with its fluorescent-green band across the chest, he looked like a garden gnome.

He declined to come inside the house.

'You good people have a busy day ahead,' he insisted. 'I'll just hand these presents over to the young man in question and wish him a happy birthday.'

Archie thought he saw Ezekiel wink as he accepted the bag, though he couldn't be sure, since Ezekiel's eyes were partly hidden beneath thick white eyebrows.

Then Ezekiel turned to Jeffrey. 'Wind's dropped. Was half expecting stormy weather after last night's gusts.'

Jeffrey shook his head. 'A tornado could have passed over us last night and I wouldn't have heard a thing.'

'A tornado?' said Ezekiel.

The air turned icy and Cecille shivered. 'It's very cold out here. Are you sure you won't come inside?'

Ezekiel was quite sure. 'The Harvey brothers are taking me out in their boat this morning. They tell me fishing's been good round Moss Rock.'

Then he wished Archie happy birthday once again and walked down the path towards his bicycle, which he'd left propped up against the garden gate. They all waited on the doorstep while he made two attempts to swing his leg over the crossbar.

'Looks like snow,' he said once he was mounted, and then with a wave of his hand he was off.

'Thanks again,' Archie called out, and soon after Ezekiel's bicycle bell rang out in reply.

'Sky looks too clear for snow,' Cecille remarked, and then she and Jeffrey walked back into the house, leaving Archie standing outside on the doorstep. He was looking up through the branches of the tree to the clear blue sky when a thick white cloud came drifting over the rooftop, and as he watched it, a single snowflake came floating down through the branches towards him. He had his mouth open ready to catch it when a strong gust of wind came whistling round the corner of the house and laughed in his face so hard he stumbled backwards through the door. Archie gave a surprised cry and a moment later the gust of wind was gone.

'What did you say?' Jeffrey was asking from inside the hallway.

'Nothing,' said Archie, straightening up.

'Must be my ears,' said Jeffrey. 'Was sure you said something.'

'Archie,' Cecille called out from the kitchen. 'Come inside before you get chilled.'

Archie shut the door and immediately the letter box blew open and a gust of wind howled, '*Soon, soon,*' before slamming shut. All was still and silent again.

He continued to stare at the letter box until a voice behind him enquired, 'All right, Archie?'

He turned to see Jeffrey watching him with a

concerned expression.

'Yes. Fine,' he replied, although the hairs on the back of his neck were standing on end. He thought about telling his father the wind was talking to him, but decided against it because he could hardly believe it himself. Perhaps he was mistaken. There was also another reason. If his mother found out, she would probably cancel his birthday tea and keep him indoors until spring. So on his way to the kitchen he managed a little playful air-punching.

'Want to see what Ezekiel brought me?'

'Sure thing,' said Jeffrey, who was keeping a watchful eye on the letter box as he listened to Archie opening his presents.

'A book on the weather!' Cecille announced. 'That's a very useful gift.'

Archie began opening his second present. Jeffrey, meantime, was keeping his eye on the letter box. With no wind blowing, not even a breeze, how was it that the letter box was slowly opening by itself, letting a ribbon of daylight fall across the faded hall carpet? It continued to open until Archie's excited voice announced, 'Boxing gloves!', at which point it fell shut with a loud clatter.

# Chapter Six

The snow continued to fall. By the time Archie's
best friends Sid and George arrived, just after two
o'clock, the rooftops, pavement and garden were covered in a thick white layer and the tree outside the
house looked like a giant white spider's web. There was
no wind, not one single unexpected gust appearing from
out of nowhere.

Both boys stood on the doorstep with a brightly
wrapped birthday gift in their gloved hands, their familiar eyes peering out from a swaddle of hats and scarves
and big padded jackets. Archie's other friend, William,
couldn't make it since he was suffering from a particularly bad case of tonsillitis, but George had no such
problem as he gave a strong whistle of approval at the
snow piled up around the house. If there was one other
wish Archie would have liked, it was to be able to
whistle – particularly as well as George.

Sid, who could almost whistle, had brought Archie a

box of six giant marbles his mum had found at a car boot sale, each one containing a miniature knight.

Archie decided the knight in silver armour with the red shield was his favourite, since it looked very similar to the cardboard knight he'd made to look like himself, hanging on the crusades mobile above his bed.

George's present was a pair of see-in-the-dark goggles, which he could personally vouch for as he'd tried them out for himself the previous night. He'd watched his younger brother, Stan, picking his nose and attaching the snot to the back of his bunk bed.

Archie took Sid and George up to his bedroom and showed them his other presents. Sid loved the boxing gloves and had a few rounds with a pillow. George thought the walkie-talkies were a particularly good idea, although he conceded not as good as a pair of Rollerblades.

'Why won't they get you some?' asked Sid, who was now scouring the packaging of the Knight of the Five Tigers computer game.

'Too dangerous,' said Archie miserably.

'So she doesn't know you skated down our slide wearing my Rollerblades?' said Sid.

'My mum says you have to experience some danger in order to grow up,' said George, who'd already fractured a wrist and ankle, and suffered concussion after falling off his Rollerblades. He also had various scars from accidents involving his skateboard, pogo stick and bike. For Christmas he'd asked for a go-kart.

Archie would have liked to have shown George and Sid the mysterious gold coin safely hidden in his magic set, but something told him he should keep it a secret – at least until he had some answers to the Uncle Rufus mystery.

The walkie-talkie on Archie's bed crackled into life and Jeffrey's voice suggested that since it had stopped snowing they should all go out into the garden and have a snowball fight.

'Maybe throw one or two in the direction of next door's barking dog,' he added softly, just in case Cecille happened to overhear.

As expected, the dog began barking as soon as they stepped out into the back garden. They couldn't actually see it because of the freshly fallen snow covering the hedge, but they knew it was close from the incessant panting, growling and yet more barking.

Sid took one look at the rustling hedge and darted back into the house.

'I don't like noisy dogs.'

'It's all right,' said Archie. 'He can't get through the hedge. He's too big.'

'How big?' Sid asked nervously.

'I've got an idea,' said George, and he scooped up a snowball and threw it, skimming the top of Jeffrey's head before it disappeared over the hedge. A moment or two later the dog gave a surprised squeal and then there was silence.

'I did it. I did it!' George was shouting triumphantly, when a large clump of snow fell out of a tree and landed on his head. He began shaking his hair wildly. 'It's freezing! It's running down the back of my neck.'

Archie and Sid were too busy laughing to help him, so it was up to Jeffrey to brush the snow from George's jacket collar. That was when he noticed a cluster of white downy feathers mixed in with the snow.

'Quickly,' George was screeching. 'It's melting!'

Jeffrey decided not to add to George's distress by mentioning the feathers, and so he packed them into a snowball and threw it aside. George, meantime, was losing no time in taking his revenge and he quickly made two giant snowballs of his own.

'Take that!' he shouted as one raced towards Archie and the other headed in Sid's direction.

The birthday snowball fight had officially begun, but Jeffrey was momentarily distracted. He looked up into the snow-laden branches of the tree, trying to work out how a handful of white feathers had come to be embedded in the clump of snow that had fallen so accurately on to George's head, but, try as he might, he couldn't come up with one single explanation. He was still thinking about it when he turned round and found himself staring at three snowballs speeding through the air towards him, all of them on target.

'What was that?' said Archie.

He was with George and Sid in his bedroom following the snowball fight and the building of a huge snowman. They were now playing his new computer game, Knight of the Five Tigers.

'Listen,' Archie whispered.

'What?' said Sid, without taking his eyes away from the computer screen. He was getting ready to destroy the Third Tiger with a flaming torch, while George looked on impatiently, hoping all the tigers wouldn't be destroyed before he had his turn.

Then the sound came again. *Tap*, *tap*, *tap*. They all turned and looked towards the window, which was frosted up with snow. Daylight had almost gone and the room was more or less in darkness but for the glow from the computer screen.

'It's only a tree branch touching the glass,' George decided.

'No,' said Archie. 'It's a sharper sound than that.' He crossed the room to take a closer look.

'This is spooky,' said Sid, standing up from the computer desk. 'I'm putting the light on.'

'Not yet,' said George, slipping into the chair Sid had just vacated. 'You won't be able to see outside if you switch the light on.'

Archie was by now standing at the window, squeezed in between a chair and the table and peering through a tiny patch in the glass that wasn't covered with snow.

'Come and see this,' he said quietly.

Something about his voice and the way he didn't move at all made the others curious.

'Maybe it's a ghost,' said George mischievously.

Sid swallowed. 'Let's go downstairs. I'm hungry.'

'Don't make a sound,' said Archie as the boys crept up behind him and looked over his shoulder. He stood aside as they bent down to look through a corner of the windowpane.

Staring back at them was a large fluorescent-green eye, and as they drew closer to the glass for a better look, it blinked.

'Is it a ghost?' asked Sid, backing away.

The sharp tapping sounded against the glass once again and snowflakes dropped away to reveal a grey beak.

'It's a bird,' said Archie.

'A big one too,' said George, and he gave a perfectly soft whistle.

The bird continued knocking on the glass with its large beak.

'It wants in. Open the window, Archie,' said George.

Archie opened the window and an icy blast of wind

blew snowflakes across the table. The bird hopped in and stood on a drawing Archie had made of King Richard the Lionheart. It had a small pouch attached to one leg.

George gulped and took a few steps backwards. 'It's got grey legs!'

'Maybe it's cold,' whispered Sid, who was holding on to the back of George's jumper.

Archie closed the window. 'I think it's a snow goose. It must have got blown off course.'

The room seemed very dark and scary now there was a huge bird on the table. Archie manoeuvred himself behind it to switch on the small table lamp and the bird stretched its wings in alarm as the room lit up.

Sid backed slowly towards the door. 'Who's going to get the pouch off its leg?' He looked at George, who was staring nervously at the bird's enormous beak.

'We need to distract it,' Archie decided. 'Give it something to eat.'

'How about the crisps your mum gave us?' George suggested. He got one out of the pack and from a safe distance tossed it on to the table. The bird snatched it up and held it in its beak. Then, remarkably, it lifted its leg as if inviting them to remove the pouch.

'It's your birthday, Archie. I think you should do it,' said Sid from his position near the door.

Archie edged closer and carefully stretched out an

arm towards the bird's leg. It didn't move, but stayed perfectly still, its large beady eye watching him as he very gently pulled at the string. The pouch fell on to the table.

The bird threw its head back and swallowed the large crisp.

'I think it wants another,' said George, who was feeling slightly braver, and he proceeded to scatter crisps on the table. Archie, meanwhile, was investigating the pouch.

'What's inside?' Sid wanted to know, and then almost jumped out of his skin as he heard Cecille's voice call up the stairs.

'Boys! Tea's ready. Wash your hands and come down.'

'Coming,' Archie shouted.

The bird panicked at the sound of Archie's voice and spread its enormous wings and took off. George looked up at it in amazement as it glided around the room. Sid covered his head with his arms and screamed.

The next sound they heard was Cecille running up the stairs and asking, 'What's going on in there?'

All three boys froze. The bird landed on Archie's bed. A faint knock sounded at the door.

Archie opened it just far enough to pop his head round the edge. 'We're telling ghost stories.'

'Who screamed?' Cecille wanted to know as she

tried to see beyond him into the room.

George appeared behind Archie.

'It was me. Sorry.'

'Where's Sid?' she asked.

'Here,' he said, jumping up and down behind George and waving his arms.

'Downstairs in five minutes, boys. Don't forget to wash your hands.'

They closed the door again and stood with their backs against it, staring at the snow goose. It was settled comfortably on the blue quilt, quietly rearranging its feathers.

'What are we going to do now?' Sid whispered. He and George both looked at Archie.

'We go down and have tea,' Archie decided. 'Give it time to rest. We'll sneak some food from the table for it to eat. Maybe once it's rested it'll fly off again.'

They all stared at the very comfortable-looking goose.

'What if it doesn't?' said Sid. 'Will we have to tell your mum and dad?'

'No,' said Archie. He was already beginning to suspect there was more to this visitation than he'd first thought. 'Not a word to them, promise?' Archie saw that both boys were staring uncertainly at the goose. 'George?'

'I promise,' said George, without taking his eyes off the bird.

'Sid?'

Eventually Sid nodded. 'But your mum's going to go bonkers.'

Archie tried to be reassuring. 'Not if she doesn't know. Act normally and then get back up here as quick as possible.'

Archie went to open the door but George stopped him. 'Show us what was in the pouch, then?'

The pouch was made of dark-brown leather with a drawstring and Archie could feel something small and hard inside. He turned the pouch upside down and let the contents drop on to the palm of his hand. A cold shiver ran through his fingers.

'It's a coin,' said George, with a hint of disappointment.

'Is that all there is?' asked Sid. 'No secret messages or anything?'

Archie looked inside the pouch to make sure. But if they were disappointed, his heart was racing with excitement. The coin in his hand looked very similar to the one he'd received through the post that morning. George picked it up and looked at it closely.

'It's a foreign coin. You can't even spend it. Looks like gold, though.'

Sid was more concerned at the large bird sitting on the bed and the way it was now looking at them as though it could understand every word that was being said.

'I'm hungry,' he announced.

Archie returned the coin to the pouch and put it in his trouser pocket. 'Now remember. Slip some food into your pockets and we'll rendezvous up here as soon as possible. We have a mission to complete.'

The boys trooped out but, before closing the door, Archie looked back into the room. Something about the bird's curiously bright-green eyes felt reassuringly familiar.

Cecille was amazed at how quickly the boys ate their tea. They were seated around a table in the living room that she had specially decorated with a white paper tablecloth and blue plastic plates and tumblers. Sausages, chicken legs and potato wedges disappeared off their plates at a remarkable speed.

'You boys certainly worked up an appetite throwing snowballs this afternoon. Anyone for birthday cake?'

Three hands shot up.

Cecille switched off the overhead light and then the Christmas tree lights in preparation for the cake being ceremoniously carried in. In the diffused glow from the hallway they waited. In the kitchen Jeffrey called for silence. From upstairs, there came a loud birdlike screech.

The boys all looked up at the ceiling.

'What was that?' Cecille asked. 'Did you boys hear something?'

'It was my impersonation of a snow goose,' said George. 'A snow goose that can't wait for some birthday cake.' He made a convincing squawk from the back of his throat and Archie and Sid made a point of laughing much louder than was necessary.

'Then wait no longer, oh, impatient goose,' said Jeffrey as he appeared in the doorway, holding the cake aloft.

'Aren't you going to light the candles, Mr Stringweed?' George asked.

'Oh. Forgot,' said Jeffrey sheepishly and he disappeared back inside the kitchen.

The three boys were staring up at the ceiling, praying there would be no more bird squawking, when Archie became aware of Cecille watching him intently, as though searching his face for evidence or clues. But she quickly snapped out of this thoughtful state when Jeffrey reappeared at the living-room door, the bags under his eyes illuminated by the flickering glow from ten burning candles.

'Strike up the band, Cecille,' he announced with great aplomb.

Cecille began singing 'Happy birthday' in a high-pitched voice, her earrings and ponytail swinging to the rhythm. Jeffrey joined in with a rich tenor voice. Then Sid and George got into the swing of it too and sang as the chocolate cake, in the shape of what was supposed to be a knight's helmet but actually looked like a deflated rugby ball, was held aloft in a blaze of flickering candlelight.

Jeffrey set it down on the table and Archie was invited to make a wish before blowing out the candles.

Sid and George watched him carefully as he closed his eyes, and they all waited in silence for what seemed like for ever.

'Bet he's wishing he gets Rollerblades for Christmas,' Sid said softly.

Cecille and Jeffrey flashed each other a concerned look just as Archie opened his eyes, took a huge intake of breath and blew all the candles out. He smiled knowingly to himself through the thin plumes of smoke.

There was much clapping while Cecille switched the lights back on and Jeffrey began cutting through the grey chocolate icing with a large knife. All thoughts of the huge bird sitting on Archie's bed were temporarily forgotten as the boys sank their teeth into the moist chocolatey layers.

Cecille raised the knife above the cake and asked, 'Anyone for more?'

Three hands shot up again.

'Can we take it upstairs, please, please?' Archie pleaded.

'We want to finish off the computer game,' said Sid

nervously, and a bright-pink spot appeared on each cheek.

'Wouldn't you rather play some party games?' Cecille asked as she cut three more slices.

'We're too old for party games, Mum. That's for babies.'

Jeffrey wrapped each of the cake slices in large red serviettes.

'There you go, boys. Don't make yourselves sick, now.'

Sid and Archie had already left the table, closely followed by George, who had to squeeze out of his chair which had been jammed against the wall.

'What's that on the back of your jumper, George?'

Everyone turned to look as Cecille pulled something free of the wool.

'Good grief, it's a feather,' said Jeffrey. He was trying to remember where he'd seen white feathers recently, and then it came to him: he had seen them that very afternoon, embedded in a clump of snow on the collar of George's jacket.

The boys, meanwhile, were all looking at one another. No one knew what to say or do. Not even George.

'I think I can guess where that feather came from,' Cecille announced.

They all turned to look at her. Her lips were slightly

pursed and her eyebrows were raised questioningly as she held up the feather to examine it. Sid's heart was pumping fast and he had to bite his lip so as not to let their secret slip.

Then she gave a knowing smile. 'No more pillow fights, please.'

The boys were so relieved they were already out of the door and running up the stairs as she shouted up after them, 'Thirty minutes till pick-up.'

# Chapter Seven

The goose was exactly where they had left it, lying on Archie's bed, except it was now curled up in a very comfortable, deep sleep.

'Maybe if we throw it some food, it might wake up,' said George as they stood looking at it.

'I've got two sausages,' said Sid. He took them out of his pocket, leaving behind a greasy stain on his best grey trousers. He tossed the sausages towards the bird. It didn't flinch.

George pulled a chicken leg and two potato wedges out of his trouser pockets, but he'd had the sense to wrap them in a serviette. He moved just close enough to place them near to the bird's head, before quickly standing back.

'And it's got three pieces of chocolate cake for pudding,' concluded Archie.

They all nodded in agreement, and each put a slice of cake on the bed beside the sausages, chicken leg and potato wedges. But still the bird slept.

'Maybe we should switch on the overhead light,' said Archie. 'That might wake him up.'

'I don't think we should startle him again,' said Sid. 'That beak looks very dangerous to me.'

'I've got an idea,' said George. 'Let's try singing softly.'

So they all sang 'Happy birthday', including Archie, until they ended up laughing so much they couldn't sing any more. The bird raised its head from under its wing at the sound of their laughter. It took a look around the room, stretched its long neck towards the sausages, chicken and potato wedges, nudged them with its beak, but didn't appear interested in eating any of it. But then it began picking up bits of the chocolate cake.

'Go down to the bathroom, George, and get some water,' said Archie. 'There's a plastic bucket in the cupboard under the sink.'

George wasn't so sure. 'What if I bump into your mum or dad?'

'They're clearing the table. Creep down, and they won't even hear you.'

Sid was looking increasingly concerned at the goose's appetite for cake. 'Do you think it's going to eat all three bits? I mean, I'd quite like to take mine home with me.'

'This is not a time to be thinking about your

stomach, Sid,' said Archie.

They both stood in silence watching the bird devour the second piece of cake and then stretch its beak out towards the third. Sid groaned with disappointment.

George came back in with the bucket of water and set it down on the floor beside the bed. The bird stretched its neck out towards it.

'Put the bucket near the table,' Archie decided. 'We need to get the goose off the bed.'

Sure enough the bird stood up, stretched its wings and glided to the floor. George picked up the bucket and set it on the desk. 'Let's get it nearer to the window.'

He took a hasty step backwards as the bird flew up on to the desk and began to drink from the bucket, while slopping water all over Archie's drawings.

'Right,' said Archie. 'I'm going to open the window.'

'Why don't we just get your dad?' said Sid nervously.

But Archie was already creeping towards the window. Very slowly he slid it open and the bird's feathers ruffled in the icy air. It stopped drinking and looked up and stared out into the darkness. Then it walked out on to the window sill. A snow flurry circled like a small tornado and the bird spread its wings and flew out into the thick white curtain of snow.

'It's gone,' said a relieved Sid. 'Shut the window.'

Archie leaned out into the cold night air and listened

for sounds of the bird – a flap of wings or a birdcall – but there was only complete silence as the snow fell thick through the tree. He looked up and saw there was no sky and he looked down and there was no earth below. He liked the icy silence, and was imagining himself to be in the centre of a large white moving cloud when he felt someone tugging on his jumper. He pulled his head back in and shook the snow from his hair.

'Quick, shut the window in case it flies back in,' Sid insisted. His eyes grew wide with trepidation as he added, 'There could be more out there.'

George was more pragmatic. 'Let's see what was in the pouch again.'

Archie shut the window and then pulled the small pouch from his pocket. Sid was more interested in investigating the remnants of the chocolate cake on Archie's bed, but he did manage to ask which country the coin came from.

'It doesn't say,' said George. 'Just got some bird on one side and . . .' he turned it over, '. . . a star on the other side.'

'Let me see,' said Archie. Where there was a dagger on the other coin he had hidden away, this one did indeed have a star.

His sense of excitement was growing. It was too much of a coincidence. Two coins, almost identical, and he'd received them both on the same day. It could only mean one thing. The bird must have been sent especially to deliver the coin to him, but by whom? And more importantly, why?

# Chapter Eight

Archie was finding it difficult to sleep. He kept rolling over on to crumbs of cake on his sheets and he could smell the cold sausages and chicken legs he'd hidden under his bed.

He looked at the time on his clock. It was almost 11.30 p.m. Outside it was still snowing. He could see the flickering shadows against the window, huge thick flakes, like goose feathers, cushioning him from the terrors of the night, but there was no wind. The house was cocooned in soft, white silence and, tired though he was, he still carried a strong feeling of expectation. He felt sure something important was about to happen in his life; that he was on the verge of a great adventure and it had something to do with the two gold coins hidden in his pack of playing cards. If this was how it felt to be ten then he liked it very much.

He was closing his eyes again when a sound like a huge clap of thunder came crashing through the house.

He sat up and switched on his bedside light. Already his father and mother could be heard talking on the landing below, and then his father's heavy footsteps were running down the stairs. Someone was banging heavily on the brass doorknocker over and over again.

Archie jumped out of bed and ran down the attic stairs towards Cecille, who was leaning over the first-floor banister.

'What's happening?' he asked.

'Sshhh,' she said as she watched Jeffrey cautiously approach the front door.

Archie started to run down the stairs, but Cecille's anxious voice called him back. He stopped four steps below her, listening to the banging that was now so loud the walls of the house seemed to shudder under the force. Jeffrey edged closer to the door.

'Who's there?' he called out, and the banging stopped.

The three of them stood still, waiting for an answer. Then a muffled voice called back from the other side of the door that only Jeffrey, standing so close, could hear clearly.

Jeffrey's voice went from an anxious shake to high-pitched incredulity as he said, 'Who?'

He switched on the outside light and a small yellow glow appeared in the window above the door.

'Who is it, Jeffrey?' Cecille hissed. 'Don't open the door.'

But he was already undoing the bolt at the top, then the bolt at the bottom and finally turning the key in the lock.

'Jeffrey!' she hissed again, and when he continued to ignore her she put her fingers together under her chin as if to pray.

The front door swung back, and through the backdrop of falling snow piled up around the doorframe there stood a tall, ghostly white figure with a cone-shaped head. It shook the snow from itself, stamped its feet and took a gangly step forward into the hall.

Archie first felt a mixture of fear and curiosity, but his father's bewildered and ecstatic expression as he stared at the stranger reassured him. Jeffrey turned and looked up the stairs to where Archie and Cecille stood.

'Look who's here?' he was saying, as though he could not quite believe it himself. 'It's Rufus. He's come home.'

# Chapter Nine

Once Uncle Rufus was inside the house and the door was closed and the hall light switched on, his head appeared perfectly normal after all, much to Archie's relief. The woollen hat he'd been wearing had become so caked in snow it had given the appearance of a strange pointed silhouette, but now that it was removed he looked relatively normal. Archie wasn't too sure about the matted hair.

Actually, once the snow had melted from Rufus's eyebrows and his red nose thawed out and his lips returned from blue to a rosy red, Archie saw how alike Uncle Rufus and his father were. The only real difference was that Rufus was a half head taller and a good deal thinner.

The sleepy dark house became busy all of a sudden: lights glowed, the kitchen fire was stoked up and the kettle was boiling. Uncle Rufus's coat and boots and strange hat were all arranged near radiators to dry off, with layers of newspaper beneath them to catch the drips. Cecille reheated the sausages and chicken legs left over from teatime and Rufus quickly ate them with an accompaniment of toast. Archie felt a jab of guilt when he thought of the food lying under his bed, but Rufus filled up on cheese and biscuits and birthday cake. He kept sighing with pleasure in between mouthfuls of food. Under questioning from Cecille, he explained how he had arrived at Edinburgh Airport that afternoon only to discover his luggage was lost, presumed gone to France. Then, after what seemed like hours sorting it out, he had caught the train north, which broke down due to too much snow on the rails, and as if that wasn't bad enough he had to wait for a replacement bus . . .

Nobody was listening by then. As Rufus talked of his difficult journey home Archie, Jeffrey and Cecille had been focusing their attention on him. The way his face moved when he spoke, the colour of his deep-blue eyes against his brown weather-beaten skin, the way he picked his food up hungrily with his fingers and, above all, the sheer unexpected strangeness of his arrival in the house so late at night.

Archie sat at the table, listening but not listening, watching the food tumble from Rufus's mouth, the drips of grease on his beard, his fingernails which were too long, and the scent of foreign travel – of adventure.

He never, ever wanted morning to come. He wanted to sit and listen to Uncle Rufus and his adventures for ever, which was just as well since no one else seemed to be talking much sense.

Cecille showed no interest at all in Rufus's travels. Her only concern was whether he would like some more cheese, if the toast was brown enough, was it sugar *and* milk he took in his tea? And Jeffrey, who would normally be snoring with exhaustion at this time of night, had pulled his chair up close to the table and was examining Rufus's every move and physical appearance as though he couldn't quite believe what he was seeing and hearing.

When Rufus decided he could eat no more, he sat back in his chair, rubbed his stomach with satisfaction and turned his blue eyes on to Archie.

'I believe birthday congratulations are in order, Archie. So how old are you now?'

'Ten,' said Archie proudly.

'A good age to be. The age of adventure.'

Archie smiled with excitement and was just about to thank Uncle Rufus for sending him the coin when he caught Jeffrey looking at Cecille, who in turn was looking nervously at Rufus.

'What are your favourite pastimes?' Rufus was now asking.

'I like playing on my computer. And I like reading

about knights.'

'You don't like being outside? How about football?'

'Archie doesn't like running much,' said Cecille.

'It makes me feel sick and I get a stitch,' he explained.

'Swimming?' said Uncle Rufus.

Archie shook his head again.

'Archie doesn't like the cold,' said Cecille.

'I have trouble with my bilateral breathing,' added Archie.

'I see you've got a good strong tree outside. Climb it much?'

'Archie doesn't like heights. It makes him dizzy,' said Cecille.

Rufus didn't ask any more questions, he just nodded his head.

'I used to like reading about knights too. You know when I was in Romania –'

'You've been to Romania?' Jeffrey suddenly interrupted.

Rufus nodded. 'And when I was there I visited a castle, and –'

'What were you doing in Romania?' Jeffrey interrupted again.

'Just visiting. Anyway, Archie, I stood in the courtyard of this castle, looking up to the high turrets surrounding me, and on the highest turret of them all stood the statue of a knight, gazing out across the countryside. And I thought to myself: that must be what freedom is. To stand high above the constraints fear puts in our way, keeping us rooted to the same old spot, stopping us from rising above the ordinary. That knight away up there was a symbol of the liberation of the spirit.'

Archie was listening attentively. He wasn't quite sure what Rufus meant but he did know it was about bravery.

'Would you like to be a knight, Archie?' Rufus asked.

Archie laughed. 'You don't get knights these days, Uncle Rufus.'

'Maybe not in clanking armour, but would you like to be brave and fearless?'

Cecille turned from the sink where she had been stacking the supper dishes, ready to be washed at some point during the following day.

'Bedtime!' she announced. 'It is definitely far too late for a ten-year-old to be up. Even knights need their sleep.'

Archie thought she spoke with a hint of sarcasm. Rufus didn't seem to notice.

'Then it must also be time for your birthday present?' he said.

Archie was just about to remind Rufus he'd already received his birthday present that morning when a plate suddenly clattered to the floor and broke. Everyone looked towards Cecille, who was staring at Jeffrey in a meaningful way, as if he should know what she was thinking. He stared back, trying to second-guess what it was he was supposed to do or say. There was a noisy screech of a chair being pushed back against the tiled floor.

'Is my rucksack still in the hall, Jeffrey?' Uncle Rufus said as he got up from his chair.

Jeffrey nodded, though his attention was still on Cecille's meaningful stare. While Rufus disappeared out the door, winking to Archie and saying, 'Back in a mo,' Jeffrey got up from the table, crossed to the sink and began picking up the pieces of the broken plate.

'Do something,' Cecille whispered to him.

'Like what, for instance?'

'Intercept,' she said cryptically, shooting a look towards the open door leading to the hall.

Jeffrey sighed and muttered some words under his breath, which sounded very much like, 'It doesn't matter now.'

Uncle Rufus came back into the kitchen carrying something wrapped in bright-purple material. He sat down again and placed it on the table in front of Archie.

'Happy birthday.'

Archie gently peeled back the cloth to reveal a glass

ball attached to a circular brass base. Inside the ball he could see small gold shapes of the moon and the sun and the stars.

'A paperweight!' Cecille exclaimed with relief.

'Nice one too,' added Jeffrey, who was peering over her shoulder.

'It stops your papers falling off your desk,' she explained.

Archie looked to Rufus for confirmation, but he just winked. Though Archie was slightly puzzled at his reaction he thanked Rufus for the gift.

'Now, off to bed,' Cecille ordered, and by the tone of her voice Archie knew there was no arguing over her decision.

'Could do with some shut-eye myself,' said Uncle Rufus. He stretched his arms above his head and gave a big wide yawn.

'I'll show you where the bathroom is,' said Archie.

'I'll make up the spare room in the basement,' said Cecille.

'I'll get you some pyjamas,' Jeffrey said.

Archie led Rufus out into the hall.

'Your room is down there next to Dad's study,' and he pointed towards the basement stairs. 'The bathroom is on the next floor.'

They walked up the stairs together, with Archie thanking Rufus again for his birthday present.

'My pleasure, Archie,' he replied. 'A paperweight is always useful.' Then he dropped his voice to almost a whisper. 'But a weatherscope is much more interesting.'

'What's a weatherscope?'

They had reached the first-floor landing and Rufus looked over the banister to make sure no one was listening. Then he took the glass ball in his hand and held it up so the gold planets glowed beneath the ceiling light.

'A weatherscope tells you when storms are approaching.'

'How does it do that?' Archie asked.

Rufus began to rotate the ball in his hand. 'The planets begin to spin. Gently at first, then faster and faster as the storm closes in.'

Archie was very impressed. 'Uncle Rufus, this is definitely my best birthday ever. Thank you for sending me the gold coin, it was very nice, but a weatherscope . . .' He gave an appreciative whistle, which was really just a squeak, but luckily Rufus didn't seem to notice. He looked far too deep in thought as he placed the weatherscope back into Archie's hands.

'A coin, you say?'

Archie nodded. 'What do the engravings of the bird and dagger mean?'

Rufus considered the question for some time. Then he smiled and said brightly, 'The coin! Ah, yes, yes. Glad you liked it. Have you got it in a safe place?'

'Oh, yes,' said Archie. 'Very safe, and the other one too.'

'Other one?'

Archie lowered his voice to almost a whisper. 'The one the snow goose brought this afternoon. Do you know who sent it?'

Rufus opened his mouth to speak but it was Cecille's voice they heard. 'GOODNIGHT, ARCHIE,' she called out from the bottom of the stairs.

Rufus agreed. 'Go to bed. It's late,' he whispered. 'Come morning we shall continue our chat.'

Cecille's feet were already running up the stairs, and by the time she reached the landing, Rufus had disappeared into the bathroom and Archie was safely in his room.

Archie was sitting up in bed looking at the weather-scope when Cecille came in to say goodnight. Usually when he'd had a late night, she'd straighten his quilt, switch off his bedside lamp and kiss him goodnight. But tonight, even though it was well after midnight, she sat down on his bed and smiled.

'So, have you enjoyed your birthday?' she asked.

'The best one yet,' said Archie. 'It's a shame Grandma and Grandpa Stringweed couldn't make it but at least Rufus arrived home. It's good to have him back, isn't it?'

She continued to smile. 'Of course it's good to have family around you.'

'When I'm older I want to go and explore the world like Uncle Rufus.'

'You do?'

Archie nodded. 'I want to be brave and fearless and have adventures.'

Cecille seemed surprised by this admission. 'Are you sure?'

'Yes, because now I'm ten I feel different.'

'In what way, Archie?'

'Braver. I think every year from now on I'm just going to get braver and braver until I'm as brave as Uncle Rufus. Then it's my dream to go and explore the world too.'

She stretched out a hand and began stroking his hair. 'We all have our dreams, Archie, and for most of us they can never be more than that.'

Archie yawned and Cecille took the weatherscope from his hands and placed it on the bedside table. 'You know we love you very much, don't you?'

'Yes,' he said, snuggling down under his quilt. His eyes were feeling very heavy, but still she continued to sit on his bed. He liked hearing her soft voice talking to him. And although his eyes were shut he continued to listen. It was a bit like getting a story read to you; sometimes you heard every word, other times when you were feeling tired it wasn't so much the story, just the quiet gentle rhythm of a voice lulling you to sleep. That was how it felt now.

'Sometimes we have to accept that our future path may be different to what we imagined,' she was saying. 'Sometimes our fate is already determined for us. When that's the case, you must try very hard not to dwell on what might have been. Instead you accept your place in the world. Happiness can come from such simple pleasures as memories of childhood and the love of family . . . bravery takes many forms.'

Archie was aware his mother had stopped talking and then he felt her lean close and kiss his forehead. But he was too tired to open his eyes.

'Goodnight, Mum,' he murmured.

'Goodnight, Archie,' she whispered, switching off his bedside lamp. Then she quietly walked towards the door.

'I'm definitely going to be an explorer, Mum,' she heard him murmur.

She hesitated.

'Sweet dreams, Archie,' she whispered. 'If only I could make them come true for you.'

# Chapter Ten

So much snow had fallen during the night that when Jeffrey came to open the front door the following morning he found it frozen solid. After a lot of kicking and pulling it eventually gave way, revealing a screen of snow stuck to the doorframe, which promptly fell in around him.

Outside, the house looked as if it were swaddled in a giant white glove. A thick layer of snow now covered the ivy-clad walls, and the branches of the tree looked like long white fingers. In some places the snow was so deep it came right over the top of Archie's wellies.

Archie and Jeffrey quickly got to work, clearing a path from the door to the front gate. With a bright sun in a cloudless sky, they had to screw up their eyes against the dazzling whiteness. They had almost dug their way out when Uncle Rufus appeared on the doorstep dressed in a pair of trousers and a jumper belonging to Jeffrey. But the most remarkable transformation was in his face, which was shaven clean of the beard he had been sporting the night before. He'd also cut his hair and, though in no particular style, it made him look a lot more normal. Archie noticed he was wearing his boots from the night before, which he now saw to be made of dark-brown animal skin – a bear's, he decided. Rufus placed his hands on his hips and stared up into the snow-covered branches of the tree.

'Amazing,' he said. 'Truly amazing.'

'Sleep well?' Jeffrey asked, as he threw aside another shovelful of snow.

'Think so,' said Rufus, between deep breaths of the chilly air. 'I recall my head hitting the pillow last night, and this morning certainly arrived unexpectedly quickly. Therefore anything in between is of little consequence.' He took deep lungfuls of air and as he blew out again he began to make a strange chanting sound.

Cecille appeared around the side of the house, wearing a fur hat with earflaps and so many layers of clothes she could barely walk, let alone carry the bucket she held in each hand. The steam from the hot water was twisting and curling up over her gloved hands, and her cheeks were pink from the cold. Her green eyes had a clear sparkle to them in the white morning light, but the sparkle soon turned to irritation as she looked at Rufus enjoying the morning air while Jeffrey toiled at snow-clearing.

She set down one of the buckets. 'Stand aside, Rufus,' she announced over the sound of his chanting. 'I'm going to wash the doorsteps with warm water. Clear the snow once and for all.'

Rufus took a gangly step to his left and found himself knee deep in a snowdrift. Unperturbed, he closed his eyes and calmly resumed his chanting.

Cecille tossed the water over the steps, and patches of stone immediately appeared beneath the melting snow.

'Plenty of salt in that water,' she said with satisfaction. 'Should keep it from freezing.'

Rufus opened his eyes and looked up into the cloudless sky. 'More snow coming in from the north.' His nostrils flared as he breathed in deeply. 'Can smell it.' Then he licked the point of his index finger and held it up in the air.

'Hmmm,' he said thoughtfully. 'I suggest we take a morning stroll, Archie.'

Jeffrey sighed and removed his gloves. Handing them to Rufus, he said, 'Use these. I'm taking a break.' He rubbed the base of his spine with his hand. 'When you've taken your walk, maybe you could finish digging us out.'

Cecille, meantime, was looking closely at something she had found lying on the bottom doorstep. 'Good gracious! Look at the size of this.' In her hand she held a large, white, soggy feather. 'Do gull feathers come this big?'

'That's a whopper,' said Jeffrey.

'Now, that's a coincidence,' said Cecille. 'George had a white feather stuck to the back of his jumper yesterday. Do you remember, Jeffrey?'

Jeffrey was nodding his head, vaguely remembering something about snowballs and feathers.

Archie's stomach rumbled with excitement. 'Can I have it?'

Cecille held the feather up out of his reach.

'Not inside the house,' she warned. 'It's probably got mites crawling all over it.' Her mountain of clothes gave a shudder of disgust.

'I won't take it inside,' said Archie, plucking it from her fingers and sticking it on the side of his woollen hat. 'Come on, Uncle Rufus, let's go and see how much snow is lying at the top of Brinkles Brae. Maybe we could build a snowman up there.'

Cecille watched Rufus's long gangly strides follow Archie down the path and out of the gate. When they had both disappeared from sight she turned to Jeffrey.

'What do you think?' she whispered.

He pushed back his hat, revealing a flushed forehead. 'I told you, Cecille, there's nothing to worry about now. The future was sealed yesterday.'

'Then why has Rufus come back? After all these

years? And he looks so *strange*. Like a *native*. And as for all that chanting, what will the neighbours think if he carries on behaving like that?'

'Rufus was always eccentric; adventurous. Not like me.' He stuck the shovel upright into the snow. 'A home-grown coward.'

'You are not a coward, Jeffrey. Rufus doesn't carry the burden you carry. Bravery takes many forms. Being a first-born Stringweed son is one of them.'

Squeals of distant laughter interrupted their conversation. Jeffrey sighed. 'And now Archie will have to carry that burden.' He looked at her. 'Do you ever wish –'

'No! Wishing is a waste of time. Wishes do not come true.'

'Pity we can't say the same of cur—'

'Sshhh,' she said, nervously looking over her shoulder. When she was sure they'd not been overheard she continued, 'We don't need wishes, Jeffrey. We're happy with what we've got.'

'Are we happy?' he asked.

'Of course we are.'

Jeffrey was looking thoughtful. 'I was just thinking back to when we first met. Do you remember?'

Cecille smiled. 'My first day at the bank? I turned up for work at 9.30 and by 9.53 we'd managed to get ourselves locked in the strongroom.'

Jeffrey smiled too, but then he returned to the memory. 'And while we were waiting to be rescued, you told me you were planning a round-the-world trip. You said you wished you had the ticket right there and then. And you said it again. You said you were *wishing* for a big adventure, so you'd never need to come back to the bank or Westervoe. You had wishes then . . .'

'I got something better than an airline ticket. I got you and Archie. And I didn't get you from making wishes. I got you from the real world. The world I'm very happy with.' She smiled. 'No more talk of wishes. Let's go inside and have a hot drink.'

Jeffrey watched her pick up the buckets and walk towards the doorsteps. 'Have you noticed something?' he asked.

She stopped and turned. 'What?'

'Listen.'

She listened.

'Still no wind,' he explained. 'Not even a breeze. And next door's dog hasn't barked once this morning.'

They stood looking at one another, contemplating the unusual silence, when it was suddenly broken by the sound of the telephone ringing.

'I'll get it!' Cecille announced, and she ran up the steps into the house without kicking the snow from her boots. Jeffrey remained where he was, listening to Archie's now distant laughter and Cecille's barely audible voice on the phone. Then she was calling to him, telling him it was a wrong number and she was going to put the kettle on.

Jeffrey looked up into the sky and watched a single white cloud drift overhead. What was it Rufus had said last night, '*rising above the ordinary* . . .' Why had he said that? When he knew perfectly well that could never be the case for Archie. Jeffrey was glad Rufus was home safe and well, but he hoped his return didn't signal trouble. Jeffrey rubbed his eyes wearily. Another headache was settling in. He kicked the snow from his boots and walked inside the house, unaware that as the door closed behind him another large white feather had drifted down out of the sky and was lying on the newly washed doorstep.

# Chapter Eleven

About halfway up Brinkles Brae, Rufus and Archie had taken a break from their walk and were making a snowman.

They had finished the body and Archie was watching as Rufus rolled the head in another layer of snow before placing it on to the shoulders. All morning he had been waiting for an opportunity to start asking important questions that would solve the mystery of the cryptic cards and presents. Yet now he had Rufus all to himself, he wasn't quite sure how to introduce the subject.

Rufus stood back from the snowman to admire their handiwork.

'A good morning's work. What do you think?'

Archie looked suitably thoughtful as he surveyed the snowman. 'We need to give him some eyes and a nose and mouth.' He looked at Rufus carefully. 'Or we could just give him a pair of goggles? Second World War flying goggles.'

Rufus was looking at him equally carefully. 'Do you have Second World War flying goggles?'

Archie shook his head. 'I don't have an old watch either. Or a torch that doesn't work. Or even a dagger.'

Rufus nodded. 'Anything else you'd like to give him, but don't have?'

Archie shook his head and looked expectantly at Rufus.

'I see,' Rufus said after much consideration. 'Then I take it you don't have a rabbit foot on a gold chain, a small hand-carved wooden flute, a gold key or a magnifying glass?'

Archie shook his head, his eyes wide with interest. 'But they're in the house. I don't know where exactly, but probably the same place as the cryptic cards.'

Rufus didn't show any reaction to the mention of the cards. Instead he began packing more handfuls of snow around the snowman's neck. Archie wasn't sure what to say or do next, so he took the white feather out of his hat and tried placing it on the snowman's head. It was just out of reach, so Rufus took it and stuck it on the top, right in the centre.

'I wonder what kind of bird that feather came from?' Archie asked. 'A snow goose, I think.'

'It's from an Icegull, actually,' said Rufus, whose voice had gone very quiet.

'I've never heard of an Icegull,' said Archie.

Rufus stroked the feather. 'A supposedly mythical bird. Protector and guardian of whoever is prepared to challenge the might of the wind.'

Archie considered what Rufus had just said while he smoothed the snow on the snowman's face.

'If it's mythical, then it's not real? And if it's not real,' he turned to look at Rufus, '. . . then how come we have one of its feathers?'

Rufus glanced over his shoulder before whispering, 'I said, "supposedly" mythical.'

'Then you think it *is* real?' said Archie. 'Does it look like a snow goose?'

'An Icegull can change its size, so it can be bigger or smaller, but what it can't change is the colour of its eyes. They are a bright fluorescent green. When an Icegull dies it becomes a green guiding light; we call them Scouts.'

'I've seen a Scout!' said Archie, and his one green and one blue eye stared at Rufus expectantly. 'And I've seen an Icegull too. It came to my window last night. It brought me a coin the same as the one you sent me, well, nearly the same, only it had a star on one side instead of the dagger, and Uncle Rufus . . .' he took a gulp of air, '. . . what's going on?'

Rufus plucked the feather from the snowman's head and fixed it back on to Archie's hat.

'Let's walk to the top of the hill. What I have to tell

you may be better understood from a good vantage point.'

As they continued their walk towards the summit, Archie noticed the snow had not fallen so heavily on the higher slopes, unlike the drifts that lay piled up around their house. The higher they climbed the lighter the snow covering, until by the time they reached the top there were only occasional patches, lying atop the dead stringy grass. They stood breathless, their faces tingling with the cold air, and looked back down on the village.

The blue waters of the bay lapped against the harbour walls, and with no wind blowing they could hear the outboard motor of a small boat in the bay. As Archie surveyed the peaceful scene he pointed out to Rufus where George lived, but as his finger swung around in the direction of Sid's house, something occurred to him.

'Why is the snow so much heavier around our house?'

'If you have something you want to protect, what do you do with it?' Rufus asked.

Archie thought of the two coins in his magic set.

'Put it somewhere safe?' he suggested.

Rufus nodded. 'Or wrap it in something soft, perhaps?'

Archie looked again at the thick layer of snow

covering his house.

'You mean the snow is protecting our house?'

'Protecting *you*,' said Rufus.

'From what?'

'The wind.'

Archie was feeling very confused. 'I don't understand.' He looked around nervously. 'What does the wind want with me?'

Rufus put a reassuring hand on his shoulder. 'I'm going to ask you to keep a secret, Archie. Just for the time being, you understand. Because what I'm about to tell you is so important that if the secret is not protected, then the curse of Huigor may never be broken.'

'The curse of Huigor?'

Rufus nodded and began to speak in a hushed voice.

'Centuries ago a knight by the name of Gustaph left Scotland to go and fight with King Richard in the crusades. He was strong and brave and fought many battles, but as the years wore on and his bravery became legendary he grew arrogant. That is when he made his one serious mistake. He believed he was indestructible, that he was in some way protected from harm, and so when the war ended, instead of being thankful that he had survived and could return home with the other knights, he went looking for further danger to prove his infallibility. On the way he met a man who offered to tell his fortune in return for food and water. The fortune-teller looked into his crystal ball and said he saw misfortune drawing closer for the knight and all future generations of his family. The knight became angry and told the fortune-teller he was a liar, a fake, because misfortune could not befall a man of noble blood who had fought for his king and was regarded as one of the bravest knights that had ever set foot in Christendom. So angry was he that he took the food and the water away.

'The fortune-teller said that if he was indeed a man of honour then he would never have called him a liar so freely, and would not have withdrawn food and water from a hungry traveller. However there was still time to retract his words. A show of humility would change the course of his family's fate.

'Enraged that a lowly fortune-teller would talk to him in such a way, the knight stood up and went for his sword, but something strange happened. The fortune-teller began chanting and held up the crystal ball to catch the glare of the sun. The light reflected back was so strong it almost blinded the knight. He tried to raise his sword but found it too heavy to lift, his arms felt weak and his legs ached. He collapsed to the ground, exhausted.

'"Arrogance," the fortune-teller told him, "must never be mistaken for bravery. Courage comes in many forms. It can be quiet and unseen. Valour is not the preserve of the rich and powerful but comes from an understanding of the world."

'For the first time the knight felt afraid. He asked why he had lost his strength and the fortune-teller told him he had placed a curse on him and future generations of his family. All first-born sons were now destined to grow up afraid of the world from their tenth birthday onwards, and as each generation carried the curse, so the family name would lose its high regard.

'The knight begged the fortune-teller to break the curse, offering him gold and jewels. But the fortune-teller told the knight he should not have assumed from his appearance that he was penniless. In fact, he came from a wealthy family and had riches of his own. Then he wrapped himself in his cloak, picked up the crystal ball and walked away into a sudden desert sandstorm. The knight was too weak to follow, and once he'd gathered enough strength, he slowly made his way back home to Scotland.'

'Why do I have to keep that story a secret, Uncle Rufus?' Archie asked. 'What does it have to do with me?'

'Because the knight's family name was Strongwood, but over the centuries as the curse took hold, we lost our land and power and the name came to be known as Stringweed.'

'You're talking about *our* family?'

Uncle Rufus nodded sadly. 'And you, Archie, as a first-born Stringweed son, are about to inherit the curse. Just like your father and grandpa.'

Archie had a sudden flash of his mother sitting at her dressing table telling his father she thought Rufus was weird. At that moment he was beginning to think that maybe she was right.

Rufus sensed his disappointment and disbelief.

'There's still time to break the curse,' he said reassuringly. 'Then your father and grandpa will have their courage restored, and generations of Stringweed courage still trapped inside Huigor will be released.'

Archie looked no more convinced.

'Has the wind tried talking to you yet?' Rufus asked.

Archie didn't answer, because a cold chill was creeping up his back under his jacket and under the wool of his hat. His eyes were wide with fear, but he felt excitement too, because Rufus knew about the talking wind. All the same, there was something he didn't understand.

'If the curse began on my tenth birthday,' Archie said thoughtfully, 'then I'm already cursed.'

'Not yet,' said Rufus. 'Nine years I have spent travelling the world, and during that time I discovered something very significant. The curse is always brought by the same tornado. His name is Huigor. He can arrive on the actual tenth birthday or very soon after.'

'A tornado?'

'This is where the challenge lies. We must find all the artefacts I sent you. They are crucial to breaking the curse and restoring the family name. They all come with the power of history. Each artefact belonged to an ancestor, a first-born male Stringweed. The magnifying glass belonged to your great-grandfather. The dagger belonged to great-great-grandfather Stanley Stringweed; the goggles were your grandfather's.'

This was exciting news for Archie.

'Grandpa Stringweed was a Second World War pilot?'

'Afraid not. The curse and bad eyesight put a stop to that. No, he wore the goggles to peel strong onions.' Rufus shook his head as if to get rid of the image. 'Anyway, is there anything you want to ask?'

At that moment there was only one thing on Archie's mind and, though he was shaking, his voice was steady.

'How do I break the curse?'

Rufus glanced over his shoulder. With the coast clear he turned back to Archie.

'You must enter and then destroy the tornado.'

'That's impossible!'

'Let us hope not. That is why we must find each of the artefacts. They look like ordinary objects, but as the curse draws near they will release a powerful and protective energy that will help you in your battle with Huigor.'

Archie was still trying to absorb this information as Rufus pointed down the hill towards Windy Edge.

'The voices you hear are rogue gusts that have broken away from Huigor. With so much snow protecting the house, they won't rattle the windows so easily or make the tree creak so noisily, and the soft snow will show you their path when they try creeping up on you.'

'How does the snow know to fall on our house?'

Rufus turned to look at Archie. 'When the time is right your question will be answered. Now, when did the wind first talk to you?'

'Friday night. It said, "He's coming".'

'Friday night?' Rufus began muttering to himself. 'Yes, that would figure. Take-off was delayed due to strong winds . . . turbulence over the Irish Channel . . .'

Archie gulped nervously. 'Shall we ask Dad to help?'

'No. He cannot help us. No, we must face this challenge alone.'

A single gust of wind rose up from out of nowhere, encircled them and was gone again. Rufus removed a glove, picked the feather from Archie's hat and balanced the tip of it on his middle finger. The feather began to spin gently and Rufus looked up into the sky, tilting his head at an angle to listen. He sniffed the air and then nodded as if to confirm what he already suspected.

'We should get back home. It's on its way.'

'What's on its way?' asked Archie.

Rufus turned to look at him, his eyes full of concern.

'The tornado. I'm afraid Huigor has found you.'

# Chapter Twelve

Sunday lunch was a nerve-racking experience. Archie kept looking at Jeffrey as he ate, trying to see if he looked different in any way now he knew he had a curse on him. But he appeared just as he always did: kind, forgetful, but still his wonderful gentle dad. Maybe being cursed wasn't so bad after all.

Archie waited until Cecille went out to the pantry to get a carton of cream and Rufus had gone to fill the buckets with coal from the shed, before asking the question that was uppermost on his mind.

'If you could do anything, Dad, what is the most exciting thing you'd like to do?'

Jeffrey looked at him over the top of his newspaper for what seemed a very long time. Archie was beginning to think he'd not heard the question, but then Jeffrey began to speak slowly and thoughtfully.

'W-e-l-l. I think flying must be very exciting. The sensation of soaring up into the sky as the sun comes up, or in the evening as the sun goes down. The North Star appearing. Or maybe to stand on the top of a mountain, looking as far as the eye can see, above everyone and everything.'

'Then why don't you do it?'

'Oh.' Jeffrey gave a short laugh that sounded more like a cough. 'We Stringweeds don't have a head for heights . . .' His voice drifted off as though he couldn't quite remember what he was talking about.

'We could go together,' Archie suggested.

'Where?'

'Up in an aeroplane or climb to the top of a mountain.'

Jeffrey was looking at him very carefully. 'Wouldn't you find that just a little scary?'

'No. How about we go next week?' Archie persisted.

'It's winter, Archie. Going up into the mountains at this time of year isn't very sensible. Too cold, I should think.'

'Spring, then?'

'Maybe.'

'Let's promise one another now.'

'I can't make that promise, Archie.'

'Then *I* promise that next spring we'll climb to the top of Ork Hill and watch the sunset and look at the stars.'

Beneath Jeffrey's smile lay disbelief.

Cecille breezed in carrying a carton of double cream. She was sniffing it suspiciously. 'I don't trust that fridge. It doesn't seem cold enough to me. Do you think the cream's off, Jeffrey?' She thrust the carton under his nose and he took a sniff.

'It's fine,' he said, raising his nose from out of the tub. He looked at Archie and gave a gentle smile, unaware that a small white blob of cream lay on the end of his nose. For the first time in his life Archie looked into that kind, familiar face and saw someone look back whom he knew wasn't truly his father.

Archie was determined to break the Stringweed curse. With the tornado called Huigor already on its way there was no time to lose, and he and Rufus would have to start making their battle plan immediately.

He was considering how to get his mother and father out of the house when the telephone rang.

'I'll get it!' Cecille announced through a mouthful of apple pie and cream, but Archie was already up and out of his chair.

She followed him into the hall. But Archie got to the phone first.

'Hello? Archie Stringweed speaking.'

'Give the phone to me,' Cecille insisted, her hand outstretched. There was a note of panic in her voice.

'Hello, Ezekiel,' Archie said, and Cecille gave a

sigh of relief.

Jeffrey appeared at the kitchen door. 'Who's on the phone?'

'Ezekiel,' Cecille whispered.

Archie thanked him for the birthday presents and handed the phone to Cecille, saying, 'Sounds urgent.'

Then he went back to the kitchen to finish his apple pie, but Jeffrey remained standing at the kitchen door, listening to the one-sided conversation, which consisted of Cecille repeating, 'I know . . . I know . . . I know.'

When the call eventually finished she relayed Ezekiel's concerns to Jeffrey. With less than a week until Christmas, the village-hall tree had still not been bought and decorated. They would also need new lights, since their only set had been returned broken by the local drama group. Ezekiel had then suggested the committee have an emergency meeting that very afternoon, and because Cecille was the committee chairwoman, naturally she would have to attend.

'I just don't know if we should spend any money on a tree and lights,' she sighed. 'There are so many other priorities. The windows must be repaired soon, before the rain completely ruins them.' She avoided Jeffrey's eyes as she concluded, 'We'll just have to accept the village-hall is going to look very cheerless this year.'

There was a quiet pause while neither of them spoke. Then Jeffrey asked, 'Are you expecting a phone call, Cecille?'

'Why?'

'You seem edgy whenever the phone rings.'

She shook her head. 'No, I don't!'

'As if you're expecting a call.'

'I'm *not* expecting a call, and I'm *not* edgy!' she insisted.

The telephone started to whine and Cecille looked down at the handset still grasped in her hand so tightly that her knuckles had turned white.

'You can replace it now,' said Jeffrey. His voice was quiet yet suspicious, and Cecille was relieved to get away from his questioning stare when he went upstairs to the bathroom to take some headache pills. But as she sat back down at the table to finish her apple pie and cream she caught Rufus watching her.

Cecille ignored him and carried on eating, which wasn't easy because his piercing blue eyes were staring at her in much the same way as Jeffrey's had been, except for one difference. Rufus's eyes were so full of reproach he might as well have stood up and said, 'You don't fool me. I know you're hiding the truth.'

Jeffrey offered to go along to the village-hall committee meeting with Cecille. He was sure his bank experience might provide some inspired financial advice, or at least some fund-raising ideas. After all, he was treasurer of the Sailing Club, the Sub-Aqua Club and recently the Deep Sea Diving Association. And a very good treasurer he was too. He attended every meeting and never missed their dinner dances.

Jeffrey and Cecille dressed in layers of outdoor clothing, while Archie stood in the hall, watching, waiting and wishing they would hurry up and leave.

'Don't get your feet wet,' Cecille told Archie as she pulled on her wellies. 'If you go outside, remember to wear your boots. You don't want to get a chill.'

Archie promised to take extra care and made a point of standing just inside the door, well away from the damp top step, to wave them goodbye. As their snow-crunching footsteps faded, the only sound left was Archie's own steady breathing.

It was so quiet he could pretend he was the only person left in the world, and therefore could practise his whistling without fear of anyone laughing. He licked his lips, filled his lungs, made the most perfect circle with his mouth and then blew. One very small shaky note appeared on his lips and was gone again, but his breath lingered and turned into a frosty white mist that began to spin, forming a long funnel shape. A chill passed across his feet, covered his toes and then crept up through his legs into his chest. He stared at the funnel shape and was reminded that somewhere out there in the distance, further than his eyes could see or his ears could hear, a powerful tornado was drawing near and the only person to help him catch it was Uncle Rufus. Uncle Rufus with his strange pointy hat and bear-skin boots.

Loud barking from the garden next door broke the snowy silence. Archie looked towards the hedge and listened to the dog behind it, which was sounding more agitated than usual. The hedge at the front of the house was much thinner than the hedge in the back garden and so he could see a black Labrador face poking through. The dog looked at him and gave a deep warning growl. At about the same time Archie noticed a movement to the side of the garden path. A fine layer of snow had formed into a shallow wave of snowflakes and was gently drifting towards him. As he continued to watch, he realised there was no breeze to carry it along; it was moving of its own accord. With this realisation came fascination. The barking dog couldn't distract him from the swirling white wave as it gathered speed and rolled over the first doorstep.

The next moment he felt Rufus's hand on his shoulder, pulling him back into the house and slamming the door shut.

Archie couldn't hide the frightened shake in his voice as he listened to the letter box rattle.

'I thought the snow was here to protect me.'

Rufus knelt down and looked at him reassuringly.

'What you've just experienced is another of Huigor's rogue breezes. Their job is to creep up and frighten you. Keep your eye on the snow, it'll show you where they are. Remember they aren't strong enough to hurt you. Don't listen to their whispers and moans. More importantly, don't be scared.'

Archie thought the rogue breezes were doing a very good job because he did feel scared. 'Rufus, I don't think I'm brave enough to battle a tornado.'

Archie was relieved that Rufus didn't seem too concerned at this admission.

'It's your decision,' he confirmed.

Then Archie remembered his father's face staring at him across the kitchen table, a blob of cream on his nose.

'I *will* challenge Huigor,' Archie decided. 'I *will* set my dad free of the curse. Then he'll be brave enough to stand on the top of a mountain and watch the sunset and the stars come up. Just like your Romanian knight, high up on the castle turret. I want to stand there with him, but neither of us will be able to do that if I fail. I'll become a coward too.'

'Your father isn't a coward,' Rufus told him firmly. 'He has never run away. There are many things he would like to do, but the curse won't let him. It fills his thoughts and plans with fears. He imagines all sorts of problems and obstacles that he cannot overcome and eventually he loses the will to fulfil them. That is Huigor's curse. A boring, safe and unadventurous life. It is Huigor's nearing presence that is making him ill. The headaches and the memory loss will disappear once the tornado blows over, but he will never be free until the curse is broken.'

Archie felt renewed determination. 'I *will* set him free.'

Rufus nodded his head. 'In that case, I'll help you all I can. This afternoon is as good a time as any to begin our search. Let's get started. We have eight gifts to find and not much time to do it.'

# Chapter Thirteen

Jeffrey's study was a gloomy basement room with one small window that looked on to the back garden. A dining-room chair, a scratched walnut desk, a filing cabinet and two wall cupboards, all of which were unlocked, took up the floor space. An armchair covered in a faded floral material was the only evidence of comfort.

Rufus was looking inside one of the wall cupboards, which was piled floor to ceiling with holiday brochures.

He pulled out a colour brochure dated 'Winter 1993'. The cover was of the snow-capped Swiss Alps, with a smiling skier leaping over a small photograph of a man and woman wearing thick jumpers and toasting one another with a glass of red wine. He examined a handful of other brochures, advertising long-haul holidays to America, the Far East and Australia.

'Dad doesn't like going on aeroplanes, or boats or trains,' Archie tried explaining. 'He says he would go on holiday if he didn't have to travel. He wishes he could just be transported there, without leaving the house.'

Rufus gave a sympathetic sigh. 'Shame. The real thing is far more exciting.'

'Have you been all over the world?' Archie asked.

'Pretty much all of it.' Rufus closed the cupboard door. He opened the one next to it, which was also stocked floor to ceiling with old travel brochures. 'OK,' he said briskly, 'let's stay focused.'

Archie's job was to keep an ear open for his parents returning home. Rufus, meantime, would carry out the search, since it would be unfair to ask Archie to pry in Jeffrey's study, but since every corner seemed to be taken up with holiday brochures and travel books it didn't take long for Rufus to put his hands on his hips and announce wearily, 'It's no good, there's nothing here.' He looked at the time on his watch. 'Almost four o'clock. We'd better call it a day.'

Archie, however, wasn't ready to give up. 'But we haven't found one single thing,' he said despondently.

Rufus began explaining the practicalities of their situation. 'We don't want to be caught snooping, do we? If we're caught, we'll either have to tell the truth about the curse challenge, which your mother would never agree to . . .'

Archie nodded in agreement.

'. . . or tell lies, which I don't think either of us wants to do.'

Archie shook his head.

Rufus tried to cheer him up. 'We'll find an opportunity to search the house again tomorrow. Your father will be at the bank and Cecille told me she's working at the charity shop in the morning.'

But for Archie tomorrow was just too far away. He wanted to keep on searching every corner of the house right there and then until they found what they were looking for. There was no time to lose.

'I think we should check out the cupboard under the stairs next,' Rufus was saying as they emerged from the basement. 'Maybe looking in the most obvious places first is the way to do it. Could be we're making it too difficult for ourselves. After all, your parents don't know we need the gifts, so they would have no reason to hide them in unlikely places.'

Archie was too disheartened to mention he'd been looking for the gifts ever since the night he had stood outside his parents' bedroom and overheard them discussing Rufus. By the time he'd crept back up to his room that night, he had made up his mind to start searching as soon as possible, but without arousing suspicion. His solution had been to offer to tidy out cupboards, explaining he needed to earn extra pocket money to buy Christmas presents. His mother thought that was a very good idea. Unfortunately she had suggested he tidy out the kitchen cupboards, which involved ploughing his way through shelves of leaking bags of flour and sugar and rice, throwing away out-of-date jars of pickles and jams, before going on to creating some kind of order in the pot cupboard. It had taken him hours and he knew for sure at the end of it that absolutely nothing was hidden in the kitchen. Well, nothing intentional.

He'd found a brochure on double-glazing, a dried-out bluebottle and a packet of plastic forks in a casserole dish. A coupon offering twenty pence off a Battenburg cake (expiry date 8th June); twenty shopping receipts at the bottom of the fruit bowl, and a tube of glue with no lid stuck to a selection of barely recognisable dusters in the cupboard under the sink.

Maybe Rufus was right – maybe they would find some of his gifts in the cupboard under the stairs – but he doubted it.

There was no point searching his parents' room either; he had done that already. Admittedly, his mother walking in and asking what he was doing had interrupted his search. She had cast her eyes suspiciously around the room while he had stood there with his mouth open, desperately trying to come up with an excuse and then the words, 'I was just looking for ideas for a Christmas present for Dad,' came tumbling out.

He'd been convinced she wouldn't believe him, but she'd hugged him and planted a big wet kiss on his cheek. 'Do you know what I see?' she'd asked, as they looked at their dusty reflections in the dressing-table mirror.

He'd given his head a confused shake. Was she referring to his face that was as red as the enormous Humpty Dumpty soft toy sitting on the top of the wardrobe?

No, because she'd smiled broadly and whispered, 'I see a wonderful and thoughtful son.'

As Archie thought back to the two of them standing together in front of the mirror, it occurred to him there was somewhere glaringly obvious he'd not thought to look. It occurred to him that he should investigate what the red-faced Humpty Dumpty might be sitting on top of.

The grandfather clock began chiming four o'clock just as the front door opened and Cecille and Jeffrey walked in, their boots covered in snow. It was already dark outside and the chill air clung to their clothes and skin.

'It's just plain weird,' Cecille was saying. 'Three streets away there's hardly any snow at all. But as soon as we walk through our gate it starts snowing again and the wind drops.'

She began kicking off her wellies, sending clumps of

snow landing on to Archie's feet. He felt it melt through his socks and wet his toes. Jeffrey pulled off a glove with his teeth while talking at the same time.

'Ezekiel said his back garden was two feet deep in snow but his front garden had only a light covering.' The glove slid off and he began removing the other one in the same way.

'Global warming,' announced Rufus. 'I remember when I was in Russia –'

Jeffrey stopped what he was doing. The glove was still dangling between his teeth as he asked, 'You've been to Russia?'

Rufus nodded and then continued, 'Floods one week and a heatwave the next.'

They all followed Cecille into the kitchen where she huddled up against the warmth of the stove.

'How was your afternoon?' she asked, scanning Archie for signs of having been outside. Immediately she spotted the wet patches on his socks. 'Archie, you didn't get your feet wet, did you? You know how susceptible you are to chills.'

He was just about to say, 'No, I didn't get my feet wet,' when an idea came into his head.

'My feet did get a little damp,' and he gave a small deliberate cough to reinforce the point.

'Go and get dry socks immediately,' she said. 'I'll make you a hot drink.'

'I'll go and fill another couple of buckets with coal,' Rufus said.

'I'll come and give you a hand,' said Jeffrey.

'No. No. There's no need,' said Rufus. 'These hands have carried pitchers of water for miles across the African plains.'

Jeffrey couldn't hide his envy. 'You've been to Africa?'

'Yes,' said Rufus. 'And that reminds me. I bumped into a man in Botswana who said he knew you. Came from Exeter. Professor somebody. Now, what was his name?' Rufus tilted his head back and stared at the ceiling thoughtfully. 'It'll come to me in a minute.'

There was silence in the kitchen as they watched and waited for him to remember the elusive name.

At last he shook his head. 'Can't remember.' He looked straight at Cecille. 'But I will. Sooner or later. In the meantime I'll go and get coal. Have you got a torch, Cecille? Looks pretty dark out there.'

She didn't move, but continued to stare at Rufus while wearing the strangest expression.

'Cecille?' he asked.

'What?' she said eventually.

'Have you got a torch?' Rufus repeated.

'On the window sill,' she said quietly. 'Make sure you put it back *exactly* where you find it. Torches need to be located quickly in an emergency.'

Rufus accepted this request without a murmur and with the torch in his hand went out into the hall leading to the back door. No one moved as they listened to the metallic clatter of the buckets, followed by the thud of the door closing. They could hear his feet outside the window crunching through the snow, following the yellow beam from the torch as he made his way to the shed at the bottom of the garden. Archie glanced at each of his parents as they listened to the fading sounds outside. Jeffrey was the first to talk.

'A man from Exeter who knows me?' His expression changed from thoughtful to puzzled. 'Do we know a professor from Exeter, Cecille?'

She was standing at the sink, busy filling the kettle, and whatever she said was lost in the sound of the running water.

'Did you say something?' he asked.

'No,' she replied without turning round. 'I didn't say a thing.'

Which surprised Archie, because he had watched her reflection in the window and her mouth had most certainly moved. What had she said that was now a secret to be kept from his father?

She finished filling the kettle and turned to see Archie staring at her.

'Have you still not gone and changed your socks?'

'I'm going now.' He got up from his chair. 'I think

I'll stay in my room and play the Knight of the Five Tigers.'

'OK,' said Cecille while taking cups and saucers out of a cupboard.

Archie ran up the stairs three at a time, stopped on the dark first-floor landing, and crept towards his parents' bedroom. The door was ajar and as he pushed it open the hinges creaked. He grimaced and stood very still, waiting for a reaction from downstairs, but when none came, he squeezed through the small gap into the room.

It was in darkness, with just a single path of light streaming through the window. Their next-door neighbour, owner of the barking Labrador, had left her outside security light on, which was a stroke of luck since it gave him just enough light to find his way around the room without the need to switch on the bedside lamp.

Archie already had a plan. He lifted the dressing-table chair, set it down directly in front of the enormous wardrobe and climbed up on it. The layers of clothes lying on the chair gave a little extra height, enough to get a grip of the enormous Humpty Dumpty and throw it on to the bed. But he wasn't quite tall enough to see over the top of the wardrobe, and in any case it was also too dark. He reached up and ran his hand blindly along the top, but there was nothing there, only large furry balls of dust sure to be full of spiders, dead and living. He stood on his tiptoes, almost toppling off the chair, and stretched his arm out as far as it would go. Then he felt something. It was a box about the length of a shoebox, but shallow, and it was just out of reach. He turned and looked around the room, his eyes settling on a dark shape hanging on the wall next to the dressing table. It was a wooden backscratcher which his mother had given his father the previous Christmas as a joke present, but its long handle with its carved hand on the end was just the tool he needed.

He took it down off the wall and was about to climb back up on to the chair when he heard Rufus's voice outside in the garden. Something in the way he was talking softly aroused Archie's curiosity. He peered out of the window and then quietly raised it a few inches.

'. . . then we'll need troop reinforcements,' Rufus was saying. He sounded anxious as he asked, 'Can you do that for me?'

Archie strained to hear a reply from whoever he was talking to, but the next sound was the clatter of the buckets as Rufus picked them up. Then the torch was switched back on and Archie watched him emerge from behind one of the trees at the side of the garden and walk towards the back door.

Archie slid the window shut. Who had Rufus been

talking to? And what was that about troops? The kitchen door slammed shut and Archie got on with the business of retrieving the box from the top of the wardrobe.

It took four or five attempts to hook the back-scratcher over the box and pull it towards him, but when he finally held it in his hands he felt a wonderful sense of achievement, which quickly vanished when he heard footsteps coming up the stairs.

Archie grabbed hold of Humpty Dumpty, threw it back on top of the wardrobe, dragged the chair back to the dressing table, and, as the footsteps neared the top of the stairs, dropped down on to his hands and knees and crawled under the bed. The outside security light was switched off, leaving him in total darkness as he tried to disentangle himself from the long bedspread that draped to the floor. There wasn't much room either due to his mother's many pairs of shoes. In addition he was trying not to breathe too loudly or call out, which was difficult, since he realised, as he lay there in the dark, that something was hiding under the bed with him.

# Chapter Fourteen

It began as a tiny pinprick of light in front of his green eye. Archie blinked several times, believing it had something to do with optical illusions and not being able to focus in complete darkness. He shut his eyes very hard and opened them again, expecting the light to have disappeared, but it was still there – only it had expanded into the size of a tennis ball. It was also floating around his head, shimmering and flickering as it drifted from one end of the bed to the other, as if examining the heavy bedcover that draped to the floor. He was tempted to crawl back out from under the bed, but the approaching footsteps were drawing nearer.

He closed his eyes and prayed that whoever was climbing the stairs wasn't on their way up to the attic. If his mother or father discovered he wasn't in his room and came looking for him, how would he explain why he was under *their* bed with the light off, clutching a box from the top of *their* wardrobe? There was also the matter of the ball of green light under the bed with him. What would his mother have to say about that?

The footsteps came to a halt outside the room, and he heard the door scrape against the carpet as it was pushed open. He hardly dared to breathe. The ball of light seemed to sense the seriousness of the situation because it had stopped fluttering and was now hovering gently by his head.

He could tell it was his mother who stood in the doorway. The footsteps were light and he could smell her familiar perfume before she pulled the door closed and Archie sighed with relief as the catch clicked shut. He listened to her walk along the landing towards the bathroom. There was a nervous moment when the perfume bottles on the dressing table rattled from the slam of the bathroom door, but then came the sound of running water in the pipes. Now was the time to make a quick escape. Archie lifted the bedcover and the flickering ball shot out and cast a path of light through the darkness towards the door. Clutching the box he crawled out from under the bed and opened the door, just wide enough to squeeze through. He glanced back in time to see the ball of light shrink to the size of a pinprick and make its escape up the chimney.

Archie ran up the stairs towards his own attic room, and by the time he'd switched on his bedroom light, shut the door and sat down on his bed, he was shaking.

It had been a close call and he would have to be more careful in future, but as he looked at the dusty old box in his hands he knew he had found the first of the eight gifts Rufus had sent him.

He untied the string and lifted the lid. Inside was something heavy and wrapped in purple velvet. He peeled back the cloth and found himself looking at a dagger.

'Wow!' he said, and he gave a tuneless whistle. The handle was in the form of two entwined snakeheads. Immediately he was reminded of something and he laid the dagger on the bed while he went to open his toy cupboard under the eaves of the roof.

He pulled a packet of playing cards out of his magic set and shook the contents on to his hand. The two gold coins lay on his palm. He looked at the engraving on one of them, a dagger with entwined snakeheads, and, as expected, it was identical to the dagger in the box. The other coin had an engraving of a star, which reminded him of the green ball of light's return. But now he knew what it was. A Scout, Rufus had called it. When Icegulls died they turned into Scouts. But where was it now?

He looked up through the skylight window as a shooting star crossed the sky. He closed his eyes to make a wish, but he knew he would have to be quick. Wishes made after a star disappeared didn't come true.

When he opened his eyes again he returned to the business of the dagger. He couldn't resist picking it up and holding it like a knight holding his sword, but as he gripped it the most unexpected thing happened. He felt a huge surge of energy sweep through him and he found himself raising it high above his head and letting out a war cry.

'Victory, victory!' he chanted.

There was a gentle knock at the door. Just as Archie hid the dagger and box under his pillow Cecille walked into the room. She was carrying a mug of hot chocolate that she set down on the bedside table.

'Having fun?' she asked. Her eyes were scanning the room and finally they settled on the computer, which was switched off. 'Don't tell me you're fed up with the Knight of the Five Tigers already?'

'I've been on my telescope,' Archie replied. 'Looking at the stars. Pluto is very strong tonight.'

'Oh, that's good,' and she gave the night sky a polite glance.

'And now I'm going to read the book Ezekiel gave me. About the weather.'

Cecille looked impressed. 'You *are* busy. I won't disturb you any more.' Then she was out the door, saying, 'Drink your chocolate before it gets cold.'

Archie wondered if his mother would be quite so impressed if she knew the box from the top of her wardrobe was hidden under his pillow. Or that he was going to challenge a tornado.

He opened the book at a page filled with a picture of a huge tornado creating a path of destruction through a small town. He began to read aloud, *'The sound of a tornado approaching is like a jumbo jet taking off. There is a strong smell of sulphur similar to rotting food and lightning inside the funnel can sometimes produce a choking smell.'*

Archie looked up at the knights hanging from the home-made mobile above his bed, and in particular the knight with the letters 'A. S.' on his silver and red armour. He reached up and flicked the knight with his finger, and, as he watched him spin helplessly, one thought kept going round and round in his head, like the spinning knight. Even if he found all the artefacts, could he also find the courage to battle Huigor?

# Chapter Fifteen

According to the church clock it was 2.26 a.m. And according to the weathervane above the clock, no wind was blowing. The vane was in the shape of a schooner with billowing sails, its bow pointing resolutely out over the roofs of the houses to the sea beyond. The village of Westervoe slept beneath the glow of the moon, and every house was in darkness but for one: the cottage belonging to Ezekiel Arbuthnott.

Ezekiel's hall light was switched on as usual, as was his bedroom light, burning brightly at a window with no curtains.

The room itself resembled a study rather than a bedroom, with maps pinned to any wall space not covered by shelves of books. His bed was positioned at right angles to the window, deliberately restricting his view, as if he was afraid of what he might see outside in the darkness. On the table beside the bed was a globe of the world, balanced on top of a large stack of books, all of them tales of adventure.

Ezekiel was sitting up in bed reading a book called *Journey into Darkness: A History of Lost Explorers*, and his eyes were magnified twofold by the strong reading glasses he wore.

Suddenly he stopped reading and peered suspiciously over the top of the book. He tilted his head to one side and listened. The sound came again, a metallic creak, like an unoiled gate. He took off his glasses, put down the book, leaned over and opened the drawer of his bedside table and, for the second time that night, took out a brass telescope. He extended it to its full length then crept out of bed, holding the telescope like a sword as he tiptoed across the floor.

He pressed his ear against the bedroom door and, because he couldn't be sure if it was up to the job, turned and put his left ear against the door instead. There were no more metallic squeaks, only the lonely silence of the night. He turned the handle slowly and peered out on to the landing.

A wind chime of glass whales hanging from the hall light was perfectly still, as was another wind chime at the bottom of the stairs above the front door. To reassure himself further, he put the telescope to his eye and looked out of the landing window. The glow from the house lit up a tree in the garden and he focused on a large wooden wind chime hanging motionless from a branch. Ezekiel was beginning to think he'd imagined the metallic squeak when he heard it again. It was a sound he knew well; the church weathervane was moving.

'I know you're out there,' he murmured, while scanning the sky through the branches of the tree. 'North Star is bright tonight,' he told himself. 'Yes, the North Star does seem *unusually* large.' It occurred to him that it wasn't twinkling like the other stars, and there was something else about it too, the shape, the green tinge, and . . . 'It *blinked*!'

As if hearing him, the silhouette of a bird with a large wingspan flew out of the tree and disappeared over the roof of the house. Ezekiel took a step back in surprise.

'An albatross?' Then he remembered something. 'Can't be. They don't have bright-green eyes.'

He forgot all about the metallic creaking and hurried back into his room to peer out of the window, but the strange bird was nowhere to be seen.

If it wasn't an albatross, he told himself, then what was it?

A cold draught crept across his bare feet, making him shiver, and he returned the telescope to the drawer and climbed back into his warm bed.

He lay against the pillows and rubbed his eyes. 'So tired,' he whispered, but he couldn't sleep just yet. The weathervane could creak and the wind chimes could chant all they wanted to during daylight, but night-time was different. Night-time was when things happened. It was quieter, so you could hear unexpected sounds that you weren't meant to hear. You could look out of your window and see movement when nothing was supposed to be moving. There was no doubt in his mind that something very odd was happening around Westervoe, but in particular up at Windy Edge. Why was so much snow piled up around the Stringweeds' house, and why was a cumulus cloud more often than not hovering over their rooftop? There was something unusual about those clouds. If you stared long enough flashes of green appeared inside them, and they always followed the same steady path towards Moss Rock and with hardly a breeze to blow them along.

And there was something else. Just the other day he'd watched Archie blown along the pavement by a gust of wind that came out of nowhere, and so fast his feet hardly touched the ground. Ezekiel decided that, as a lifelong friend of the family, it was his duty to keep a close eye on young Archie, particularly since all these strange occurrences coincided with his tenth birthday and the return of Rufus Stringweed.

# Chapter Sixteen

Archie was having trouble sleeping. His head was buzzing with a thousand thoughts, mostly about tornadoes and finding the seven missing artefacts.

Downstairs the grandfather clock chimed three o'clock.

He yawned loudly, rolled over on to his side and closed his eyes. A moment later he rolled over on to his other side and his eyes popped open again. He decided that since he was fully awake he might as well do something useful. He switched on his bedside light and took the dagger out from under his pillow.

He hoped that by focusing on it he could come up with an idea of where to search for the seven other presents. When this didn't work, he went over to the table by the window and drew a map of the house, indicating every cupboard in every room.

He discounted the bathroom cupboards that were overfilled with tubes and potions and bottles of sickly perfumed substances. As for the medicine cabinet, well, it was just too narrow to hold anything but a few cough-mixture bottles, headache pills and his father's tonic and vitamins. He put a large red cross over those cupboards. He sat looking at the map and his pen hovered over the cupboard under the stairs and the spare bedroom Rufus was sleeping in. Surely Rufus would have thought to search his own room, but to be absolutely sure he'd ask him in the morning.

Archie sighed. It would all be so simple if he could ask his father directly where the presents were, but Rufus had been quite insistent that his father would try and prevent them breaking the curse if he suspected anything.

'I wish, I wish, I knew what to do.'

He was so preoccupied with worrying that he was unaware of a small movement outside the window. Flakes of snow that lay piled up on the window ledge were drifting upwards in small spiralling waves against the glass. Then a voice laughed softly.

Archie sat up straight and looked around the room. Had that laugh come from behind him, beside him or above him?

'Who's there?' he asked.

'*He's coming*,' said the voice, so close it appeared to be inside his head, and so soft and breathless he wasn't sure if he had heard the words at all. The room suddenly felt cold and the hair around his brow lifted slightly, as if caught in a gentle breeze. Then the mobile above his bed moved, sending the knights marching into a hesitant circle. Archie reached for the dagger and a strong surge of bravery flowed through him.

'Who's coming?' he demanded.

There was more soft laughter. '*Huigor*,' said the whisper.

Archie watched as his map of the house rose up from the table and floated to the floor. He squeezed the dagger handle.

'I'm not afraid of Huigor.'

The voice laughed again. '*We shall see.*'

He felt the cold air circle him and then it was gone. The window gave a single rattle and the snow flurry settled back on to the window ledge. Archie looked across to his weatherscope and saw the planets inside it were spinning. He was still holding the dagger, which gave him the courage to say again, 'I'm *not* afraid,' but he almost leapt from his chair when he heard a different, louder voice speak to him from under his bed.

'Archie? Archie, don't be afraid. Can you hear me?'

He gripped the dagger and peered under the bed. Lying on the floor was his walkie-talkie handset and the voice coming from it belonged to Rufus.

'Receiving you loud and clear,' Archie quickly replied.

'Keep your voice down,' Rufus instructed. 'Get down to the basement as quickly and quietly as you can, and watch out for the creaky stair.'

'Roger,' said Archie. 'Over and out.'

He held on to the banister and when he came to the third stair from the bottom, he grabbed the stair-post and swung himself to the floor. He stood still and waited for any movement from his parents' bedroom. Unusually his father wasn't snoring. When he was sure they were still asleep he tiptoed along the hall carpet and then ran down to the basement.

The door to Rufus's room opened. He was standing there fully dressed, wearing his bear-skin boots, pointy hat and coat, and with his rucksack slung over one shoulder. He put his index finger to his lips and then indicated to Archie to come inside. Once the door was shut, the Scout appeared from behind it and spread its green glow around the room. Rufus didn't seem surprised in the least. His surprise and concern were directed at Archie.

'What's that in your hand?' Rufus wanted to know.

Archie held up the dagger. 'I found it on top of Mum and Dad's wardrobe. I went searching while you were out getting coal. It's one of your gifts, isn't it?'

'Anything else you want to tell me?' Rufus asked.

'The planets inside the weatherscope are spinning.'

Rufus nodded. 'Anything else?'

'A rogue breeze got into my room. But I wasn't scared; the dagger helped me be brave.'

'Did it say anything?'

'First it laughed and then it said Huigor was coming.'

Rufus began pacing the small room, his expression a mixture of worry and concentration. The Scout paced back and forth with him, hovering just above his shoulder. Archie watched and waited, taking in the outdoor clothes and the rucksack on his shoulder.

'Where have you been, Rufus?'

'Nowhere. Yet.' He was still pacing and looking intently at the floor.

'Are you meeting the troops?' Archie asked. 'Can I come with you?'

Rufus stopped pacing and the Scout came to a halt behind his head, so that when Rufus turned and looked at Archie he appeared to be wearing a green halo.

'What do you know about the troops?' he asked, his eyes wide with surprise.

'Nothing,' said Archie quickly. 'Except, I overheard you talking to someone in the garden. Who were you talking to?'

'Maybe you misheard me. Sometimes I talk to myself.'

Archie knew he'd not made a mistake. 'You were behind the tree,' he persisted. 'The torch was switched off.'

'You really do keep your eyes and ears open, don't you? I'm impressed.'

'Can I come with you?'

'That was the intention.'

Rufus was looking him up and down and Archie realised how unprepared he must look, standing there in his bare feet and faded cotton pyjamas.

'My boots and coat are by the kitchen door,' he said. 'I'll get trousers and a jumper from the airing cupboard.'

Rufus nodded. 'Hurry. We must get back before morning.'

Archie had no idea where they were going as they slipped out the door into the back garden. It felt very cold outside, so cold he couldn't quite catch his breath, and when he did it felt as if he'd swallowed a lump of ice. He shivered and the Scout slipped inside Rufus's rucksack.

'You all right?' Rufus whispered and Archie nodded furiously, just in case Rufus used the cold as an excuse to leave him behind. They walked slowly around the house to minimise the sound of their footprints crunching in the deep snow, Archie stepping into Rufus's footprints, which was difficult considering the length of his stride. But as they made their way down the path towards the front gate, two eyes suddenly appeared through the hedge separating them from next-door's garden. There followed a low growl and a loud frosty bark.

'Oh, no,' Rufus hissed. The dog growled again while trying to push its way through the hedge.

'It's going to wake everyone up,' Archie whispered.

But Rufus was already crouching down in front of a gap in the hedge, his eyes level with the dog's eyes. It stopped barking immediately and gave only one small whimper before turning and walking away.

'How did you do that?' Archie asked when they were through the gate and walking up the hill.

'Little trick I picked up from nomads on the savannah,' Rufus murmured. 'Doesn't work quite so well with lions.'

Archie had never been outside in the dead of night before. The latest he'd ever been out was 11.30 p.m., but that had been by accident. On that occasion they had run out of petrol on the way back from a birthday dinner for Cecille. The two of them had sat in the car for an hour while Jeffrey set off into the night to get help. He'd pulled his collar up against the cold wind and in only four or five short footsteps he'd disappeared into the darkness and Archie had felt an overwhelming fear that he might never see him again.

But now it was his turn to set off into the night with Rufus. Archie dug his hands into his pockets and through the thick padding of his gloves felt the reassuring handle of the dagger. He gripped it and didn't feel in the least afraid of any rogue breezes that might creep up on him.

The Scout reappeared out of Rufus's rucksack to light the way ahead and, to amuse itself, changed shape between a beam of light and a flickering green ball.

On and on they walked, up and over the top of Brinkles Brae, past the snowman they'd built that morning, across moorland, until arriving at the edge of an abandoned Second World War airfield.

'Where are we going, Rufus?' Archie asked, because his legs had begun to ache and his toes had turned numb. He had also lost feeling in the end of his nose and his stomach was starting to tell him that it would rather enjoy a small snack.

Rufus stopped walking. He was breathless and clouds of vapour spilled from his mouth as his warm breath hit the icy air. It took a moment or two before he felt ready to speak and when he did, his words created smaller intermittent pockets of mist.

'Not far now, Archie. We're almost there.'

They climbed through a huge gap in a very broken-down perimeter fence and walked towards a building that had walls but very little roof. Rufus took Archie's hand as they walked around the side of the building and then they came upon the entrance, which was three times the size of the whole front of Archie's house.

Archie was beginning to feel nervous of this big, dark building that was falling to pieces, but the flickering Scout shot past them and expanded into a welcoming blaze of light, illuminating the entire building and the single item contained within it. Archie gave a surprised gasp and looked up at Rufus, who was smiling proudly.

'Archie,' he said, raising his arm and pointing towards the bright red aeroplane that stood before them, 'meet Monika.'

# Chapter Seventeen

Archie's first question to Rufus was, 'Where did you get the aeroplane from?' His second question was, 'Where are we flying to?'

'I picked the aircraft up in Ireland,' Rufus told him. 'It's a Cessna. 1939. And we're paying a visit to Moss Rock.'

'Can you land an aeroplane on Moss Rock?' Archie asked, trying not to sound nervous.

'This little beauty will land just about anywhere,' said Rufus. He opened his rucksack and took out a pair of flying goggles. 'I went on a searching expedition tonight too,' and the Scout spread its glow to give Rufus a green-tinged smile.

Archie could hardly contain his excitement. 'The Second World War flying goggles! You found them!'

'They were in the coal shed,' Rufus explained. 'Wrapped in a tea towel and wedged in a gap above the door. You'd never have known they were there unless you managed to stick your head in and do a hundred-and-eighty-degree twist.' He rubbed the back of his neck and did a pretend grimace. 'Haven't had to do a contortionist act like that since I found myself hanging upside down from a eucalyptus tree in Eastern Australia. A koala bear was involved, if I remember rightly.'

'You've been to Australia?' Archie asked, full of admiration for his intrepid uncle.

'Yip,' said Rufus. 'Though I made a point of avoiding gum trees on the second visit. Now, climb up and let's be on our way.'

Archie had never been in an aeroplane before. He'd never been on a train either, or a boat. Because Jeffrey didn't like travelling very far from home, summers had been spent on the beach a few miles along the coast, close to where his Grandma and Grandpa Stringweed lived. Now here he was, wearing the flying goggles and setting off for Moss Rock.

Rufus fired up the engine, flicked on the lights and they trundled out of the old hangar. They swung around to the left, heading for the runway, and Archie felt the aeroplane vibrate as they picked up speed. The noise of the engine was deafening as they accelerated, so fast it made him bounce and rock from side to side as they raced into the night. Then he felt himself being pushed back into his seat as the aeroplane tilted upwards and they were rising up into the air, higher and higher towards the moon and the stars. In his excitement he forgot all about his cold feet and growing hunger. And he didn't even notice that a wet drip had formed on the end of his nose until it fell on to his sleeve.

If only Sid and George could see him now. If only the whole world could see him now.

Archie looked at Rufus, ready to tell him that this was the most exciting day of his life, but Rufus seemed very busy with the business of flying the plane. His head was moving around, looking out of one window and then the other, searching for something. It was very dark and Archie hoped he knew where he was going since they could see nothing much apart from the stars.

Then all of a sudden two green balls of light appeared close to the aircraft.

'Aha,' Rufus said, sounding relieved. 'Our navigation system has arrived,' and he gave the Scouts a welcoming wave.

The next moment they were descending and Archie raised himself up in his seat for a better view out of the window. They were flying quite close to the sea, and in the glow of the aircraft lights it resembled a black moving mass tinged with a dirty yellow colour, but much scarier were the rocks looming out of the darkness. He could never have imagined how big cliffs were once you got near to them, or how menacing the beady eyes of hundreds of seabirds could look, staring back from the narrow ledges.

The aeroplane gave a lurch and Archie held on to the edge of his seat as the wings began swinging from side to side. He closed his eyes and tried not to feel scared, and then he remembered his dagger. He put his hand in his coat pocket and clasped the handle tight and that wonderful warm sensation of bravery ran through him again, all the way down to his toes. The aeroplane gave another, stronger, lurch and Archie opened his eyes to see they were approaching a grassy landing strip lit by Scouts. It was not a smooth landing; the force of the brakes pushed him forward in his seat and the aircraft was thrown around so violently Archie was sure it would break in half. It was only when they came to a standstill that he dared let go of the dagger handle.

Rufus switched off the engine and smiled broadly at Archie. 'You OK?'

Archie nodded and pulled off his goggles. 'Are we at Moss Rock?'

'We are, but no time for sight-seeing.'

Rufus helped Archie out of the aeroplane. 'It's only a short walk from here. Stay close.' Then he switched on the torch he had taken from his rucksack.

Archie could smell the grass they walked on, which felt spongy and soft beneath his boots, and he could hear the sea moving against the cliffs, somewhere out there in the darkness. But apart from the path of light from the torch, he could see nothing of the landscape around them. If they came to Moss Rock again he would remember to take the see-in-the-dark goggles George had given him for his birthday.

Rufus had been right though. They didn't have far to walk before they came to a large rockface, looming up out of the darkness. A hundred small fluorescent-green lights suddenly appeared around the entrance to a cave and Rufus switched off the torch. Once inside Archie could hear dripping water and the presence of some kind of living creatures, but his eyes wouldn't adjust to the darkness. Then came the beat of wings above his head and so close that he felt the wind on his cheeks. A thousand small green lights were suddenly flicked on, followed by more beating wings. Archie immediately thought of giant bats and he gripped Rufus's arm.

'Nothing to worry about, Archie,' Rufus said quietly. 'You have friends here.'

A Scout shot past, followed by another and another and another, each of them exploding into a blaze of light. Archie saw he was standing in a vast cave, bigger and higher than a cathedral, but more astonishing was the heaving mass of Icegulls covering the ground around him and filling the ledges all the way up to the cave ceiling. The silence was unexpectedly broken as they stretched their necks upwards and in time to the beating of their huge wings gave a deafening rallying cry while their green eyes stared at him in expectation. Rufus bent down close to his ear.

'Meet the troops, Archie.'

# Chapter Eighteen

As suddenly as the squawking had begun it stopped, and the sea of birds folded their wings and fell silent. Those perched up on the ledges settled down and those on the ground around him stood perfectly still. Archie felt as though they were waiting for something to happen. He looked at Rufus, who was staring expectantly at the cave entrance. A flap of wings made Archie turn round as an Icegull as big as Rufus's plane flew into the cave and glided above them, round and round, casting a huge circling shadow. The birds on the ground moved aside to make a clearing and the Icegull descended in a straight line to land in front of Archie and Rufus. Archie tried hard not to feel afraid, but the bird's beak looked about the size of their coal-shed and as white as the feathers covering its body. But it was its staring green eyes that really worried him; they were as big and as dazzling as the headlamps on the snowplough Sid's dad drove.

Rufus and the bird were now staring at one another, eye to eye. Neither moved and neither made a sound. This went on for what Archie thought was a long time. Taking his eyes off the giant bird for a moment, he looked around at the rest of the flock and found they were all staring directly back at him. He took a small step closer to Rufus and reached for his hand. Rufus squeezed it reassuringly, and he found himself being led closer towards the bird until it towered over him, like a huge marble statue but for those glowing watchful eyes.

'We have news for you, Archie,' Rufus said, his voice echoing throughout the cave. 'The Scouts send word that Huigor is mid-Atlantic. His path is erratic, but we expect him to blow in after two sunsets.' Some restless squawking sounded from one of the higher ledges and Rufus waited until all was quiet again before continuing, 'We also know that Huigor is travelling under water and is creating a giant tidal wave. Therefore it's essential we keep him out of the bay and draw him in along the cliffs further down the coast.'

There was more squawking from the birds, as if voicing their approval at this information.

'What must I do?' said Archie, and the restless birds became still again.

The enormous Icegull tilted its head down towards Archie, making him take a nervous step backwards as the huge eye closed in. But Archie saw only kindness in the eye and felt warmth from the feathers and wasn't afraid, even when a voice that he couldn't hear with his own ears began talking deep inside his head. As he continued to stare into that glowing green eye he knew the voice belonged to the bird. He was reading its mind.

'Do not be afraid,' it was saying. 'Huigor lives on fear. Show him bravery and he will weaken. The strength of your defiance will return him to dust. When that moment comes, Huigor will be destroyed.' The eye drew closer, the voice softer. 'You have many friends. They will make themselves known when the time is right, but only you, with the hand of courage, can break this curse. We shall guide you and watch over you, but once you enter Huigor's path we are powerless. Take with you the knowledge that your heart is many times stronger than his.'

The bird raised its head again, spread its wings and then soared straight up towards the ceiling. The Scouts began to shrink, taking their light with them, and the giant bird disappeared into the darkness above.

'Time to go,' said Rufus.

The Scouts shot past them, one after another, and the birds on the ground moved aside, creating a clear path leading towards the cave entrance. Those birds perched high on the ledges had already disappeared into the growing darkness, and, as the final Scout shot out of the cave, only a few bright-green eyes peering through the black could be seen as one by one the birds closed their eyes.

Once outside the cave, Rufus took the torch from his pocket and switched it on. He looked to the horizon.

'Better hurry,' he said. 'It's getting late.'

They climbed back into the aeroplane and Rufus handed Archie the rucksack.

'There are some biscuits and chocolate in there. Help yourself. You deserve it,' he added with a smile.

The little green runway lights suddenly flickered in the plane's headlamps, marking out the route the aircraft should take. Archie didn't feel so nervous this time of the bumps and rattles and the way the plane swung from side to side as it raced along. In fact he was in the process of unwrapping a large bar of chocolate which he'd found in the rucksack when, with a bump and a rattle and another bump, they were up in the air again and heading for home.

As they flew through the night sky, just above the sea and close to the cliffs, Archie wondered how on earth he was supposed to show bravery towards Huigor. He had never been allowed to be brave; in fact he didn't know how to be brave. Perhaps he was going to have to confide in George, because George, who had suffered two fractures, concussion and various cuts and bruises resulting from his many precarious adventures, was the bravest person he knew – after Rufus, of course.

Archie took another bite of the chocolate and settled back in his seat. He was feeling very tired now, and he remembered with a weary groan that once they landed at the airfield they still had the long walk home across the moor and back down the hill. He wished he could just fall asleep there and then and wake up in his own bed. He blinked hard to stay awake, trying to focus on Rufus's head, which kept moving backwards and forwards and from side to side as he stared anxiously out of the window down to the sea below. Small white tips had appeared on the top of the waves that had not been there when they flew over earlier.

'Wind must be getting up,' Rufus said, but there came no answer from Archie, who had finally fallen asleep with a half-eaten chocolate bar melting in his hand.

# Chapter Nineteen

The first thing Archie was conscious of was the chiming of the grandfather clock; then, as his head emerged out of the quilt, he blinked against the bright daylight, which made him suspect he had slept very late indeed. He gave a long sleepy yawn and licked his lips. They tasted of something sticky and sweet. Something familiar. Chocolate! All of a sudden everything came back to him. How he'd been sitting in Rufus's aeroplane on the flight home from Moss Rock eating a chocolate bar. His eyes opened wide at the memory, particularly the cave full of Icegulls. Even more incredibly he had read a giant Icegull's thoughts, which was how he had come to discover that Huigor was now mid-Atlantic and would blow in tomorrow, sometime after sunset.

Archie gulped nervously. How on earth was he supposed to battle a tornado that was right now drumming up a tidal wave? He wasn't sure if he felt up to the job. It was all very well the Icegull telling him to be brave, but just how brave would he have to be?

He sat up in bed and discovered he was fully clothed. Then he discovered he couldn't actually remember going to bed. Try as he might, he had no recollection of walking home across the cold dark moor from the airfield or of the trek down the hill to the house. Rufus must have carried him all the way.

The time on the new watch Grandma and Grandpa Stringweed had sent him for his birthday was just after nine o'clock. Archie got out of bed and walked downstairs on wobbly legs. When he came to the creaky stair he grabbed hold of the stair-post and swung himself to the floor, landing in front of the grandfather clock. It was making a strange whirring noise, as if it wanted to give a good cough but couldn't quite drum up the strength.

Then Archie heard a scuffling noise coming from the under-stairs cupboard. The door was open and he found Rufus inside, crouched down, pulling old shoe-boxes and coats aside as he searched every corner with the torch he had been carrying the previous night. He smiled when he caught sight of Archie's sleepy, pale face.

'Morning,' he said. 'How are you?'

'Great,' said Archie, fighting back another yawn, and he did a little air-boxing to prove how great he felt. 'Find anything?' he whispered.

Rufus switched off the torch, emerged out of the cupboard and stood up straight. He was very tall indeed.

'Nothing in there, I'm afraid. And it's OK, you don't need to whisper. There's no one here. Your dad's away to the bank and your mother's gone into the charity shop for a couple of hours. So we've got plenty of time. Fancy some breakfast?'

In the kitchen Rufus poured Archie a glass of milk and produced a plate of toast that had been keeping warm on the stove.

'I'm sorry I fell asleep last night,' said Archie. 'And I'm sorry you had to carry me home.'

'Oh, I didn't carry you home,' said Rufus cheerily. 'You got a lift from a couple of Icegulls.'

'I did?'

'Snuggled you up among those feathers with a blanket and you were warm as toast. Butter?' The knife was already poised over the dish.

'Jam, please,' said Archie. 'Weren't you worried I might fall from the back of the Icegull?'

'They expand themselves to whatever size is necessary. Made to measure, you might say. You looked very comfy, I can tell you. Good service too. Dropped you off right in front of your bedroom window. All I had to do was open it and haul you in.'

Archie looked wide-eyed. 'Do you think someone

might have seen us?'

'No chance. The gulls drummed up a bit of a snow flurry to conceal us.'

'How did they do that?'

'An Icegull can turn its breath to snow.'

Archie looked out of the window to the thick snow lying in the back garden.

Rufus nodded. 'That's the Icegulls' work. They tend to travel in flocks that look like large clouds. That way they avoid detection. But if you look really carefully you see flashes of green from their eyes. Most people don't bother looking closely at the clouds.'

'Is that a flock of Icegulls?' Archie was pointing to a large cloud drifting towards Windy Edge.

Rufus walked over to the window to take a closer look. 'Yes.' As he watched it drift overhead he murmured, 'That's an unusually large flock.'

Archie was unaware of Rufus's concerned expression as he began to munch his toast. 'What are we going to do about the six gifts, Rufus? We only really have today to find them if Huigor's blowing in tomorrow.'

Rufus turned back to the table. 'I know, I know. I've been thinking about that.' He took a scrap of paper out of his trouser pocket and picked up a pen that was lying on the table. 'Now, let's see. We've got the dagger and the goggles.' He ticked the items with green ink and Archie thought of the Icegull's green eyes. Rufus gave a long sigh as he looked at the list. 'That leaves the torch, the magnifying glass, the key, the rabbit foot, the flute and the pocket watch.'

'It's a lot of things to find, isn't it?' said Archie, suddenly not enjoying his toast and jam any more.

Rufus looked into Archie's worried, pale face and adopted a more positive approach. 'Well, we've got the best part of the morning to have a good old nose around.' He picked up the pen and carefully balanced the point on the tip of his index finger.

Archie was impressed.

'Is there anything you can't do, Rufus?'

'Course there is, just can't think of it at the moment.'

But Archie's moment of distraction was short-lived.

'Have you searched your room, Rufus?'

Rufus nodded and returned the pen to the table.

'Clean sweep. Absolutely nothing under all that dust. So that just leaves the box room upstairs and the living room. Which one do you want to take?'

'I think I should do the box room,' said Archie. 'Mum gets nervous when I'm around her glass-fish collection.'

'Fair enough.' Rufus brushed the toast crumbs from Archie's jumper. 'Let's get started, then. I feel lucky today!'

'So do I!' said Archie. And he scampered up the stairs on all fours like an enthusiastic dog.

He charged into the box room and was confronted with the enormity of his task. The floral carpet was barely visible beneath boxes and boxes of bric-a-brac. The pink bedspread was covered in piles of old clothes and overflowing carrier bags.

Archie wished he'd opted to search the living room. But he set to work, starting with the big chest of drawers just inside the door. The two small top drawers contained old cables, tarnished keys, instruction manuals, three pin plugs and a rusty penknife with a tartan handle. He then worked his way through the big heavy drawers full of old bedlinen that smelt of mothballs. From there he searched a rail of clothes covered in polythene and even climbed through to the other side where he came face to face with a fireplace. On the mantelpiece was an old dried-out child's painting that consisted of five red splashes of paint, beside which his mother had written, 'An aeroplane by Archie, aged 4'. Also on the mantelpiece was a small blue car with a wheel missing, a pink comb and a half-eaten packet of mints.

Next he searched through the bags of baby clothes stacked up inside his old cot that also contained a couple of broken fan heaters. By the time he came to the small cabinet beside the bed where the photo albums were kept, he was getting bored, and also a little tired after his late-night visit to Moss Rock. He sat down on the floor and began flicking through an album that was dedicated to his first year of life. Downstairs the phone was ringing and not long after he heard Rufus tell the caller that Cecille wasn't at home.

Archie didn't pay much attention to the phone call because he was too absorbed with the photo album. The first page of photos was of his mother sitting up in the hospital bed holding him, his tiny face like a large strawberry peering out of a blue shawl. Another photo showed him lying beneath the Christmas tree next to the huge red-faced Humpty Dumpty soft toy. Archie flicked through the photographs, stopping to look at one taken on the day of his christening. A large group was gathered on the church steps and standing centre-front were his mother and his father, who was holding Archie in his arms. Archie was kicking his legs and cry-ing, though everyone else was smiling, including Ezekiel Arbuthnott, standing in the back row, his head looking as if it was resting on Grandpa and Grandma Stringweed's shoulders. His other grandparents were there too: Grandpa and Grandma Caine, both looking thin and frail, holding each other's arms as if to stop themselves from falling down.

Rufus was almost unrecognisable in his suit and short hair. He was standing next to Cecille, who was holding on to her wide-brimmed hat to stop it blowing away. It was a happy and relaxed photograph in contrast to those taken on Archie's first birthday.

In all of those Rufus looked miserable as he watched Jeffrey, Cecille and Archie blowing out the single candle on the birthday cake. In another he was scowling at Grandpa Stringweed, who was showing Archie how to use a spinning top. In the only photograph of Rufus and Archie together, he finally managed a smile as Archie fed him chocolate biscuits, but in the background Grandpa Stringweed looked on uneasily.

As Archie continued to flick through the photographs he became aware that Rufus's voice had gone quiet. His words were barely audible as he spoke on the telephone. 'Are you sure?' Archie heard him say.

Archie put the album to one side and crawled across the floor towards the door to listen.

'Then that changes everything,' Rufus was now saying. 'It won't leave us much time . . . is it possible to do it without them? . . . No, thought not.'

Archie crept closer and the floor beneath him creaked. Rufus stopped talking. Archie held his breath, then he heard Rufus tell the caller he had to go and Archie crawled back into the room and carried on looking at the photographs.

'Find anything?'

Archie looked up to see Rufus standing at the box-room door.

He shook his head. 'Nothing.' He returned the

album to the cabinet. 'How about you?'

'Not a thing. Even checked the chimney.' Rufus showed him his hands, which were covered in soot. 'Let's have a conference in the bathroom while I clean up.'

By the time Rufus had scrubbed and rinsed, Archie felt ready to ask the question that was on his mind.

'Rufus? Why did you go away on my first birthday?'

'Oh, I'd decided to leave a long time before then.'

'But why that day?'

If Rufus was surprised by the unexpected question, he didn't show it.

'The night before your birthday I was up in Grandpa Stringweed's attic looking for Christmas decorations, when I came across a wooden casket. Inside were all the artefacts. At the bottom of the casket I found the dagger. With it was a note saying it was to be handed down to every first-born Stringweed son. When I asked Grandpa why he'd not given it to Jeffrey, he said there was no point stirring up the past, "what must be must be". I knew then it had something to do with the curse. You see, no one ever talked about it. I think Grandpa had convinced himself that if it wasn't mentioned it wasn't true. I took it upon myself to give you the dagger as a birthday present. Grandpa was angry. Then your dad joined in. They told me it wasn't mine to give and the curse wasn't any of my business. I disagreed. As your godfather I thought it *was* my business. So, I packed all the artefacts in a bag and off I went. I was determined to do something. I'm sorry I missed your second birthday, but that was a particularly tricky time. After that I sent an artefact each year to their rightful heir – you.'

Rufus continued to scrub his nails but he became very quiet, as though remembering his adventures over the years. His head was bent down low and because Archie was standing so close he noticed a long scar on the back of Rufus's neck. He imagined something very terrible had happened to him.

'Did you miss us, Rufus?'

'Yes, I did.'

'I think Grandma misses you. She cries when Mum or Dad mentions your name. Grandpa doesn't say anything, he just goes for a long walk.'

Rufus was watching the warm tap water run over his perfectly clean hands. He seemed to be deep in thought, but then he turned the tap off, turned to Archie and said briskly, 'Let's get back to business?'

Archie agreed. He had enough information, for the moment anyway.

'The way I see it,' Rufus was saying, 'we have to get inside your father's head. Try and figure out where he would have hidden the presents.' He went to dry his hands, but there was no towel.

Archie pointed to a door directly opposite the bathroom. 'In the linen cupboard. Top shelf.'

The linen cupboard smelt of moth balls. It had deep shelves and was lined with wood, making it very dark inside. Archie switched on the cupboard light which flashed and made a popping sound.

'There's a spare light bulb in here somewhere,' he said, rummaging around in a cardboard box at the bottom of the cupboard.

Rufus pulled a towel from the top shelf, dried his hands and then, resting a foot on the bottom shelf, raised himself up to replace the light bulb. As he twisted around to hand the old bulb to Archie he noticed a rolled-up tea towel resting on a deep ledge on the inside of the doorframe.

'What do we have here?'

He jumped back down. The floorboards beneath the carpet shuddered and a layer of dust rearranged itself.

He unwrapped the towel to reveal a small, carved flute. 'Clouds gather to the music,' he murmured.

'There's something else in there,' Archie told him.

Rufus unwrapped the towel further and out of the folds emerged the gold-plated magnifying glass.

'Doorframes seem to be a reoccurring theme. First the goggles above the shed door and now these.'

'I bet you're going to suggest that we examine all cupboard door frames,' said Archie.

'That's *exactly* what I was going to suggest.'

Archie was already running up the stairs to the attic. 'Might as well try my bedroom first.'

The first thing Rufus noticed when he walked into Archie's room was the weatherscope beside his bed. He eyed it suspiciously. If Huigor was still more than a day away, why was it spinning so fast?

Archie was already inside his cupboard, which was quite small being near the eaves of the house, and it didn't take him long to find a rolled-up handkerchief lodged above the doorframe. It was one of Jeffrey's handkerchiefs and something was wrapped inside it. He handed it to Rufus, who peeled back the dusty cotton to reveal a rather ordinary small black torch with two buttons – one red, the other green.

Archie couldn't help chanting excitedly, 'Yes, yes, yes!' but as he went to hold it Rufus maintained a tight grip.

His expression and the tone of his voice turned serious as he explained, 'You must not use the torch until the time is right and you are ready to do battle. As Huigor draws near its power will become active, triggered as the lost courage of your ancestors is reawakened. Do you understand?'

Archie nodded. 'I understand.'

'Good,' said Rufus. Then he wrapped the torch in the blue towel along with the flute and magnifying glass and returned them to the ledge above the door for safe-keeping. 'Now, that just leaves the key, the rabbit foot and the watch to find.'

Archie produced his map of the house and they began their search of every single cupboard. When they had finished they had found no more gifts.

Rufus tried to sound optimistic. 'The pocket watch is solid gold, and I don't believe for a minute your mother or father would have thrown anything that valuable away. The key is also gold, and the chain that holds the rabbit foot. So, where do you keep something valuable that no one will find?'

'In a safe?' said Archie.

'Exactly. And is there a safe in this house?'

'No.'

'Exactly. So . . . ?' Rufus was staring at Archie, waiting for the answer he so obviously knew.

Archie stared back, trying to make his tired and fuzzy brain come up with the right answer. Rufus was nodding encouragingly and then the answer popped into his head.

'Dad's bank!' he shouted excitedly. 'He's hiding them in a safe at the bank!'

# Chapter Twenty

'Very peculiar,' Ezekiel Arbuthnott was saying to himself as he tapped the barometer that hung on his hall wall. What he saw worried him enough to tap the glass again. The barometer hands wobbled a little but remained steadfastly pointing at a small white sticker he had placed on the glass with the words 'hurricane-force winds'.

'Very peculiar,' he said again and crossed over to the living-room window.

Out in the bay the sea was calm and a large white cloud moved sedately across the sky towards Moss Rock. There was nothing at all to suggest a hurricane was on its way. Ezekiel picked up his binoculars from the window sill and scanned the horizon. A fishing boat was returning to harbour, followed by one or two seagulls dipping and diving for fish scraps thrown overboard. He swung the telescope around to the right and caught sight of a school of porpoises playing in the sheltered waters of the bay.

'Very peculiar,' he said to his grey-striped cat, Marley, who was quietly sitting on a table beside him. He lowered the binoculars. 'Fancy some fresh air, Marley?' But as Ezekiel opened the window the fat cat gave a loud miaow in protest and jumped down to the floor. Ezekiel listened to its low growl as he shut the window, then walked over to a big armchair next to the fire and bent down as far as his stiff bones would let him. Beneath the chair Marley's frightened green eyes stared back at him.

'What's up, old boy?' Ezekiel asked. 'Something give you a fright?'

The cat growled and curled up tighter.

Ezekiel made a decision. 'I think I need to take myself out for a bicycle ride.'

Out in the hallway he put on his heavy black coat, flat cap and thick gloves. His bicycle was propped up against a scooter, and he grabbed the handlebars and pushed it out through the front door into the chilly morning air. The door slammed behind him, and he had taken only a couple of steps towards the gate when he was reminded of something. He turned and stared at the wind chime that hung from his garden tree. It was absolutely still. He looked up, squinting into the bright sunlight, and watched another white cloud moving across the blue sky.

'Very, very peculiar.'

He swung his leg over the bike crossbar and wobbled uncertainly down the path, ringing his bell as a warning to anyone approaching his garden gate, which was just as well because someone just happened to be walking up the pavement at that very moment.

'Good morning, Ezekiel,' she said. She was slightly breathless because she was carrying two bags of shopping, and was wearing a very large padded red jacket. Ezekiel didn't immediately recognise her because she was also wearing a sheepskin hat with earflaps that covered her head and half her face. In fact, it wasn't until she smiled and said, 'I thought our meeting yesterday went very well,' that he realised who the stranger was.

'Good morning, Cecille,' he said. 'Yes, we had a very good meeting and I have to say that husband of yours came up with some brilliant thinking. With a bit of luck we'll get enough donations of old lights to illuminate the whole village.'

'Here's hoping,' said Cecille. 'I've put notices up in all the shops. All we can do now is wait.'

Ezekiel looked up at the white cloud moving across the sky. 'You'll excuse me if I hurry away. Got some urgent business to attend to,' he said mysteriously.

Cecille looked up into the sky too. 'Lovely morning,' she said. 'Not a drop of wind and the snow's almost gone too. Except for around our house. Still piled up around the walls. Don't understand it.'

Ezekiel flicked his eyes from the sky to look at her. 'You say your house is still surrounded by snow?'

'Yes,' she said. 'Must have been an unusual direction of wind last night. Blew it all our way. I suppose that's why the house is called Windy Edge.'

'Wasn't always called Windy Edge,' said Ezekiel.

'It wasn't?' said Cecille.

'Oh, no,' said Ezekiel. 'It once belonged to a woman called Bella Simm. In those days it was called Ocean Breeze. Long time ago now, but in her day she sold fair winds to sailors.'

'She sold winds?' Cecille repeated, not quite believing what she was hearing.

'Fair winds,' he corrected her. 'That is, until the night of a great storm when one of the boats returning home was sunk just outside the bay. Everyone blamed her, accused her of being a witch. After she left the village the house was renamed Windy Edge. But it wasn't her fault, you see.' Ezekiel looked thoughtfully at Cecille for a moment before speaking again. 'Something to do with a curse,' he said, and he looked so deeply into her eyes her legs turned to jelly.

'A curse?' she whispered. Surely he wasn't referring to *their* curse. Nobody was supposed to know.

But Ezekiel didn't elaborate any more. He just climbed back up on to his bike as if a curse was the most normal thing in the world.

'Yes,' he said. 'You want to change the name of your house. It's a magnet for wind, that place.'

Cecille tried to disguise her anxiety by laughing off his words of warning. 'Nothing can change the wind. If it's going to blow, it's going to blow.'

'Perhaps,' said Ezekiel. He looked up into the sky again as another white cloud sailed overhead. 'I really must be going.' He rang his bell and waved as he set off down the hill. 'Hurricane's coming,' he called out as he tried not to wobble.

But Cecille didn't hear him. She was too busy watching a large white feather float down out of the sky and land gently across the toe of her boot.

# Chapter Twenty-one

The bank, where Jeffrey was manager, was situated on the north side of the village square, between the newsagent's and Mrs Grieve's bed-and-breakfast establishment. A small patch of grass in the centre of the square was taken up by a very large Christmas tree – about fifteen feet tall – and propped up in a large wooden barrel, supported by ropes, attached to two fencing posts.

Archie and Rufus walked up to the bank doors just after 11.00 a.m. and once inside found themselves at the end of a long queue of people waiting to be served. Archie sighed.

A voice close by misinterpreted his sigh. 'Not bored by the school holidays already, Archie?'

It was Karen, one of the bank employees. She was pinning up a notice about Christmas and New Year opening times on to one of the main doors. Her eyes looked enormous behind the strong lenses of her glasses, but then she noticed Rufus and she gave him his very own smile. He responded by showing a strong interest in the notice and even offered to push in one of the drawing pins for her.

At about the same time the security door opened and Mr Ratteray, the assistant bank manager, who was also George's father, walked out.

'Excuse me, Mr Ratteray,' said Archie, 'do you think I could see my dad for a minute?'

Mr Ratteray looked at Archie with the kind of preoccupied expression usually worn by someone dealing with an urgent problem, but then he was smiling and looking like George's dad again.

'Wait here,' he said. 'It's a busy time of year, but I know your father always makes time for you.' And after tapping out the security code he disappeared back through the door.

While they waited Archie was conscious of the attention Rufus's strange appearance was attracting. Some of the older customers were whispering to one another while unashamedly staring at his boots. Karen didn't seem in the least concerned by Rufus's hat or the fact he was wearing a Second World War flying jacket. Maybe it had something to do with her poor eyesight or the fact she never took her eyes off his face. Archie was glad when his father appeared at the security door, beaming and gesturing for them to enter.

Once inside Jeffrey's office, with the door firmly closed, Rufus took over.

'The reason we're here, Jeffrey, is because I need a safety deposit box and I'd rather you dealt with it. The items I want safe-keeping are of a delicate nature.'

'What do you mean by "delicate"? There are restrictions as to what is allowed in these boxes, Rufus.'

'When I say delicate, I mean . . . rare.'

'I see,' said Jeffrey. While he considered this information, he sat staring at a fountain pen he was rolling around in his fingers.

Archie and Rufus waited. Out in the corridor they heard a girlish laugh. Jeffrey stopped playing with the pen and looked at Rufus.

'Do you plan to visit Dad?'

Rufus was surprised at this unexpected question.

'It had crossed my mind,' he said calmly.

Jeffrey looked at Archie. 'I got a phone call this morning from Grandma. Grandpa's been taken to hospital. It's OK. Nothing too serious. Just a precaution.' Then he turned to Rufus, who was looking at him questioningly. 'Bad headaches. Hallucinations. Albatrosses, apparently.' He rolled the pen some more. 'He's been asking about you.'

Rufus nodded. 'I'll go and see him this afternoon.'

This seemed to satisfy Jeffrey, and with his mood lightened he placed the pen on his desk and stood up.

'Now that's settled let's get the paperwork sorted out. Then we can go down to the basement and put these "rarities" into a box.'

Archie had never been down to the bank basement before. He followed Rufus, who was following Jeffrey, along a cold, narrow, dimly lit corridor. There were no carpets on the floor, only squeaky grey linoleum, and the walls were painted a dull mustard colour. At the end of the corridor Jeffrey unlocked a metal door, and inside the strongroom switched on an overhead fluorescent light, which took a moment or two to spring into life. Archie was able to see about twenty small safes built into one wall, all of them locked.

'This is exciting, Dad,' said Archie. 'I wish we had one of those boxes to keep our valuables safe.' He kept his eyes on his father all the time, searching for some kind of clue, but Jeffrey didn't say a thing as he unlocked safe 338, and lifted out a strong metal box that he handed to Rufus.

Archie was determined not to give up. 'Owning something valuable doesn't mean it's worth lots of money,' he persisted. 'It could be something you don't want to lose. Or something you might really need in the future. Isn't that right, Dad?'

Jeffrey was looking at him now. Really looking, deep into his eyes.

'Is something worrying you, Archie?'

Archie shook his head. 'No.'

'You slept very late this morning. You feeling all right?'

Archie nodded.

Jeffrey bent down and brought his face close, which meant Archie could actually look over his shoulder and see what was going on in the room. The Scout had flown out of Rufus's rucksack and was now hovering in front of the wall safes. Rufus was placing something in his deposit box when the Scout began fluttering wildly in front of safe 333.

Archie felt his father's fingers on his cheek, guiding his face round to concentrate on what he was about to say next.

'Your mum told me something this morning,' Jeffrey began. 'She told me she found the backscratcher she gave me last Christmas lying on the floor by the window. Have you been in our room?'

Archie felt his face and his ears and his neck burn red. He nodded and gulped before saying, 'I . . . I . . . was looking for my presents.' Immediately he felt ashamed at telling his father a lie. But he decided it was only half a lie, because he had been looking for a present, only it just happened to be one of his birthday presents from Rufus and not his Christmas present. All the same, his father was still staring deep into his eyes.

'If you need to talk to me about anything, you know you can.'

'I know,' said Archie.

Jeffrey nodded and then he smiled and stood up straight again.

'Sid and George were in the bank this morning. Said they were drawing out some of their savings to buy Christmas presents. Have you bought your mother her present yet?'

Archie shook his head. Jeffrey put his hand into his trouser pocket and pulled out a twenty-pound note. 'Not much time left. Maybe you should think about doing some Christmas shopping. I know your mum has taken a fancy to a rather large chocolate frog in the bakery window.'

'Thanks, Dad,' and Archie threw his arms around Jeffrey's neck and gave him a great big hug for just being his dad.

'Finished,' Rufus announced from behind them. He slung his rucksack back on to his shoulder and Archie noticed the Scout had disappeared again.

As Jeffrey put the deposit box back into the wall safe, Archie wanted more than anything to tell him that in just one more day the curse of Huigor would be broken for ever, but instead he said, 'Do you still want to go to the top of Ork Hill in the spring and watch the sun set?'

Jeffrey finished locking the safe and turned to face him.

'Climb up Ork Hill? Did we arrange to do that? You know I'm not too good with heights, Archie.' He saw the look of disappointment on Archie's face. 'Course we'll go up Ork Hill,' and he gave a reassuring smile. 'Just as soon as the weather improves.'

But no amount of smiling could hide from Archie that his father had forgotten. And no amount of smiling could make Jeffrey feel better about it. He couldn't shrug off the feeling that he was a disappointment to Archie.

By the time Rufus had finished his business and he and Archie were walking towards the main door of the bank, Jeffrey was feeling extremely agitated, though he didn't know why. He stood on the bank steps watching them cross the square. Then he saw Rufus put a re-assuring hand on Archie's shoulder and he recognised what he felt – jealousy. He had the strongest feeling that Rufus and Archie were in some way involved in a secret pact. A subterfuge he had no part of and, perhaps more worryingly, something they did not *want* him a part of. As he waved goodbye he felt an unexpected fear, one he had never felt before. Could it be that Archie preferred Rufus to him?

When they were back outside the bank Archie said to

Rufus, 'I don't like telling Dad lies.'

'Only one more day,' said Rufus. 'Then you won't need to tell him another lie, ever.' He decided to cheer him up. 'Do you want to hear the good news?'

'What?'

'The Scout found your dad's deposit box.'

'I know,' Archie sighed. 'It's number 333.'

Rufus nodded. 'There's every indication that there's gold inside it.'

'The watch, the rabbit foot and the key?' Archie asked with new enthusiasm. 'How do we get them out?'

'Ah,' said Rufus. 'That's the bad news.' He looked around, checking they couldn't be overheard. 'You don't know any bank robbers, do you?'

Archie shook his head and looked worried.

'Thought not,' said Rufus. 'But not to worry. We're just going to have to come back when the bank closes and do a little night work. At least we know the layout of the basement and which is your father's safe.'

Archie was just about to ask Rufus what he had put into his own safety deposit box when a slushy snowball hit the back of his neck. He spun round, shaking the snow from his collar, and saw Sid and George trying their best to hide behind the Christmas tree, even though Sid was wearing a distinctive orange jacket and George a purple and yellow ski hat.

'Why don't you go and spend some time with your

friends, Archie?' said Rufus. 'Do some Christmas shopping.'

Archie didn't look too sure.

'Don't worry about a thing,' said Rufus. 'Leave it all up to me.'

Another snowball landed close by.

'OK,' said Archie.

'Just keep your eyes and ears open,' Rufus advised him. 'Watch out for rogue winds and don't take unnecessary risks.' He looked at his watch. 'Let's rendezvous at Windy Edge at 3.00 p.m. and set our plan of action for tonight. Now go and have some fun.'

Archie didn't need too much encouragement and he ran towards the two figures laughing behind the tree. If he had stopped and given a backwards look he would have seen Rufus walking along the pavement in the direction of Windy Edge, his head bent low, hands in his jacket pockets and looking very worried indeed. He would also have caught sight of Ezekiel riding by on his bicycle, keeping a watchful eye on the clouds as he cycled down to the harbour. And he might just have seen a particularly strong gust of wind rise up out of nowhere and send the church weathervane spinning full circle.

# Chapter Twenty-two

Sid and George still hadn't got round to doing their Christmas shopping. George found wandering around the shops boring and Sid just couldn't make up his mind what to buy. With a total budget of twenty pounds and six presents to find, his choice was limited. By the time they met up with Archie they had been hanging around waiting for something to happen.

'Who's that you were with?' George wanted to know.

'My Uncle Rufus.'

'Looks a bit strange.'

'He's an explorer.'

Sid was impressed. George pretended not to be.

'Where's he been?

'Everywhere.'

'Has he been to Norrie Bews's boatshed?'

Archie didn't think so.

'Another window's blown in,' George told him. 'Want to have a look?'

Archie shrugged and said, 'OK,' while behind him he heard Sid give a worried sigh.

Norrie Bews's boatshed was a wooden hut with a curved tin roof. It stood at the head of a boat-launching slip and the most unusual thing about it was the colour: a dirty, flaking purple, with a thick layer of tar beneath the paint. The story went that when Norrie Bews got too old to build rowing boats he locked up the shed one night and never set foot in it again. Over the years the window frames had rotted and some of the glass had been blown in, but because Norrie was a distant relative, George felt quite entitled to break in now and again.

This was how he did it. On one side of the boatshed was a padlocked door opening on to a paved pier. On the other side of the shed was a ten-inch ledge that dropped down to the sea. If it was low tide and you fell, you hit the pebble beach. At high tide you fell straight into a sea that was so deep you couldn't see the bottom. It was high tide.

Archie and Sid stood watching George ease himself along the narrow ledge, push aside some wooden planks and disappear inside the shed.

'He's just showing off,' Sid complained.

They waited and then George appeared at a window close to where they stood. His face looked distorted and grey behind twenty years of grime, but his eyes came into sharp focus as he peered out of a hole in the glass.

'Bet your Uncle Rufus wouldn't be scared to come in.'

Sid looked anxiously at Archie. Archie stared at George. 'Who said anything about being scared?'

'I'm staying here,' Sid decided. 'That shed's haunted.'

Archie stepped on to the narrow ledge. Up ahead George's head appeared through the loose planks.

'Scared?'

Archie shook his head. He was determined not to lose his nerve, but as he edged closer to where George was waiting for him, a familiar cold chill gripped the back of his neck. 'Oh, no,' he said to himself, but there was no time to turn back. He held on to a rusting window-sill and closed his eyes. From around the corner of the shed the wind came rushing off the sea towards him, blowing his jacket hood across one side of his face. He felt his fingers being pulled from the window and his trousers flap against his legs. All he could do was keep his head down and wait. He could hear Sid telling him to hold on above the sound of the sea rising up and slapping the pier close to his ankles, and then he heard the wind laugh.

'Go away!' he told it. 'I'm not scared of you!'

The next instant he felt George's hand on his arm and the wind died. Together they edged towards the hole in the shed wall and crawled inside.

'Where did that wind come from?' George asked as he looked through a window on to the flat calm sea.

A loud knocking made them both jump. At the opposite end of the shed Sid was peering through the broken window. He put his mouth to the hole in the glass and shouted, 'I told you there were ghosts. They were stopping you getting into the shed.'

'You don't get ghosts in the morning,' said George, but even so he gave the gloomy shed a sweeping glance. So did Archie. There wasn't much to see: a few dusty planks of wood; a rotting canvas sailor's bag; a work-bench piled high with old newspapers, rusting nails and a mallet. There was the smell of wood, decay, neglect and of unknown times long gone. For Archie, ghosts of some sort lingered. He didn't intend staying long and, unusually, George had the same idea. George picked up the mallet. 'Let's see if we can open the door on to the pier. Then we won't have to go back along the ledge.'

The door was padlocked on the outside, but the bolt holding it shut had grown loose over the years. George began hitting the door and splinters of rotting wood flew out.

'One more whack should do it,' he was saying, when they heard the high-pitched wail.

George stopped hammering and turned to look at Archie. 'What was that?'

170

'It's the ghost,' said Sid through the broken window. 'It's back!'

'I'm getting out of here,' said George, and he began kicking at the door with his foot.

Behind him he heard Archie say, 'Oh, no.'

George turned, and what he saw made him drop the mallet. Archie's hair was rising up from his scalp and his eyes were darting around as if searching for something he couldn't see. But worse was to come. A strong gust of wind lifted the newspapers from the bench and started blowing them around inside the shed.

'Gho . . . o . . . ost,' George said, and he began kicking at the door, over and over again in terrified desperation. When it still wouldn't open he dashed across the shed towards the open planks in the wall and climbed out on to the ledge. Archie tried following him, but the wind pushed him backwards into the mass of blowing newspapers. He went to pull the dagger from his coat pocket, but the rogue gust pinned his arms to his sides and he felt himself being spun round on the spot. As the wind grew stronger, the faster he went, until he was spinning like a top.

Sid gave a horrified yell through the broken window, but Archie couldn't hear him. His ears were filled with a piercing wail that was the wind's voice. *'Be warned . . .'* he heard it say. He tried calling out to George, but he could hardly breathe. He was beginning to think the wind was never going to let him go when he stopped spinning. He was so dizzy he could hardly stand, and he couldn't focus properly either. Everything was still going round and round, including Sid's horrified face staring at him through the window. Out of the corner of his eye he saw the newspapers take the shape of a wave and he knew the wind wasn't finished with him. He found himself being pushed roughly across the shed, with his arms still pinned to his sides. This time he screamed.

George had managed to safely negotiate the ledge. Though his first instinct was to run, he wasn't going to leave Archie behind. Particularly now he was screaming for help.

Sid was still peering through the broken window. 'It's going to bash him against the wall!'

'Come on!' said George. 'We've got to get the door open.'

They ran around the shed and were met with the sound of an almighty crash as the doors burst open. Moments later Archie was blown out in a maelstrom of newspapers, staggering disorientatedly and heading dangerously close to the edge of the pier. George grabbed his arm and Archie found his own hand pulled back just far enough to reach the dagger in his pocket.

He gripped it and the wind screamed angrily. He was spun round once more, the shed door slammed shut and in another piercing wail the wind was gone. Archie was left reeling at the edge of the pier. His vision was double, his ears were ringing and he felt sick. As he began to refocus, he was aware of a man standing watching him from the other side of the harbour, and as the man slowly lowered a pair of binoculars from his eyes, Archie saw it was Ezekiel. Archie took a shaky step forward and heard a warning gasp from Sid and George. He realised he was now balancing precariously on the edge of the pier. He staggered backwards and turned to see George and Sid staring at him, both wearing a look of absolute terror.

'Run!' said Sid, and his wellington boots slapped against his legs as he tore up the pier towards the safety of the shops.

George stood his ground, but a low moan from inside the shed soon changed his mind.

'Let's get out of here!' he shouted.

Archie didn't argue. He would have preferred a ghost to the rogue wind that had just tried to push him into the sea, but he couldn't tell George that. He began to run, as fast as his unsteady legs would carry him, up to the top of the alleyway to where Sid was waiting for them, wide-eyed and scared.

'See! I told you there were ghosts.' Then, to cover up the fact he was the first to run away, Sid announced, 'I saw its face staring at us through the shed window. It was like a skeleton with bits of skin hanging off it.'

That did it. There was a brief scuffle as all three jostled to get as far away as quickly as possible. They raced along the street towards the safety of the Sweet Stuff shop and it was agreed they would never go near Norrie Bews's boatshed again, but for Archie that was the least of his fears. The rogue gust had been much stronger than any of the other gusts and its force far scarier than he could have imagined. Clutching the dagger had helped him escape this time, but how much protection would it give against the full might of a powerful tornado?

# Chapter Twenty-three

Cecille had learned a worrying piece of news in the charity shop that morning. She was still thinking about it as she placed the bags of shopping on the kitchen table, walked back into the hall and called up the stairs.

'Archie?'

When no answer came Cecille climbed up to his bedroom, but she found it empty. To distract herself from worrying she picked up an old dusty handkerchief lying on the floor and laid it on top of a pile of clothes on the chair. She was about to run downstairs again when she noticed the paperweight on the table by the bed. The gold moon and star shapes inside it were spinning. She picked it up and shook it, expecting the planets to spin faster, but they continued at the same steady pace. Shivers crawled up her spine.

Cecille ran back down to the kitchen and looked out of the window. The only semblance of human life was the snowman looking back at her from the thick layer of snow covering the ground. The only sound to be heard was next-door's barking dog.

She walked back into the hall. 'Rufus?'

Her voice seemed to echo throughout the empty house. What was it Ezekiel had said? A house once lived in by a woman who sold fair winds to sailors. A woman who had been branded a witch. Shivers crawled up her spine again.

Then the telephone rang, and Cecille gave a nervous jump. Still shaking, she answered it and her face froze as she listened to the voice at the other end. She tried interrupting the caller.

'I've already told you . . . No! I forbid you to talk to Jeffrey. Revealing information of that nature will benefit no one. Our lives are difficult enough already . . . What difference can it make? The future is sealed . . . What do you mean you wish I would listen? Wishes solve nothing . . . If you call again I shall report you to the police. *Goodbye*, Professor Himes.'

She put down the phone and discovered a large black mark on the palm of her right hand. Immediately she swung round and looked through the open living-room door to the fireplace which was laid, ready to be lit that night. Clumps of soot lay on the kindling. She wiped the handset with the sleeve of her coat and began pacing the hall, giving the phone an uneasy glance as though afraid it might ring again. When the grandfather clock chimed 11.45 she yelped nervously. To stop her heart pounding she took a deep calming breath and resolved to put the call out of her mind – and the fact that someone with sooty hands had been using the phone while she'd been out. That someone, she decided, could only be Rufus. Why had he been messing around with the fire? There was also the matter of the backscratcher she'd found lying on their bedroom floor. She'd assumed Archie had been snooping, but could it have been Rufus?

The grandfather clock whirled and wheezed and clanked. 'Have to get that fixed,' she said. Then she took a look around the peeling paintwork in the hall, the faded wallpaper and the worn carpet. 'Everything needs fixing,' she sighed.

That's when she noticed the open door to the cupboard under the stairs. She pushed it, but when it wouldn't close she opened the door fully and looked inside. What she saw made her heart miss a beat. *The cupboard had been tidied.*

The bag of shoe polish was hanging on a hook and all the shoes and wellies were placed side by side *in matching pairs.*

'Somebody's been snooping around in here,' she said to herself. 'And I know who that person is.'

She tiptoed downstairs to the basement and knocked

gently on Rufus's bedroom door.

'Rufus? Are you in there?'

Silence followed, so she opened the door. At first she just popped her head into the room and took a look around. His bed was made although two unfinished glasses of water were on his bedside table. The room had a pink glow to it, from daylight shining through the unopened red curtains. She told herself she wasn't snooping but that the room needed airing. She went in, opened the curtains, and they promptly slid off the curtain rail. She clicked her tongue in irritation before sliding the window open a few inches. Then she picked up a glass from the bedside table and gave the room another sweeping glance. What was she looking for? She didn't know, any more than she knew what Rufus had been searching for in the under-stairs cupboard; because she felt sure he was the culprit. Who else would have tidied it up? Then a thought crossed Cecille's mind. Had Archie been searching with him? Was Archie part of this conspiracy? Anxiety gripped her stomach.

She had to do something and that something was to open the bedside-table drawer. Inside was a brown leather-backed book the size of a paperback. It had to be a diary. She put the glass back down on the table and picked up the book, while wondering what she might read if she dared to open it. But first she would take another quick look around the room, just in case she found anything else of interest.

Cecille opened the wardrobe, which was empty. All the clothes Rufus had borrowed from Jeffrey were piled up on a chair. She got down on her knees and looked under the bed and felt completely foolish when she found nothing more than a torn sock. To make matters worse it was pink with red hearts on it and belonged to one of her nieces, which meant it had been lying there since last summer. She was just getting back up on to her feet when she heard the front door slam.

'Archie,' she said, her voice full of relief as she ran out of the room and up the stairs. 'Archie?' she called hopefully.

But it was Rufus who stood in the hall, and he was alone.

'Where's Archie?' she asked, trying to keep the panic out of her voice.

'He went off with a couple of his friends.'

'What friends?'

'I don't know. He didn't introduce them.'

'You left him to just walk away with strangers?'

'Not strangers . . . friends.' Rufus was demonstrating how tall they were by holding his hand against his chest but Cecille was ignoring him.

'Where were they going?' she demanded.

'I don't know. But they looked nice kids.'

'You didn't ask where they were going?

'They can't go far in a village this size.'

'You abandoned Archie?' The level of Cecille's voice was rising, but it was the look in her eyes that troubled Rufus. He had seen some strange and disconcerting sights on his travels around the world but he had never seen a woman contain so much anxiety. He thought if he could just get her to listen to him he might be able to calm her down with his eye stare, in much the same way as he'd managed to calm the barking dog next door.

'Cecille, don't you think you might be over-reacting?'

But Cecille was having none of it; she wouldn't even look at him as she tossed her head first one way and then the other as the tirade continued. Definitely a savannah lion, thought Rufus. She was still wearing her furry hat with the earflaps and they were flying all over the place each time she moved her head.

'Why have you come back, anyway?' she demanded. 'Nine years and then POP!' At this point the flaps shot up straight above her head like a pair of rabbit ears. Rufus might have considered laughing if she'd not been so angry. Her voice had also developed a very disconcerting shriek.

'You appear from out of nowhere,' she was saying. 'No warning. Why can't you arrive for a visit like nor-

180

mal people? Why does it have to be the dead of night?'

'Eleven thirty, I think –' Rufus tried to say.

'And no luggage either. Oh, far too conventional for the likes of you. No, instead we have to have some cock-and-bull story about it going to France. Well, I've got news for you.' She wagged her head knowingly. 'The airport was closed on Saturday, so you couldn't have flown in. That great long story was a great long lie. Start to finish.'

One of the flaps on her hat had become lodged across the top of her head. Rufus tried very hard not to think of her as some kind of furry animal caught down-wind. To add to his discomfort he also had the problem of trying not to laugh. Cecille seemed to interpret his lip-biting silence as an indication of some kind of guilt, and she raised her chin in indignation.

'So come on, Rufus, own up. Why are you here? What's in it for you? What are you hiding?'

If Cecille was expecting Rufus to be unnerved by her outburst she was mistaken. He was infuriatingly calm.

'There's always somebody hiding something. Isn't that so, Cecille?'

Her voice dropped. 'What are you talking about?'

'I remembered the name of the man from Exeter. The one I met in Botswana. Who said he knew you.'

She didn't reply but Rufus knew through her silence that she remembered clearly.

'Well,' he continued. 'Now let me get this right . . . his name is Professor Neville Himes. He runs a small company tracing family trees. After we were introduced he asked if I was any relation to Cecille Caine, who was married to Jeffrey Stringweed of Westervoe, Scotland.'

Still Cecille showed no reaction, though Rufus did think her cheeks had turned a deeper shade of pink.

'Well, it seems you had asked him to trace your family tree and in doing so he discovered we Stringweeds and you Caines have something in common.'

'What's this got to do with my family? What are you saying? Why are you trying to frighten me with all your weird ideas?'

'No one is trying to frighten you. What you fear is the truth.'

'Truth? That's rich coming from you!'

'Professor Himes phoned me this morning. He told me he had made it perfectly clear to you what you must do.'

'I don't know anyone by that name –'

'I believe he has tried explaining to you the reason behind your overprotective behaviour towards Archie. It's in your blood; you can't help it. But you *can* help him by acknowledging the past and speaking the truth. No one can do it for you. You see, the curse is affecting you too –'

'Curse? I don't know what you're talking about. I'm

not listening to this,' Cecille said dismissively.

'It's in Archie's interest that you listen, and as his godfather, I –'

'Archie has a *real* father. And a very good one too. Anything he needs he gets from Jeffrey. He was here doing his fatherly duties all those years you were off holidaying across the world. Weren't too bothered about your godfather duties then, were you?'

Rufus stared at her. 'And what about your duties as a mother? Do they include sacrificing your son's future because you refuse to acknowledge the past?'

'I don't need your advice,' snapped Cecille. 'If you're really concerned about Archie's welfare, go out and look for him. If he *has* gone missing I'll hold you responsible. You can take the Land Rover, and don't come back without him.'

Rufus thought that was probably the most sensible thing to do. It would give Cecille time to calm down and also to finish snooping around in his bedroom. He held out his hand towards her.

'The car keys are on the hook behind the door,' she sniffed.

Rufus continued to hold out his hand. Cecille looked at it and then at her own, which still held the torn pink sock that had been lying under the bed downstairs for at least six months, but it was the item in her other hand that finally rendered her speechless with embarrassment. She took four stately steps forward and, without looking Rufus in the eye, placed the leather-bound diary in his palm. Then she turned and walked away in an equally regal manner into the kitchen. She stood just behind the kitchen door and waited while Rufus went downstairs to return the diary to his room and then walked back upstairs again.

'Speak the truth, Cecille,' she heard him say. 'Help Archie rise above the ordinary.'

Only when he had picked up the car keys and the front door had slammed shut behind him did Cecille allow herself to collapse on to a kitchen chair, and to vent her frustration she clasped the sock between her teeth and ripped it like some mad long-eared animal.

# Chapter Twenty-four

George and Sid had recovered from their ghostly encounter at Norrie Bews's boatshed. George had bought himself two packets of toffees and as he opened the second packet he felt his usual bravado return. Sid, being on a tight budget, was still sucking the one toffee George had offered him, while wishing he hadn't been the first to run away. Archie, meantime, was keeping a nervous eye open for any more rogue gusts of wind.

They were standing in front of the baker's shop window, admiring a large chocolate frog. George gave a whistle of approval, for it was indeed a very handsome fellow. It was covered in green shiny foil and sat majestically on a green felt leaf, wearing a rather smart red velvet waistcoat and a golden crown at a jaunty angle. Archie could see why his mother liked it.

George and Sid waited outside while Archie went in, because Mr Ashburn, the baker, had barred them from the shop earlier that morning for meddling with the decorations on top of the Christmas cakes.

'Bad luck for two days if you catch sight of his gold filling,' Sid said as Archie walked into the shop.

The shop was so small that any more than six customers and you had to queue out on the pavement regardless of the weather. A glass display case, which also served as the counter, ran the entire length of the shop. Inside were eight different kinds of loaves, sliced on the premises if requested, five different kinds of bread rolls and the usual pancakes and scones, but cakes were Mr Ashburn's speciality. Framed certificates of baking excellence hung on the walls behind the counter, and a large colour photograph of Mr Ashburn presenting the Prince of Wales with a cake on a visit to the shop in 1982 hung above the till.

'Morning, Master Stringweed,' said a much older Mr Ashburn than was evident in the photograph. 'What can I get for you today?'

'I'd like the chocolate frog with the gold crown,' said Archie. Then he remembered his manners and added, 'Please.'

Mr Ashburn smiled, but thankfully kept his mouth closed, thereby hiding any evidence of the gold-filled tooth. He wasn't a young man and he wasn't particularly slim, but he managed a complicated upper-body twist that would have had a champion ballroom dancer green with envy as he fished the frog out of the window display and placed it on the counter in front of Archie. He straightened his bleached white apron and smiled another closed-mouth smile beneath a neatly trimmed grey moustache.

'A fine specimen of an amphibian,' he said, tapping the frog's head gently. 'Seventy per cent cocoa solids. Came all the way from France, that frog. The only one in the shop. Yes, a superior mould of chocolate for those of a discerning taste. Not that you get many of them round here.' He flicked a disgusted glance towards Sid and George, who had their faces squashed up tight against the window. Then he turned his attention back to his beloved chocolate frog. 'And I do believe there is a surprise gift inside for the lucky recipient.'

'It's for my mum,' said Archie.

'For your mum, is it? In that case . . .' and Mr Ashburn twisted and stretched his arm into the window display again and fished out a small chocolate angel wrapped in gold paper. 'With my compliments. Every mum is an angel on Christmas morning.'

'Thank you very much, Mr Ashburn.'

'A pleasure, Archie. Always a pleasure to serve you. Unlike those two scallywags out there. You want to keep away from that pair until they learn some manners.' And he made a big show of waving them away from his window.

'That'll be seven pounds ninety-nine. You'll be wanting a carrier bag too, I suppose?'

Archie nodded and watched him place the chocolates carefully in the bag. Then he waited as Mr Ashburn began to count out the change from the twenty-pound note into the palm of his hand.

'Seven pounds and ninety-nine . . . and one pence makes eight. And a pound makes nine and another pound makes ten.'

The ten-pound note he held to ransom in the air just above Archie's hand.

'Be sure to pass on my season's greetings to your father. The greetings of a small business should never be underestimated by the financial services. Remember, Archie, the bakery is the heart of a small community.'

Archie didn't have a clue what he was talking about but he nodded anyway. Mr Ashburn smiled again and this time an uneven set of teeth appeared between his lips and the moustache. Archie quietly said, 'NO!' to himself, but Mr Ashburn's mouth spread into an even wider smile and a glint of gold flashed from out of the top left side of his mouth. Archie groaned inwardly with disappointment. Two days of bad luck was the last thing he needed. So disappointed was Archie in catching sight of the elusive gold tooth that he hardly felt the ten-pound note fall into his hand.

'Yes, Archie,' Mr Ashburn was saying, 'you be sure

and tell your father that frog came all the way from Paris, France.' And he flashed another gold-toothed smile.

George and Sid were leaning against the chemist's shop window when Archie caught up with them. Blue, red and gold ribbons adorned the inside of the glass, which was edged with coloured flashing Christmas lights, while a plastic Santa Claus waved and nodded between bottles of perfume on the one side and aftershave on the other. Archie noticed that Santa's beard had fallen loose at one side. It just reminded him of his own newly acquired bad luck.

'Did you see it?' Sid asked excitedly.

'Twice,' said Archie desolately.

George gave one of his accomplished whistles and Archie's desolation was complete.

'Double bad luck,' whooped Sid and he danced in a circle, his arms above his head.

Archie put his hand in his pocket and his fingers touched the dagger handle. He felt a surge of bravery run up his arm and into his chest. It wasn't fair that George could whistle when he couldn't, and he didn't like Sid dancing in triumph as a result of his own double bad luck.

'No!' Archie shouted above the whooping and dancing.

Sid stopped dancing, his arms still above his head. 'What?'

'I'm not putting up with any more bad luck. I'm not letting anyone tell me I've got bad luck. I'm not!'

'It was only a joke, Archie.'

'You shouldn't make jokes about bad luck. It's serious. Anything could happen when you give people bad luck. They could have an accident. Or die.'

'Only if you believe it,' said George. He was chewing on a toffee and was in the process of unwrapping another. 'Everyone knows bad luck doesn't really exist.'

'How do you know?' asked Archie. 'What do you know about bad luck?'

'It's only superstition. My gran told me people who believe in bad luck make bad luck.'

'Really?' said Archie hopefully. 'So is it the same for curses? They only exist if you believe in them?'

'Curses?' said George and he thought about it for a minute as he pulled the toffee free of his teeth. 'Aaaaaah, I'm not sure. But I would definitely think so. Why?'

'Nothing,' said Archie quickly. 'Just wondering.'

A thick spray of dirty slush covered his boots as a bicycle wheel skidded to a halt directly in front of him. It was Brian Bain, younger brother of Stewart, who worked at the bank. Brian stretched out a leg and placed his foot on the wall next to Archie's head to balance himself while remaining seated on the bike.

'What you kids up to?' he asked before taking a swig from a can of fizzy drink.

'Nothing,' said George.

'What you got in the carrier bag?' he asked Archie.

'My mum's Christmas present.'

'What is it?'

Archie was just considering telling him to mind his own business when . . .

'It's a chocolate frog,' said Sid, who didn't want any trouble.

'What kind of Christmas present is that?' Brian spat a mouthful of saliva over his shoulder in disgust. 'I'm getting my mum a sandwich toaster.' He took another swig of something orange that fizzed and crackled in the tin, then he wiped his mouth on the sleeve of his fleece. From the layer of encrusted stains, it looked as if he had wiped a week's worth of breakfast, lunch and dinner on it. After another over-the-shoulder spit he asked Archie, 'What you getting your dad?'

'Don't know.'

'Can I make a suggestion?'

'If you want.'

'When you go down to Porky Simpson's to get your turkey, ask him to make up a big bag of guts for your dad as well.'

He took a last swig from the can, dropped it on the

pavement next to Archie's feet and threw his head back to laugh loudly at his own wit. Archie curled his fingers into a tight fist and was ready to use it when a huge lump of black slime with a greenish tinge landed on Brian Bain's face. The laughing stopped abruptly and Brian threw his bike aside while he retched and spat and retched and spat.

'What was that?' he screeched as he finished wiping the slime on to his sleeve.

'Bird shit,' said Sid, marvelling at the size of it.

George was trying not to laugh. 'An ostrich by the look of it.'

Archie, meanwhile, was looking up into the sky, carefully watching a huge white cloud like a giant iceberg looming over the rooftops above them. It was a strange-looking cloud that seemed to shimmer and flicker with flashes of green and it turned the air icy cold as a huge grey shadow fell across the village. Archie uncurled his tight fist and opened his hand in time to catch a single falling white feather.

# Chapter Twenty-five

Rufus was approaching the bottom of the hill in Jeffrey's old Land Rover. He was about to turn left on to Main Street, which ran along the sea front, when a huge cloud drifting out across the bay distracted him. The cloud was brilliant white and as Rufus stared at it he caught odd flashes of fluorescent green.

'The reinforcements are arriving early,' he said to himself. 'The signs are not good.' So preoccupied was he that on turning the corner he found himself heading towards a rather unsteady Ezekiel riding his bicycle on the wrong side of the road. Rufus braked hard. Ezekiel wobbled some more. Rufus veered the car to the opposite side of the road. Ezekiel toppled off the bike. Rufus jumped out of the car, and by the time he reached him, Ezekiel had managed to raise himself into a sitting position, his bike lying beside him with its wheels spinning at a leisurely pace.

'Are you OK?' Rufus asked. 'Anything broken?'

Ezekiel shook his head and began mumbling incoherently.

'Tell me again,' Rufus said. 'But a bit slower this time.'

Ezekiel looked up at him. His hat was slightly askew and he had a patch of dust down the side of his cheek, but it was the look of nervous excitement in his eyes that concerned Rufus the most.

'It's coming,' he wheezed.

'What's coming?' Rufus asked.

'Tornado,' Ezekiel gasped. 'Tonight.'

Rufus decided to ignore the comment and carefully raised Ezekiel on to his feet. Once he was sitting in the front seat of the Land Rover Rufus fixed the bicycle on the roof rack. Then they set off along the narrow street, but when they pulled up at the medical centre Ezekiel was quite adamant that he wasn't going in.

'I haven't let a doctor near me in thirty years. If I go in now I'll never get home alive.'

Nothing Rufus could say would make him change his mind, so they drove onwards towards the village square, where Rufus could turn the car around. That's when he noticed Archie, standing in front of the chemist's with Sid, George and Brian Bain. He stopped the car and wound down the window.

'Where are you going?' Archie asked Rufus. He was looking suspiciously at Ezekiel's dirty face and then at

Rufus's concerned expression. He couldn't help but notice the bike on the roof rack too.

'Ezekiel took a tumble from his bike,' Rufus explained. 'I'm taking him home.' Then he noticed the fluorescent-green stain on Brian Bain's cheek. 'What's that on your face?'

'Giant bird droppings,' said George, laughing. 'This big,' and he spread his hands wide.

Brian Bain was furious at being laughed at, which worried Sid. To calm the situation he announced, 'Being dropped on by a bird is supposed to be good luck.'

Brian didn't look any happier, especially now that Rufus was leaning out of the car window for a closer look and saying, 'You've been targeted.'

'Targeted? What do you mean?' Brian demanded.

'I'd stay inside for a day or two if I was you,' Rufus told him. 'Good chance of it happening again.' Then he turned his attention back to Archie, who was smiling at the prospect of Brian being targeted again.

'Better jump in,' Rufus advised. 'Your mother sent me to find you. Looks like we're both in trouble.'

Archie's smile disappeared. 'Why do I have to go home?' he complained.

'Archie's mum never allows him to go anywhere without her,' George announced. Then he turned to Brian. 'She thinks he's still a scared baby.'

'Like his dad!' said Brian.

'I'm not a scared baby!' said Archie. 'I'm a lot braver than you are because I'm going to break the cur—' Archie stopped as Rufus gave a surprised gasp.

'Break what?' asked George. 'What did you say you're going to break?'

Archie realised he'd almost given away the secret. 'Nothing,' he said sheepishly. 'I'm going home.' He got into the back seat and just before pulling the door shut said, 'I'll see you later.'

'If your mammy lets you, scared baby,' Brian was shouting as the car pulled away.

Rufus looked in the car wing mirror. Brian Bain was laughing again, holding his stomach and swaying theatrically. Sid looked very unimpressed and George was now looking guiltily towards the moving Land Rover. Brian carried on laughing, throwing his head back and opening his mouth wide just in time for another huge lump of bird droppings, bigger than the last one, to land smack in his mouth. Rufus smiled with satisfaction.

'I *hate* Brian Bain,' Archie announced very loudly. 'I am never, ever going to speak to him again in my whole entire life. Or George Ratteray.'

Rufus was just about to say something appropriately reassuring when an unexpected voice spoke up from the front passenger seat.

'They'll soon come running.'

Ezekiel eased himself round in his seat and his hat fell further over his face so that he was looking at Archie with only one eye.

'You only get the one shot at it.'

'One shot at what?' Archie asked.

'Breaking the curse.'

All thoughts of Brian Bain and George were gone as Ezekiel continued to hold Archie's attention with his staring eye.

'I've seen that tornado with me own eyes, and let me tell you . . . it's *mean*.'

Goosebumps ran all the way up Archie's neck and across his scalp. He looked at Rufus's reflection in the rearview mirror and said, 'He knows about Huigor?'

Rufus nodded and pulled the car up in front of Ezekiel's house.

Between them they lifted the bike down from the roof rack and helped Ezekiel inside. Archie waited while Rufus propped the bicycle up against an old green scooter at the bottom of the stairs. Through the living-room door he could see a very large cat lying asleep on an armchair beside the fire. It opened one suspicious green eye, had a good look at them all and then closed it again.

'What did I tell you?' Ezekiel was saying as he tapped the barometer with the tips of his fingers. 'The needle's dropped again. Expect hurricane-force winds.

That barometer's never been wrong in forty years. And that's not all. The cat won't go out and there's clouds crossing the sky without a drop of wind. And fishermen down at the harbour say nothing's moving near Moss Rock. Even the gulls have gone. I went over to the beach and the seaweed is bone dry. There's a storm coming all right. But it's the tornado you've got to watch out for.'

Rufus's expression gave nothing away as he stared at the barometer. He tried tapping it with his own fingers but still it continued to point at the white sticker with the words 'hurricane-force winds'.

Rufus turned to Ezekiel and asked, 'What do you know of the tornado?'

'Follow me,' said Ezekiel, and they trooped into the living room. Every surface was covered in books, charts and maps. Ezekiel cleared a space on the table by the window, hooked a pair of reading glasses around his ears and took a large scrapbook from out of the table drawer. He opened it to the first page, which contained a newspaper cutting with a photograph, dated 15th June 1976. The headline read: 'FISHING BOAT MYSTERIOUSLY REAPPEARS AFTER 17 YEARS.'

Rufus began to read the article.

'*Mystery still surrounds the reappearance of the* Megan Star, *which disappeared on a fishing trip seventeen years ago. The boat was found floating two miles north of Moss Rock late on Saturday night. Police are not discounting the theory that its reappearance may have some connection with the freak weather conditions that hit the area that evening.*

*'Local teacher Ezekiel Arbuthnott, who had been fishing in the vicinity at the time of the tornado, told the* Courier, *"I believe the* Megan Star *was sunk by the same tornado seventeen years ago."'*

Ezekiel shook his fist at the newspaper cutting.

'That tornado had no business being there in mid-June. It blew up from out of nowhere. Picked up the boat from the bottom of the sea and tossed it around like a feather.'

'But that's impossible,' said Rufus.

'Saw it with my own eyes. I'd been out near Moss Rock picking up creels and was heading back. The sun had set, but I got a good look at it rearing up out of the water without so much as a splash. When it was gone, there was the *Megan Star* on the surface. Put the outboard motor on full and chased the tornado inshore.' Ezekiel looked at Archie. 'It spun around the house your grandma and grandad lived in at the time. Thought it was going to take the roof off.'

'You say it came out of the water?' said Rufus incredulously.

'That's right. Like a big ugly black sea snake.' Ezekiel pointed to the newspaper article. 'They thought I was crazy. But nobody else could come up with another explanation.'

He pulled out a home-made chart from under a pile of papers, spread it open and pointed to a date in black ink.

'March the seventh, 1916. A freak tornado hits Westervoe. Two days after the tenth birthday of Stanley Stringweed. That was your great-grandfather, Archie.'

He pointed to another date on the chart. 'Twenty-fifth of May, 1946. Tornado hits the day after your grandpa's tenth birthday, and the last time it struck: thirteenth of June, 1976. The day of your father's tenth birthday. All of them first-born Stringweed sons.'

Ezekiel looked at Archie over the top of his glasses. 'Then I remembered something very odd happening to your grandpa. We'd been out on the cliffs looking for gull eggs on his tenth birthday. He was scrambling over them rocks like a spider. The next thing I know, he won't come out of the house because he's frightened of the wind. Says it's talking to him. After that he was nervous of everything. And your dad? He was swimming around in the open sea like a fish one day, but wouldn't dip his big toe in once he turned ten. I reckoned you Stringweeds were cursed. And it had something to do with the wind.'

Ezekiel looked at Rufus. 'That's why you've come back, isn't it? You're going to sort it out once and for all, and I'd like to offer you my assistance.'

Rufus was impressed. 'You've certainly done your homework, Ezekiel, and I congratulate you, but how do you think you can help us?'

'I can keep an oil light burning and I can say a prayer for you.'

'Aaah,' said Rufus, who was trying hard not to sound ungrateful, while realising he would have to go back to Plan A, which was that night's bank robbery.

'Yes, you'll need a lamp burning when the tornado appears tonight,' Ezekiel concluded.

'No. Not tonight,' said Archie. 'Tomorrow. After sunset.'

'Oh, no,' said Ezekiel. 'Most definitely tonight.'

Archie looked at Rufus, who was nodding thoughtfully. 'There are indications to that effect.'

'Was that what the phone call was about this morning?' Archie asked.

Rufus showed no surprise that Archie knew about the call. He just nodded his head. 'And I saw troop reinforcements flying in towards Moss Rock. They're a day early.'

'But it can't be tonight!' said Archie. 'It can't be. I'm not ready!'

# Chapter Twenty-six

Cecille had made up her mind. She would give Archie another thirty seconds and if he'd still not walked through the door by then she was phoning Jeffrey. Another ten seconds passed, by which time her concern was almost unbearable. She picked up the phone and dialled the bank.

'Jeffrey? Archie's gone missing.'

'He can't be missing,' he said wearily. 'He was here in the bank with Rufus a couple of hours ago.'

'Doing what?'

'Rufus opened a safety deposit box.'

'A safety deposit box? What's *he* got to keep secure?'

'I don't know what he put into the box, Cecille,' said Jeffrey in his bank manager's voice. 'As you know, it's confidential.'

She shrugged off the remark. 'Where could Archie have gone after leaving the bank? Rufus came home on his own, all vague as usual, saying Archie went off with "some friends".'

'Sid and George came in this morning and drew money out to buy presents. The three of them are probably doing their Christmas shopping right now.'

'Probably! I need to know for sure.' Her voice was starting to rise again. 'You're not concerned he's gone missing? Especially now he's cursed and with no one to protect him.'

Jeffrey decided to be reasonable. Offering practical advice was the only approach to take when Cecille became overanxious about Archie's safety.

'Why don't you phone George or Sid? Chances are he's at one or the other's house.'

Cecille was silent just long enough for Jeffrey to congratulate himself on averting another crisis; then she spoke again, only this time her voice was harder.

'And while you're on the phone, can I ask what we plan to do about Rufus?'

'Do?' said Jeffrey, rubbing away the beginning of another headache. The subject of their conversation had changed so rapidly he'd not a clue as to what she was talking about.

'Is Rufus staying with us for Christmas? Have you asked him what his plans are? Why he's here at all? Have you told him your father is in hospital?'

'Has something happened?' Jeffrey asked.

There was another pause and when Cecille spoke

again there was a quiver in her voice.

'We had an argument,' she sniffed. 'About half an hour ago.'

'Where is Rufus now?' said Jeffrey as the headache settled behind his eyes.

'Out looking for Archie.'

Jeffrey sighed. 'OK. I'll be home in twenty minutes. Make me a corned-beef sandwich. Wholemeal, and go easy on the butter.'

He put down the phone. 'Why is nothing ever straightforward?' He sighed and reached into his desk drawer to take the last remaining painkiller.

By the time Jeffrey walked up the hill it was nearly 1.15 p.m. He had been so deep in thought that it was only on reaching the gate to the house that he realised the weather was starting to turn. It was colder than ever and the bitter air made his throat ache. His headache continued to throb. A gust of wind blew straight through his body and he shivered. He could almost believe he was coming down with flu, yet he felt stronger and more energised than he had for quite a while. Not only that, his memory appeared to be improving.

He would allow himself exactly twenty minutes to reassure Cecille about Archie's well-being; they were just too busy at the bank for him to be away for any length of time. Besides, he had a lot on his mind, particularly the phone call he'd received just before leaving his office.

As Jeffrey opened the front door to Windy Edge and walked into the hall, he gave a silent prayer that Rufus and Archie had returned and therefore Cecille would be in a calmer state of mind.

'Is that you?' he heard her call from the kitchen. Then she was in the hall, looking at him expectantly, and, bizarrely, wearing her fur hat with the earflaps.

'Are they back yet?' he asked.

She shook her head and the look on her face told him she was near to tears. He decided to take control.

'Cecille? Did you receive a phone call this morning? Around 11.45?'

She took a few moments to consider his question, before giving a very definite, 'No.'

'Are you sure?'

She continued to stare at him. 'Why do you ask?'

'I tried calling. The line was engaged.'

'Oh, yes,' she said quickly. 'I remember now. A wrong number.'

'We seem to get a lot of wrong numbers. Who were they looking for?'

Cecille gulped. 'I didn't recognise the name.'

'And no one else called?'

'No.'

'You're quite sure?' he persisted.

'No one else called,' Cecille confirmed.

They continued to look at one another. Jeffrey hoped his insistent stare would draw her on the subject of the phone call. Cecille, however, was quite adamant she had not received any other call that morning at 11.45.

Eventually Jeffrey changed the subject. 'Did you phone George and Sid?'

Cecille nodded, relieved the questioning over phone calls was over. 'George and Sid both said Archie went off with Rufus and Ezekiel in our Land Rover.' A horrible thought suddenly occurred to her. 'I bet Archie wasn't even wearing his seat belt! And did I mention Ezekiel's bicycle was on the roof rack? And one other thing. Rufus was apparently very interested in the colour of bird droppings on Brian Bain's face.'

'What?' said Jeffrey, sounding confused.

'Exactly!' Cecille was now saying. 'And he's also been tidying the under-stairs cupboard and poking around in the fireplace. Now, is that the behaviour of a responsible person?'

'There's probably a perfectly rational explanation to all this –' Jeffrey started to say.

'Something weird is going on,' Cecille interrupted. 'And there's only one way to find out what it is.'

'How?' he asked.

Cecille turned and ran downstairs to the basement.

Moments later she was back and walking towards him with a leather-bound book in her hand.

'What's that?' he asked.

'Rufus's diary.'

Jeffrey looked horrified as she put it in his hand. 'I can't read that.' He thrust it back at her.

'He's *your* brother. You read it. If Archie is in danger we are entitled to know.' She replaced the diary firmly in his hand.

Jeffrey didn't look any more convinced. 'What am I supposed to say when Rufus walks in and finds me with it?'

'He won't, because you are going to sit in the kitchen reading it, eating your corned-beef sandwich, while I keep watch from the front-room window. If he turns up I'll do this.' She put a little finger into each corner of her mouth and let out a shrill whistle.

Jeffrey jumped and in the distance a dog began to bark.

'Where on earth did you learn to whistle like that?'

Cecille didn't answer but gave him a gentle push towards the kitchen. 'Start reading and please be quick about it.' Then she was gone in a flash of brown ear-muffs disappearing around the living-room door.

Jeffrey settled himself down at the kitchen table and took a bite of his corned-beef sandwich that was made from white bread and was over-buttered. He stared at the brown leather book lying beside his plate. Confidentiality was his business, so to open Rufus's diary and read his personal thoughts was a violation of trust. But then again there was the question of Rufus's bizarre behaviour, and he had to think of Archie too – particularly Archie. Jeffrey found himself torn between respect for privacy and his family's interests, but of course there was no contest and he put his sandwich back down on the plate and opened the book.

Cecille, meantime, was settling down for her vigil by the living-room window. She had pulled up a chair and was peering through the tinselled branches of the Christmas tree, looking ever more like a hunted animal. She stared out on to the snow-covered garden, half of her wanting Archie and Rufus to walk up the garden path at that very moment, and half of her wanting them to stay away just long enough for Jeffrey to find out what Rufus Stringweed was really up to.

# Chapter Twenty-seven

Rufus and Archie walked down Ezekiel's garden path in respectful silence. They had left him asleep in his armchair by the fire, trying to catch up on the sleep he'd missed the night before. Rufus looked up at the swaying branches of the tree and the wind chime's irregular notes.

They climbed into the Land Rover and Archie fastened his seat belt. As they drove up the hill, Rufus looked in his wing mirror and saw the church weathervane suddenly swing from north to south to north again. And though it was still early afternoon, the sky was darkening with the weight of thick grey cloud.

When they arrived at Windy Edge two minutes later, Archie caught a glimpse of Cecille peering through the front-room window from behind the Christmas tree. As he climbed out of the Land Rover he saw her put her fingers in her mouth, and even more surprising was the piercing whistle she most certainly gave before turning away into the room. Archie stood staring at the window.

As if everything wasn't bad enough already, he had to discover that even his mother could whistle, and so strongly and clearly that she'd made the dog next door bark.

A cold rush of wind came whistling up the hill, reminding him of his encounter with the rogue gust that morning, and he ran up the garden path.

Overhead, an eerie laugh sounded through the tree branches. 'Wind's getting stronger,' Archie heard Rufus say as yet more banks of grey cloud crossed the sky.

'Where have you been?' came Cecille's anxious voice. Archie looked up to see her standing at the open door staring at him, hands on her hips, wearing her furry hat. 'I have been out of my mind with worry,' she added as he brushed past her into the hall.

'I wish you'd stop treating me like a baby,' he said angrily.

She was so surprised she could only stare at him as he kicked off one boot and then the other, finally throwing his coat on the floor next to them.

'Where have you been?' Cecille asked again, only this time she looked accusingly at Rufus.

'Nowhere,' said Archie in a preoccupied voice. Then he picked up his carrier bag containing the chocolate frog and began climbing the stairs.

'What have you got there?' Cecille asked, quickly shifting her focus from Rufus to the carrier bag.

'Nothing,' said Archie.

She watched him climb the stairs, his shoulders drooping under the weight of his worries.

'How are Sid and George?' she asked.

'Fine.' He carried on climbing.

'Would you like a corned-beef sandwich?'

'I'm not hungry.'

He took the remaining stairs two at a time until he reached his room. Just before he shut the door he heard Rufus say, 'I'd quite fancy a sandwich, Cecille.'

Archie collapsed on to his bed and lay there, staring out of the window at the tree, watching the branches moving closer towards the glass. The wind was rising and quickly. Would Huigor really arrive that night just as Ezekiel had said he would?

Maybe he should do some training. Archie got up from his bed, pulled on his boxing gloves and started sparring. Then he caught sight of himself in the wardrobe mirror. The big red gloves dangling from his thin arms seemed to accentuate exactly how he felt: tired and far too weak to be fighting a tornado. The strength of the rogue breeze inside Norrie Bews's boatshed had told him that. He pulled off the gloves, threw them into a corner and fell back down on his bed. He wished everything would go away. He wished Rufus had never come back and he wished he'd never heard of Huigor, but more than anything he wished there was no such thing as a curse.

Someone knocked on his bedroom door. 'Can I come in?'

Before Archie could answer Jeffrey's head peered around the door.

'OK?' he asked. 'Your mum says you don't want lunch. That's not like you.'

'I'm not hungry.'

'Not even for a corned-beef sandwich?'

Archie gave a small smile, enough to encourage Jeffrey to come in and shut the door. He was carrying a plate of sandwiches, which he set down on the bedside table.

'Why aren't you at work, Dad?'

'Couldn't resist the prospect of a corned-beef sandwich.'

Archie smiled again. Jeffrey crossed to the window and looked out.

'Wind's getting up. Colder too.' He bent down and looked through the telescope, focusing and refocusing on the distance. Eventually he stood up and blinked over and over again. 'Those clouds keep going out of focus. Must get my eyes tested.' He turned to look at Archie. 'So, did you go Christmas shopping with George and Sid?'

'Yes. I got Mum the chocolate frog. Oh, and Mr Ashburn said to be sure and wish you the very best of the season's greetings. He also mentioned some stuff about the bakery being the heart of the village.'

Jeffrey nodded. 'True, but a heart needs blood to flow through it.'

Archie was beginning to think he would never understand the grown-up world. No one ever seemed to say what they meant, and everyone spoke in a code that only other adults understood.

A sudden gust of wind rattled the window and then a voice, like a low moan, said, '*Archie.*' He sat up straight on his bed and listened. Another gust of wind hit the window and he heard his name again.

'Feeling all right, Archie?' his dad was asking.

He nodded as he stared out of the window, watching the tree swaying. The wind began to laugh.

'*Soon,*' it wailed, '*soooooon.*'

Jeffrey looked over his shoulder to the window as the branches brushed against the glass. 'Strange sounds the wind can make.' He turned again to look at Archie. 'Could almost believe it was talking to you.'

Archie looked at him. 'What do you think it's saying?'

Jeffrey tilted his head to listen.

'Not sure. But let me tell you what happened on my tenth birthday.' Jeffrey moved the clothes piled up on the chair to one side. Lying on the top was a dusty handkerchief with the letter 'J' embroidered on one corner. A handkerchief he immediately recognised as his own. He glanced towards Archie's cupboard as he sat down. Then he collected himself and began his story.

'I celebrated my birthday with a bad case of chicken pox and slept most of the day. When I woke up a storm was blowing. Anyway, I was lying in my room, listening to the wind, and I realised it was saying my name. When I told your grandpa, he said I was just hallucinating with the fever. He said the same thing had happened to him too when he was a boy, but he reckoned it was the wind blowing in the pipes.' Jeffrey continued to look at Archie. 'Have you ever thought the wind was talking to you?'

'Yes,' Archie whispered.

'What did it say?'

Archie looked at his father's intent expression. 'It said . . . it said . . .' Then he remembered Rufus telling him to keep everything a secret. 'It said too many corned-beef sandwiches are bad for you.'

Jeffrey smiled gently and went back to telling his story.

'Yes, it was a particularly severe case of chicken pox. I never did feel the same afterwards.'

'What was different?' Archie asked.

'It felt as if someone had told a joke that everybody in the world understood except me.'

'Did anyone call you a scared baby?'

'Oh, all the time. But then again I was. Everything frightened me. The dark, the wind, heights, open spaces, small spaces. Tried not to let it, but it didn't make any difference.'

'George Ratteray called me a scared baby today and I am never going to talk to him again,' Archie announced. 'And Brian Bain . . .' he hesitated, '. . . he said you're a coward.'

Jeffrey gave a knowing nod. 'The biggest cowards are afraid of anyone who thinks or sees things differently from themselves. Being part of a pack makes them feel strong. We Stringweeds learn to live with ourselves and that's our strength.'

'I don't think you're a coward,' Archie told him.

Jeffrey gave an uncertain smile. 'Maybe one day I'll surprise everyone and become fearless like Rufus. Travel across the African plains and visit Romanian castles.'

'Would you like that more than anything in the world, Dad?'

'I've got the whole world right here.'

And to prove his point, Jeffrey came and sat down on the bed beside Archie and hugged his shoulders. At that very same moment there came the unmistakable crack of a chocolate frog breaking into many, many pieces.

They both shouted, 'Oh, no,' and stood up quickly to view the devastation. The carrier bag and its contents were flattened into the shape of Jeffrey's bottom. Archie looked inside the bag and, as expected, the frog was no longer recognisable as the gold-crowned king of amphibians. He put his hand inside and drew out a crumpled little red waistcoat.

'Don't worry,' Jeffrey was saying. 'I'll get another on my way back to the bank.' He was trying to sound as hopeful as he could, but Archie knew it was no use.

'Mr Ashburn didn't have another. It came all the way from Paris, France.' He said this while looking at a small glass star inscribed with the words 'Make a wish' that he'd found at the bottom of the bag. The surprise gift the frog had contained.

Right at that moment Jeffrey wanted to explain to Archie why he had been such a disappointing father, but that would mean revealing the truth about the Stringweed curse, and, judging by Archie's careworn demeanour, now wasn't a good time to add to his worries.

Instead, he simply said, 'I'm sorry.'

'That's OK,' said Archie, unaware that Jeffrey was apologising for a lot more than a broken chocolate frog.

Another strong gust of wind came rushing towards the house with a high-pitched wail that sounded like a heartless laugh. They both looked towards the window, where a layer of snow was being whipped up from the window ledge.

'Weather's turning fast,' said Jeffrey. 'Better stay inside. I have to get back to work.' Then he left the room, saying, 'Remember to eat your sandwich crusts.'

Cecille must have been waiting on the first-floor

landing because she began talking softly the moment Jeffrey ran down the attic stairs. Whenever his mother talked softly to his father it usually meant one thing – they were talking about him. Archie stood at the open bedroom door and listened.

'What did he say?' she was asking.

'Nothing much,' said Jeffrey. 'I think he's just tired.'

Archie was about to shut the door when he heard his mother say something that made him stop.

'What did you do with Rufus's diary?'

'Ssssh,' Jeffrey hissed and began speaking so softly Archie could only just make out the words, '. . . in my pocket . . . work late . . . Rufus visiting Dad.' There followed a lot of rustling as they walked down the stairs to the hall, where he put on his coat, but Archie caught a few more words: '. . . keep Archie inside, we don't want him . . .' Then his voice rose as he shouted, 'Rufus, I'm leaving now. Do you want a lift to the bus stop?'

A gust of wind roared around the house and the noise of the windows rattling drowned out all other sounds until the front door slammed. Archie ran to his window to watch Jeffrey and Rufus walk down the garden path. Rufus was pulling on his pointed hat and he held a sandwich between his teeth. Jeffrey was striding ahead of him, his long black coat flapping in the wind as he buttoned it up. Pockets of snow were curling up around his legs and then a particularly strong gust of wind pushed him towards the parked car. Rufus looked up at the attic window as he closed the gate and waved. Archie waved back but his smile was for his father, watching him from the front seat of the Land Rover. He squeezed the wishing star that he still held in his hand.

'I'm going to get your courage back, Dad,' he whispered. 'I'm going to get it back and then no one will ever call you a coward again.'

But what was his father doing with Rufus's diary? As Archie watched the Land Rover pull away in a cloud of exhaust fumes he realised the diary was sure to contain information about Huigor. If his father discovered how they intended to break the curse he would certainly try to stop them. He had to warn Rufus.

He was pacing the room trying to come up with an idea when a shrill screech made him look towards the skylight. He put the glass star in one of his zip trouser pockets and climbed on to his bed. He pushed the window open and the force of the wind almost pulled the lever out of his hand. He gasped, trying to hold on to it with both hands, as something soft and white brushed his cheek, and then, using all his strength, he shut the window again.

Archie turned to see a windblown Icegull looking at him from the top of his computer screen.

'I need you to take a message to Rufus,' he told it. 'Urgently!'

He quickly got paper and a pen and began to write a note, careful not to give anything away, just in case it got into the wrong hands. He decided all he needed to write was:

*Red alert, return to base. A.*

Archie folded up the piece of paper and put it in the pouch the coin had come in, then he placed it inside the gull's beak. This time he slid open the window that looked out on to the tree. As the bird took flight it suddenly occurred to him he'd not told it where to go.

'The hospital,' he shouted, but his voice was lost in the folds of the curtain that blew across his face. He shut the window and looked out through the waving tree branches and across the rooftops to the white-tipped waves beyond the bay. He looked up at the thick grey cloud speeding across the sky and listened to the roar of the wind. 'Huigor *is* coming tonight,' he said out loud, and a cold breeze circled the room.

Archie took a thick jumper from out of his wardrobe and from the top shelf a small red rucksack. The time on his watch was 1.57 p.m. All he could do now was wait and hope Rufus got the message. In the meantime he would prepare the best he could for Huigor's imminent arrival.

Archie sat down and made a list of the items he intended to put into his rucksack.

A spare torch

The carrier bag containing the broken chocolate frog (for sustenance)

Three corned-beef sandwiches wrapped in holly and ivy serviettes (for more sustenance)

His night-vision goggles from George

His marbles from Sid

Rufus's birthday gifts: magnifying glass, flute, torch, dagger (which was still in his coat pocket downstairs)

The flying goggles? Were the goggles in Rufus's rucksack or were they still in the plane? That was something he would ask Rufus when he got back.

He decided to take the two gold coins also and he put them in his trouser pocket with the zip for safekeeping. He was trying to decide what else he might need when he heard Cecille's footsteps on the stairs and her voice calling up to him.

'Archie! George is on the phone.'

He hid the rucksack under the bed just as she walked into the room.

'It's very cold in here,' she said with a shiver. She glanced around the room and saw the uneaten sandwiches on the bedside table, and then she noticed the stars and moon inside the glass globe were spinning faster than ever. She shivered again. 'Have you had the window open?' Before Archie could reply she was repeating, 'George is on the phone.'

'Well, I don't want to speak to him,' and Archie flopped down on his bed and turned his back on her.

'Are you not feeling well?' she asked. 'Don't you want your sandwiches?'

'I'm OK,' Archie was saying. 'I just don't want to speak to anybody.'

She thought she heard him give a small yawn.

'I'll tell George you're busy and to phone back later. Why don't you take a nap?'

'I'm not tired,' he mumbled into his pillow, and this time he gave a loud yawn.

Cecille had already decided he was exhausted and she closed the door quietly behind her as though expecting him to have fallen asleep already. Archie opened his eyes and lay where he was, listening to her feet running down the stairs and her distant voice on the phone to George.

He decided he would rest until Rufus returned – best to have a clear head when they made their plans – but his brain was buzzing with images of Icegulls, red aeroplanes, green balls of light, broken chocolate frogs, and being laughed at by George and Brian Bain, but most of all he couldn't stop thinking about Huigor, who was close to delivering his birthday present of the Stringweed curse. With time running out he still didn't have all the artefacts he needed, and, as he lay listening to the wind wailing and moaning, he hoped Rufus would return soon.

# Chapter Twenty-eight

By the time the bus drove the seven miles to Breckwall and dropped Rufus off outside the hospital gates it was 2.20 p.m. The daylight was almost gone, hidden by the weight of thick grey cloud low across the sky. The wind tore at his hat and spots of rain hit his face as he walked up to the hospital entrance. An automatic door slid open and he was blown inside along with an empty crisp bag and a small whirlwind of dust.

Rufus found a sign pointing to Ward 19 and followed the scent of antiseptic. At the entrance to the ward he took a moment to survey the scene before him. The ceiling lights were all switched on, making the sky outside look worryingly dark. Red and gold paper chains were looped across one wall and a plastic snowman was stuck to one of the swing doors. It was stiflingly hot. Six beds were lined up on each side of the ward, each with pale blue bedcovers and curtains of varying shades of yellow and orange. Rufus's eyes scanned the groups of visitors gathered around the beds until he spotted a small plump woman at the other end of the ward, wearing a bright-red jumper. He recognised his mother immediately by her hair, which hung straight to the chin as it always had, but it was now the colour of soapstone. She was seated at the bedside of an elderly man, whose eyes were closed. As Rufus drew near he saw how old age had turned his father's hair as white as an Icegull's wing and his skin pale and grey. Perhaps his father sensed Rufus approaching because his eyes opened and then they were looking at one another.

If he was surprised at Rufus's dishevelled appearance he didn't show it; neither did his mother, who stood up and said in a matter-of-fact voice, 'You picked a day to come home. Last week we had bright sunshine. Didn't we, Dad?'

His father gave a small nod of his head. 'Fixed the greenhouse door.'

Rufus hugged his mother and kissed her cheek before pulling up a chair and sitting down.

'How are you feeling, Dad?'

His father closed his eyes in pain. 'The headaches are bad. Making me see things.'

'What things?'

'Green lights. Giant white birds on the garden gate.' He gave a weak smile and closed his eyes.

Rufus felt his mother lean over and whisper in his ear.

'Hearing things too. Says the wind's talking to him.' Then she went over to the window, leaving them to talk.

His father opened his eyes again. 'Got your postcard. Tokyo, was it?'

'You would have liked Japan, Dad. The cherry blossom was in full bloom.'

'We had a good flowering year too. And the year before. Pity you missed them.'

'Had some pressing business to see to.'

'Is this business done?'

'Almost. Got a few ends to tidy up tonight.'

The wind rattled the window beside the bed. Rufus felt his father grip his hand and pull him close.

'Does Archie know? Is that why you've come home? To tell him?'

'To help him. Listen, Dad. Archie's not cursed yet. The pain you feel is the curse closing in. When the curse breaks the headaches will disappear. You'll feel as good as new.'

'Do what you have to do,' he whispered. 'Don't let Archie miss out the way me and Jeffrey did.'

A particularly strong gust of wind buffeted the window and soon after a flash of lightning lit up the sky. Everyone in the ward stopped talking and waited for the sound of thunder. When it came there was a flurry of movement as visitors stood up and prepared to leave, anxious to get home before the storm set in. Rufus looked at his father. His eyes were closed again, and this time he seemed to have fallen asleep. Rufus turned to his mother, who was standing looking out of the window.

'I need to get back before dark. Will you be all right?'

She didn't appear to hear and Rufus was ready to ask the question again, only a little louder, when she spun round and stared at him. She was shaking.

'What is it, Mum?'

'He sees things,' she whispered.

'I know.'

'Giant white birds. Fluorescent-green eyes.'

'Yes.

'One just flew past the window.'


Rufus stood at the bus shelter scanning the sky and the rooftops for a glimpse of the Icegull. Why wasn't it congregating on Moss Rock with the rest of the troops? Could it have been blown off course? Was it injured?

The wind was so strong the bus shelter was shuddering as if it might take off and blow away. A single-decked bus pulled up and Rufus searched the sky once more for the Icegull before climbing aboard.

He took a seat at the front in order to have a clear view of the sky and the road ahead. The bus made two more stops and then they were out in the countryside driving straight into the wind. The driver was using all his strength to keep the bus on a straight path as it rocked from side to side in the strong gusts; some of the passengers nervously clutched the seats in front. Rufus was thinking it odd they had not met one other vehicle on the road when he saw a large white ball come hurtling out of the sky towards them.

There was no time to shout out a warning. Something very large hit the windscreen, followed by another loud thump as it rolled up and hit the bus roof.

The driver slammed on his brakes and Rufus grabbed the safety rail around his seat to stop himself shooting forwards. One or two passengers gave startled shouts and then the bus came to a halt.

'Everyone OK?' The driver's voice was shaky as he stared at the windscreen. Rufus was staring at it too, as were a group of passengers who had come down to the front of the bus.

For a few moments no one spoke. The only sound was the moan of the wind. Then the driver said, 'What is *that*?'

The entire windscreen was covered with the imprint of a huge bird wing. One or two large white feathers were wedged into the windscreen wipers.

'Could be a swan,' said one of the passengers.

'Whatever it was, it was big,' said another.

'Lucky the windscreen didn't break,' said the driver.

They all continued to stare at it until a voice demanded, 'Open the door! I must get out. Open the door *now*.' Rufus was pulling on his rucksack and trying to squeeze past the crowd of people filling the bus aisle.

'Nothing could survive a hit like that,' a passenger told him.

'Open the door,' Rufus persisted.

A shaft of light suddenly lit up the windscreen and a man appeared at the side of the road waving a torch. He was wearing a long beige raincoat that billowed in the wind like a parachute.

The driver opened the door and the man rushed in on a gust of wind.

'A bit draughty out there,' he said, his coat deflating. He spoke in short gasping sentences. 'Tree down on the road. No traffic moving in either direction. Fire engine's out on another call. Could be in for a long wait.'

He looked through the windscreen to point in the direction of the fallen tree.

'What's that?' he asked, leaning towards the imprint on the glass.

'A swan hit us,' two passengers said at the same time.

'Lucky it didn't come through the windscreen.

Could have killed us,' said the driver.

The passengers all nodded in agreement and made suitably serious comments on what a lucky escape they'd had.

The driver looked over his shoulder to where Rufus had been standing. 'Where's that guy that wanted out?'

A cold rush of air from the back of the bus made everyone turn in time to see Rufus push open the emergency door and jump out into the storm.

The driver shook his head. 'I thought he looked a bit crazy.'

Rufus ran back along the road, helped by the wind pushing him from behind. He had taken a torch from his rucksack and he shone sweeping arcs of light across the road, up into the swaying trees and into the undergrowth. He was about to retrace his steps when there came a high-pitched wail from the wooded area beside him. He leapt across a ditch and ran into the dark undergrowth. Up ahead he could see what looked to be a large snowdrift around the base of a tree. As he approached he switched off the torch.

The Icegull lay belly down, its wings spread wide, its head twisted back across its body, its neck broken. Rufus knelt close to the bird, sheltering it from the strong wind ruffling its feathers. Its beak was open and he carefully removed the pouch from inside it. The gull opened its eyes and let out a piercing cry that soared up through the branches of the trees. Rufus began to chant softly, while watching the fluorescent glow in its eyes grow dim. The bird's body began to shake and when it opened its beak again it made no sound. Soon after the last green pinprick of light in its eyes flickered and died. A flash of lightning lit up the wooded area and Rufus saw quite clearly that it was dead. Very gently he cradled its head, stroking the feathers as he straightened its neck. Then he opened the pouch and removed the piece of paper. He switched on the torch and read the message from Archie: *Red alert, return to base. A.*

Rufus stood up and looked around. Behind him was the dark empty road. On three sides was the wooded area with tree branches swooping down towards him like giant spider legs. Time was precious and passing fast, but still he waited. Something rustled in the grass close by. He kicked the undergrowth, sending a huge rat running towards the ditch at the side of the road. Still he waited. It was now fully dark, the wind was rising and he was cold, but he couldn't leave yet.

Rufus continued to stay guard over the bird until he saw what he'd been waiting for. The colour was slowly draining from its feathers, turning them transparent, and when the transformation was complete the feathers were filled with an iridescent glow. The bird began to move. It raised its head and the green light returned to its eyes. It stood up and enveloped itself with its out-stretched wings. Then it began to rise and as it did so it formed a perfect circle of white light with two small green lights at its centre.

The outer white circle began to shrink and the two green lights fused together and expanded until all that was left of the Icegull was a flickering green ball the size of Rufus's hand. Rufus watched it float upwards through the waving branches and then it was gone, like a small green shooting star crossing the sky.

Rufus threw his rucksack over his shoulder and hurried back towards the road. The lightning strikes were becoming more frequent and the wind was gaining strength. Huigor could blow in any time and he was still a long way away from Windy Edge. He had to get back to Archie and to the bank before it closed, but with the road blocked by the fallen tree he would need a miracle to get him there in time.

# Chapter Twenty-nine

Archie had been sitting at his bedroom window for almost two hours, waiting for Rufus to return home. They had agreed to rendezvous at 3.00 p.m. and it was now 3.58 p.m.

He opened his bedroom door and warm air from the hall soothed his cold nose and hands. He tiptoed downstairs, listening for Rufus's voice, but the only sound to be heard was laughter and clapping coming from the television in the kitchen.

Archie stood in the hall, staring at the coat stand. Rufus's coat wasn't hanging up, nor were his boots lined up next to the door. He tiptoed towards his own coat, still lying on the floor where he'd left it. He took the dagger from the pocket and transferred it to his trouser pocket, then jumped with fright as the grandfather clock gave a single off-key chime. Something was most definitely wrong with the clock. As he prepared to walk back upstairs Archie gave it a closer look. That's when he noticed the small keyhole in the door to the pendulum. It was glowing Icegull-green.

He opened the door and the Scout inside spread its light, revealing the key to the clock face hanging on a small hook close to the pendulum, but, more importantly, it cast its light upon a brown envelope taped to the wooden casing.

A roar of laughter and clapping from the television gave Archie the cover of noise he needed to stop the pendulum swinging, rip the envelope from the casing and hide it up his jumper. Then he picked up the key from the hook and used it to open the clock face. The Scout had shrunk to the size of a grain of rice and it floated away through the front-door keyhole.

Lying inside the clock-face casing was another key, a very peculiar-looking one: long and thin with a single arrowlike spike, and it was made of gold. It had to be the missing key they'd been looking for. He put it in his pocket, closed the clock face, and was shutting the door to the pendulum casing when he heard his mother say, 'What are you doing, Archie?'

Cecille was standing half in and half out of the kitchen, and the red apron she wore was splashed with flour.

'The clock was making a strange noise,' he told her.

But she was more concerned about him than the clock.

'How are you feeling?' she asked, walking over and putting the palm of her hand on his brow to check his temperature. 'You slept a long time,' she said, looking into his eyes for signs of illness.

Archie didn't correct her. There were more important things on his mind.

'Is Rufus home yet?' he asked.

'No,' she said, feeling the glands on either side of his neck.

'Where is he?'

'He went to visit Grandpa in hospital.'

'When will he get back?'

She glanced at the clock. 'I thought he'd be home by now. But we're talking about someone who walked out the door one day and didn't return home for nine years. So who knows when he'll be back?'

This was all very bad news for Archie. 'Don't say that. He can't be away tonight. He can't. He can't.' And he turned and ran upstairs.

'Archie?' Cecille called up to him. 'I was only joking,' and as if to reinforce the point there came another round of applause and laughter from the TV.

Archie sat on the bedroom floor, his back against the door holding it shut, just in case Cecille followed him upstairs. He listened for the sound of her footsteps, and when there were none took the gold key out of his pocket and laid it on the carpet next to him. Then he pulled the brown envelope out from under his jumper and opened it. Inside were seven postcards, all with the same drawing on the front. A white bird with spread wings, exactly like the engraving on his two gold coins.

'Icegulls,' he whispered.

That was where he had seen the symbol before: on the card he'd received from Rufus on his fifth birthday, accompanying the flying goggles. On the back of each card were the words 'Happy Birthday' and an inscription written and signed by Rufus.

Archie flicked through the cards: the inscriptions read: *Run with the speed of the wind*; *Unlock the prison of fear*; *He who has vision sees beyond the horizon*; *Look into the eye of the storm*; *The ice awaits the warmth of the glow*; *Do not measure time, let the hands find the path*; and lastly, *Clouds gather to the music*. He remembered that Rufus had said something about clouds and music when he'd found the flute that morning.

Archie's mind was made up. He put the key back in his pocket, got his rucksack out from under the bed and put the envelope containing the cards inside it. He also packed the items on his list, with the exception of the flying goggles. Not having them was a problem, but not half as big a problem as Rufus not returning home. He decided he would have to get into the bank on his own while the doors were still open.

He slipped on a jacket and zipped it up, put on an

old pair of trainers found at the bottom of his wardrobe and with the rucksack slung over his back he climbed up on to the table and opened the window.

It was a bit like sticking his head into a wind tunnel. Archie's hair was blown back off his face one moment, stuck up at right angles the next, before collapsing around his eyes. The curtains flapping around his face made it doubly difficult to see as he eased himself out on to the window ledge. The wind was so strong he could hardly breathe as it tried blowing him back into the room and then in the next instant suck him out again, but Archie had listened to it often enough to know that it came in strong advancing waves that then retreated, quickly followed by smaller gusts. He waited for one of those smaller gusts, which gave him just enough time to reach out and cling on to the drainpipe, hook his arm around a tree branch and pull himself on to it.

He wrapped his arms and legs tightly around the branch and told himself he would be fine if he didn't look down. Another strong gust rocked the tree and he closed his eyes and waited, wishing the squall would hurry up and recede so he could ease himself along the branch towards the trunk. But the gusts just kept coming and he was tossed around as if the branch was trying to shake him off.

Archie opened his green eye and there on the bedroom

window sill, staring back at him, was an Icegull. It stood absolutely still against the battering wind, its unblinking eyes fixed on Archie's precarious position.

He didn't dare shout for help. He couldn't risk someone overhearing. But if the Icegull wasn't there to help him, then what did it want?

The wind suddenly retreated and Archie eased himself towards the trunk where the branches were thicker and stronger. The tree was lit up by the house lights, enabling him to choose branches that would take him via the safest route to the ground. Nobody could call him a scared baby now, he said to himself as he scrambled down the last few feet and jumped into a snowdrift.

He looked back up to his bedroom window and saw that the ledge was full of Icegulls, with one or two flying around inside his room. The slanting roof above his window could have been mistaken for having another covering of thick snow if it wasn't for the many pairs of green eyes staring down at him.

The birds were completely motionless and silent in the angry wind, never flinching as it tore at their feathers and buffeted their bodies. All around him he could hear garden gates slamming, windows rattling and the dog next door barking. He could also hear the distant roar of the sea as it pounded the harbour wall. Huigor was drawing closer.

# Chapter Thirty

Archie set off at a run, as fast as he could, down the hill towards the village. Once or twice he had to hold on to a lamp post to stop himself being blown to the ground or pushed backwards, and although he was beginning to feel exhausted he knew he had to keep going. He'd seen bank break-ins on TV, but they always consisted of blowing holes in the walls with dynamite or getting in through windows with metal-cutting equipment. The only way he was going to get in was to walk through the front door.

By the time he reached the village square, one of the bank tellers, Stewart, who happened to be Brian Bain's much older brother, was just starting to close the doors. Stewart was also the local football-team goalkeeper, and he was using all his muscle power at that moment to close and bolt one of the heavy double doors against the wind. Archie wasn't interested in football but he had been fascinated to hear a team supporter say that

Stewart had two left feet.

'My dad's expecting me,' said Archie above the noise of the wind, and Stewart waved him inside. As luck would have it another of the tellers, Karen, who earlier that day had briefed Rufus on the Christmas and New Year opening times, was just coming through the security door.

'Hello, Archie. Didn't get blown away?' she asked with a smile.

Archie swallowed hard and was just about to give a nervous shake of his head when a loud bang made them both jump. Stewart had finally bolted the second door shut.

Karen resettled her black-rimmed glasses on to the bridge of her nose.

'Oooh, Stewart, you gave me a fright,' she said with exaggerated fear.

Stewart pushed blonde strands of hair away from his forehead and straightened his tie.

'I think we should get away as soon as possible,' he said breathlessly. 'Sounds like a serious storm is blowing up out there.'

The prospect of leaving work early with Stewart propelled Karen out of Archie's way, and he took advantage of her distraction to dash through the security door seconds before it slammed shut. Luck was on his side and he found himself alone in the corridor.

At the far end, on the left, was his father's office, but it was the second door on the right he disappeared through.

It was dark inside the stationery cupboard, with the only light coming through the keyhole and a small gap at the bottom of the door where it didn't quite reach the carpet. Archie scrambled around in his rucksack and brought out the torch and then settled himself down in a corner next to boxes of photocopying paper. The time on his watch was 4.45 p.m. He would know the bank was empty when the corridor light was switched off. In the meantime he could only hope that no one would open the cupboard door before then.

As Archie sat there, listening to passing footsteps, occasional voices and the sound of telephones ringing, he began to feel bored and then hungry. He took the corned-beef sandwiches from his rucksack and ate them while keeping watch on the light shining through the keyhole. Just as he was about to eat his crusts a shadow moved across the keyhole and he switched off his torch. Someone was standing in front of the door, blocking the light from the corridor.

'Are you ready to leave, Stewart?' he heard Karen say. 'Mr Stringweed is hanging on for a bit longer. He said we should just go and he'll set the alarm.'

'What's he up to in there?' he heard Stewart ask softly. 'Had his door closed all afternoon.'

'Not sure,' Karen was whispering, 'but when I went in just now he was reading a book. Looked like a diary. He snapped it shut when he saw me staring at it.'

'Been behaving very oddly since he came back from lunch,' Stewart said, as he considered this new information. 'Went straight down to the basement. Met him on the stairs coming back up with something hidden under his jacket. Very suspicious.'

'You don't think he's stealing, do you?' asked Karen, enjoying the sudden drama.

'Old Weedy? Stealing? Don't be daft. He hasn't got the guts.'

'Ssssh,' Karen sniggered.

Archie was just about to jump up and shout, 'Don't talk about my dad like that,' when he remembered he wasn't even supposed to be there. He was so angry that someone with two left feet was criticising his dad that he let out a high-pitched whine.

'What was that?' he heard Karen say.

He held his breath.

'Probably the wind,' said Stewart. 'Or the ghost of Pirate Bloodeye.'

Karen laughed. 'I don't believe any of that stuff.'

Archie wasn't sure what frightened him the most at that moment – the ghost of Pirate Bloodeye haunting the bank, or the sound of Stewart locking the cupboard door.

'Story goes his ghost has been seen down in the basement,' Stewart said as he removed the key from the lock.

'I'm never going down to the basement again on my own,' Karen was saying as they walked back along the corridor. 'Not unless you come with me,' she added with a giggle before the security door swung shut behind them.

Archie was left alone again, locked inside a very dark and silent cupboard in a haunted bank – and not one person in the whole world knew he was there.

# Chapter Thirty-one

Rufus calculated he was approximately four miles from Westervoe: a long way when walking on foot into a headwind. For every step forwards he found himself blown back two. To make matters worse, the torch battery was running low, he was tired and cold and not a single vehicle had passed him by.

He was trying not to feel despondent but to stay hopeful, when through the incessant roar of the wind he was alerted to a new sound. He couldn't hear it too clearly because of the wailing wind, so he stopped walking and stood on the edge of the kerb and listened.

Was it a tractor? Or was it thunder? But it couldn't be thunder, because he could feel the earthly vibration of whatever was travelling in his direction. A flash of lightning lit up the road and he saw a huge black horse galloping towards him, its hooves drumming against the grass verge. Rufus stood his ground, stretched his arms out either side of his body and waited. The horse was bearing down fast, and when it seemed as if they would collide it came to a halt directly in front of him and reared up on to its hind legs, its hooves pawing the air above his head. The whites of its eyes stared at him in terror from beneath its blowing mane and it opened its mouth and snorted and whinnied loudly. Rufus reached up and caught hold of a rope trailing from the horse's halter and smiled. His miracle had arrived.

Using his eye-staring technique he calmed the horse down, and after a few gentle words of encouragement it allowed him to stroke its back. It wasn't wearing a saddle, which meant it would be an uncomfortable ride, but to Rufus, who had once ridden thirty miles bare-back on a donkey, this was luxury, and he swung himself up on to the horse and set off at a gallop towards Westervoe.

# Chapter Thirty-two

Jeffrey's office door at the bank was closed. He was seated at his desk, head in his hands, staring at the cover of Rufus's diary. His hair was tousled and the shadows beneath his eyes were darker than usual. He looked as if he had been sitting in that same staring position for quite some time. Eventually he turned his tired eyes up towards the clock on the wall, and although a piece of holly had fallen down to cover the number twelve, he could tell it was six o'clock.

Jeffrey stretched his arms wide, stared at the ceiling and gave an enormous sigh, just as the overhead light began to flicker. He watched the fluorescent light fluctuate between being very dim and very bright, and then, after a particularly half-hearted flicker, he found himself in complete darkness. He became aware of the deep roar of the wind outside his window and the fragments of voices breaking through it; people outside in the square were shouting to one another.

Jeffrey had been bent over the diary most of the afternoon and had become so engrossed in the information filling the pages that he hadn't noticed how fiercely the wind had risen. He picked up the phone to call Cecille, but discovered the phone lines were down as well as the electricity supply. That meant the storm was a lot more serious than he had first thought.

He remembered the small torch he had taken to carrying around since the night the Land Rover had run out of petrol and he pulled it from his overcoat pocket and switched it on. Then he gathered his belongings together.

He put Rufus's diary into his briefcase, locked his desk drawers, put on his coat and walked out into the corridor. As he passed the stationery cupboard he halted, and turned round again. He could have sworn he had seen a glow of light coming from the keyhole. He took a deep breath to calm himself and turned the door handle. To his relief it was locked.

'A trick of the light, most probably,' he said. 'Made by my own torch,' he told himself as he hurried on down the corridor, through the heavy security door and out into the main foyer of the bank. With the electricity down he'd be unable to set the alarm; instead he would have to lock up the old-fashioned way with just his set of keys.

There were two sets of doors to lock before he was

standing out on the street. A couple of oil lamps in one or two windows either side of the square gave off small pools of light, and at a few other windows he could see the flickering of candles and torches being carried from room to room. Otherwise he stood in near-darkness. He looked up to the sky and saw occasional moonlight through pockets of fast-moving cloud, but what he had not expected was the ferocity of the wind.

As Jeffrey walked towards the Land Rover he could hear the distant crash of something metallic falling to the ground, followed by glass breaking. From somewhere down near the harbour came the sound of a car alarm, wailing over and over again like an injured animal.

He got into the car and started the engine, still thinking about what he had discovered within the pages of Rufus's diary. If the information was accurate, then in approximately twenty-four hours a tornado by the name of Huigor would blow in and deliver the Stringweed curse. But from what he could see, all the indications were that a severe storm was already closing in. Could Rufus have got it wrong?

The diary had also told him his memory loss and headaches were caused by Huigor's ever-nearing presence and his health would improve once Archie was cursed, yet he felt stronger and more clear-headed with every passing minute. He put his foot down hard on the accelerator and willed the old car to move faster. He had to get back to Windy Edge and confront Rufus about the diary; in particular the information concerning Archie and the part he would play in the breaking of the Stringweed curse.

All around him he could hear the wind laughing and screeching, taunting him just as it had done all those years ago – only this time it wanted Archie. If Rufus's diary was correct, and Archie still wasn't cursed, then he had to get home and protect him before Rufus and Huigor got to him first.

# Chapter Thirty-three

Cecille was in a remarkably happy state of mind. The third batch of mince pies was in the oven, she was listening, undisturbed, to another TV quiz and, best of all, Jeffrey would soon be home to reveal the contents of Rufus's diary.

At that moment, in the warmth of the kitchen, even though a draught was blowing from somewhere, she felt quietly contented. That is, until she became aware of the banging door.

The kitchen window had been rattling off and on for most of the afternoon and the back door had taken to giving an occasional thud, but now an upstairs door was banging loudly. Just as she got up to investigate, the television suddenly died on the spot. At the same time, the entire room went black as the power failed and the only immediate sounds to be heard were the last few electrostatic gasps from the TV. Cecille blinked, trying to adjust her eyes to the new darkness, and then a rectangular patch of grey on the opposite wall came into focus; it was the window, and she shuffled towards it, holding the edge of the table for guidance and support.

A torch was always kept in the same place on the window sill for power failures, and she ran her fingers along the ledge behind the curtain, searching for it. A flicker of irritation made her sigh. It wasn't there. Obviously Rufus had not returned it to the exact position on the left-hand side after he'd borrowed it to go out and get coal. She remembered quite clearly telling him how essential it was to know where torches were kept at moments such as this. She sighed again as she made a mental note to have another word with him about safety in the home. Then she told herself it was ridiculous to feel stressed by Rufus, particularly when her real concern was for Archie, upstairs and all alone in the dark. He'd not called out or tried to come down, which was strange, but perhaps he'd fallen asleep again and was blissfully snoring through the crisis.

The house had turned unusually silent, as though it was watching and waiting for the beam of light from the torch to be switched on. Without the cheerful background banter of the TV Cecille became more aware of creaks and bangs and the howling wind, but beneath it all, or perhaps above it all, there was a new unfamiliar silence. She finally located the torch in the centre of the window sill, obscured by the leaves and berries of the

Christmas Cherry plant.

'It's all right, Archie, I'm coming,' she called out. 'I've got a torch.'

She switched it on and shone it around the kitchen into all those dark corners that could hide who knew what.

'So very silent,' she said to herself as she walked out into the hall, catching the grandfather clock in the beam. She stood and stared, realising the source of the unfamiliar silence. The clock had stopped ticking at four minutes past four that afternoon: exactly the time she had last seen Archie.

She ran up the stairs, the torch beam leaping ahead from stair to stair, creating strange flashes of light on the walls.

'Archie? Can you hear me?' But the only answer to her question was another loud bang of the door.

She wished Jeffrey was there with her, or even Rufus – anyone, in fact, because Archie's silence told her something was very wrong. As she ran up the last flight of stairs towards the attic, the torchlight shone on to his closed bedroom door. It was rattling violently within the frame and a draught blowing under the door was so strong it lifted the hair from around her face. She grabbed the handle and turned it, but something heavy and strong on the other side was holding it closed.

She banged on the door with her fists.

'Archie? Can you hear me?' she shouted. 'Archie? Are you in there?'

The wind gave another high-pitched shriek that echoed through the house, but it was nothing compared to the scream she gave as a hand reached out of the darkness and grabbed her firmly by the shoulder.

# Chapter Thirty-four

Cecille shrugged herself free of the hand that gripped her shoulder, but a second hand grabbed her wrist as she prepared to strike the intruder with the torch.

Then a familiar voice said, 'Stop! It's me.'

Jeffrey's face loomed close. 'Is Archie all right?' he asked. 'His window's open and the curtains are blowing around outside.'

Cecille was still shaking as she said, 'The door won't open. Something is holding it shut. There's no answer when I call to him.'

'Where's Rufus?'

'I don't know. He's still not back from the hospital.'

'Stand aside,' said Jeffrey. He gripped the door handle and, with his shoulder raised, threw his full weight against the door and burst into the room. Something soft hit his nose. 'What the . . .?' he began to say as the light from his torch picked up a wall of swirling white feathers.

Cecille gasped as she followed him into the room. 'White feathers!'

'Icegulls,' she heard Jeffrey say as the door slammed shut behind them. He grabbed a feather and examined it closely in his torchlight. 'They shed feathers before a battle,' he said softly, as though reading aloud.

'You read the diary, didn't you?' Cecille asked.

Before Jeffrey could answer, a veil of feathers blew across her face and into her mouth.

'Archie?' Jeffrey called out through the swirling feathers. 'Are you in here?'

He flashed his torch on to the empty bed while Cecille began to search every corner of the room, their torchlight revealing the devastation caused by the wind. Clothes had been blown on to the floor, the wardrobe door was swinging open and posters were hanging off the walls. A curtain had been partially ripped from the rail and was caught up in a tree branch.

Cecille leaned out of the window, screaming Archie's name into the roar of the wind. Jeffrey shone his torch on to the tree and then down into the garden, but even as he searched the darkness, he knew Archie wasn't there; his car headlights had shown him that. He untangled the curtain from the tree and closed the window and the swirling feathers began to float towards the floor. He had taken one step towards the door when he felt something crumple beneath his foot. Lying on the carpet amid the feathers was Archie's home-made mobile.

Jeffrey picked it up and saw all the knights had been crushed but for one, Archie's favourite, the black and red knight with the initials A. S. written on the shield. The fact it had survived intact persuaded him it was a good omen to finding Archie safe and well.

'Look at this,' Cecille was saying. She was holding the weatherscope and the planets inside it were spinning so fast they were now a golden blur. Though she was trying very hard to stay calm, her eyes were wide and questioning. She looked up into Jeffrey's concerned face. 'You said the birds were preparing for battle. What battle? What did the diary tell you?'

'Archie knows about the curse,' Jeffrey told her. 'Rufus told him.'

Cecille went very quiet while listening to the wind beating angrily against the window. What else had the diary told Jeffrey? This was a situation she had no control over, and when she spoke again her voice was no more than a scared whisper.

'What are we going to do?'

And then, to her surprise, Jeffrey threw back his shoulders and said in a very un-Jeffrey-like voice, 'We're going to go out there, and we're going to find him.'

# Chapter Thirty-five

From inside the stationery cupboard Archie could hear the wind wailing. It never seemed far away, as if it was following him. A cold draught blew in under the door, sending shivers up his legs, and he huddled deeper into his coat to keep warm. He ate another corned-beef sandwich and looked at the time on his new watch. It was exactly ten minutes since he'd heard Jeffrey leave his office and slam the security door shut.

Now he was alone with only the dark and quite possibly the ghost of Pirate Bloodeye to keep him company.

Archie dusted the crumbs from his clothes, packed the remainder of the uneaten sandwiches into the rucksack and slung it on to his back. He turned the door handle and immediately remembered it was locked. He told himself that there was no need to panic just yet, because in his trouser pocket was the strange-looking key he'd found inside the grandfather clock. He felt sure the key was the answer, but it was too narrow and wobbled in the lock as he tried to turn it. Then his finger found a small notch on the key stem. When he pressed it small arrow-shaped pins shot out from the end of the stem to fill the lock exactly. He recalled the words on one of the cards Rufus had sent him: '*Unlock the prison of fear*'. He turned the key.

'Yes!' he whispered as the door opened. He pressed the notch on the key again and the small arrows retracted into the stem. If the key fitted every lock in the bank then the job he had to do would be straightforward. Knowing this made him feel better.

He shone the torch along the corridor, hoping he wouldn't pick out the ghostly figure of Pirate Bloodeye lurking in a dark corner, but with the coast clear he walked quickly towards the light switches at the top of the stairs that would take him down to the basement. But when he flicked on the switches, the corridor and the stairs remained in darkness.

'Oh, no!' he said as he flicked the switches again. 'A power failure!' He would have to go down to the basement with just the torchlight to show him the way. He looked over his shoulder at the blackness stretching behind him. He looked down the stairs to the darkness stretching ahead, but he couldn't give up now. 'I'm not afraid, I'm not afraid,' he kept telling himself as he began to descend the stairs. But he *was* afraid of the eerie wailing and moaning coming at him through the pipes and the ventilation grilles. Was it the wind or was something else making that low groaning sound?

When he reached the bottom step he shone the torch along the full length of the corridor, took a deep breath and ran towards the strongroom, his trainers making an odd slapping sound against the linoleum floor. By the time he reached the metal door he was shaking so much it took a couple of attempts to find the notch on the key to release the metal arrows. But to his relief the door swung open and he walked inside.

It was cold and there was the damp smell of night. Archie waved the torch around to light up the shadows before walking over to safe number 333: his father's safe. He opened it with the key, feeling a mixture of fear and excitement as he set the metal deposit box down on the floor and then trepidation as he lifted the lid.

It contained a series of envelopes of differing sizes, which he gathered up in his hands until he came face to face with the bottom of the box. There was no watch and no rabbit foot on a gold chain. He let out a disappointed groan and in his frustration threw the envelopes to the floor, tears creeping into his eyes.

To comfort himself he took a large piece of the broken chocolate frog from out of his rucksack, tore away the wrapper and put the whole piece in his mouth. Even as he ate it he felt sick. Not just because of the chocolate but because he had no idea where else to look for the watch and rabbit foot.

Meanwhile that strange wailing in the corridor was growing louder and the roar in the pipes was now like an express train. He began picking up the envelopes. Each of them had his father's handwriting in ink identifying the contents: house insurance, car insurance, health insurance, and about half a dozen labelled life insurance. Then he came across a plain brown envelope containing something round and hard – like a coin, or could it possibly be a watch? He put his hand inside and pulled out a gold medal on a rainbow-coloured ribbon. Attached to it, by a safety pin, was a small certificate presented by Westervoe Community Council to Jeffrey Stringweed. It was dated 12th May 1976: one month before his father's tenth birthday. Archie began reading the details.

*'For an act of unselfish bravery resulting in the saving of the life of thirteen-year-old Herbert Bain, Quoybanks, Westervoe . . .'*

'Herbert Bain?' Archie said. 'Stewart and Brian Bain's father? My dad's a hero!'

He continued reading, '. . . *by diving in and returning him to shore, where he did carry out life-saving resuscitation resulting in his full recovery.'*

Archie looked again at the gold medal. Had the Scout mistaken it for the watch when it examined the box that morning? Though he was proud of his father's past act of bravery, right then he needed the watch and rabbit foot more than anything. It was while he was trying to imagine what Rufus would do in this situation that he came up with an idea. He returned everything to the box, locked it inside the safe, then moved along to safe number 338. Whatever Rufus had put inside his own box might give him a clue as to what he should do next.

Using the gold key he opened the safe and a ball of green light shot out. Archie smiled briefly at the comforting presence of the Scout and returned his attention to the security box. It contained a small wooden casket held shut by a brass combination lock. He shook the casket and it rattled, but without knowing the combination number he couldn't open it. The security box also contained a roll of parchment paper, held together with red ribbon. He untied the knot and as he began to unroll the paper his eyes opened wide in surprise. The words 'Stringweed Family Crest' were written in large letters across the page. He unrolled the parchment further to reveal an illustration of a dagger appearing out of a castle turret and the Latin words '*Semper fortitudo*' on a banner held aloft by two eagles.

'*Semper fortitudo*,' he said softly as he unrolled the parchment further to reveal the Stringweed family tree.

Beneath it was a great deal of handwritten text in

black ink. The letters were small and decorative, making it difficult to read in the torchlight, but Archie deciphered enough words to make him wide-eyed at the knowledge laid before him. He was still trying to absorb this new information when he heard the crash of glass breaking somewhere inside the bank. Soon after came the sound of the strongroom door slowly creaking open.

Archie's thumping heart began to thump louder. 'Captain Bloodeye?' he whispered as he waited for the awful apparition to appear at the door. When it didn't, he quickly returned the parchment and casket to the security box and locked it inside the safe. It was time to get out of the bank. The watch and the rabbit foot weren't there and now he needed to find Rufus. The Scout, meantime, was hovering above his open rucksack as though trying to tell him to look inside.

Archie caught sight of the night-vision goggles George had given him for his birthday, and he put them on. He also grabbed the knight marbles he'd got from Sid and put them into the same jacket pocket as the golden key.

'Ammunition,' he told himself.

He felt a lot happier now he had the Scout for company, and with the night-vision goggles he felt much more secure about being in the dark. All the same, he decided to keep the torch switched on until he was safely back outside.

Archie was ready to leave the room when the door flew open and crashed against the wall. Fear and surprise kept him rooted to the spot. He stood staring into the empty dark space beyond the door. It was filled with a strange wailing that was drawing closer. The Scout disappeared behind the door. Archie understood its message and he switched off the torch and hid there with it, hardly daring to breathe. He put his hand into his trouser pocket and pulled out the dagger. Immediately he felt a strong surge of courage, which he would need, because the wail in the corridor was now like a battle cry – the same threatening wail he'd heard that morning in Norrie Bews's boatshed. The rogue wind was growing stronger and more ominous and it was outside in the corridor, blocking his escape.

He put the torch in his jacket pocket to free up his hands and then, clutching the dagger tightly, shouted, 'I'm in here!'

There was a piercing screech and the wind came hurtling into the room. The Scout shot up and over the top of the door while Archie slipped around it, intending to pull it shut, but the wind grabbed him and he felt himself thrown to the floor, unable to move against the weight that was pressing down on his chest. He looked for the Scout and saw the wind had pulled it into the shape of a fluorescent-green claw that was now speeding towards him. In the next instant the dagger was plucked from his hand and carried upwards towards the ceiling.

'*Huigor cannot be defeated* . . .' he heard the wind say. '. . . *Do you concede?*'

'No!' he gasped, and the claw pointed the blade in his direction.

Archie reached into his jacket pocket and, as the dagger came hurtling towards him, he threw the marbles and, though he didn't mean to, the gold key too. There came the sound of glass clashing against metal, and perhaps it was the effect of the see-in-the-dark goggles, but it seemed to Archie that the knights were no longer inside the marbles, but were spinning around the dagger with their swords and lances, striking it, knocking it out of the claw's clutches. It fell to the floor with a clatter. He stretched his hand out towards where the dagger lay on the floor and the gold key fell into his outstretched palm.

'*Semper fortitudo,*' he found himself saying.

Immediately the wind released its grip and spiralled towards the ceiling with the claw at its centre.

Archie grabbed the dagger and scrambled to his feet but the claw was already flying towards him again.

He pointed the dagger. '*Semper fortitudo!*'

The wind gave an agonising screech and subsided, leaving the claw hovering midair.

Archie staggered backwards towards the door.

'*Do you concede?*' a voice asked over his shoulder.

He spun round. 'Never,' he said into the darkness.

The wind's strength quickly returned. '*Be warned,*' it moaned. '*Huigor will suck you up and cast you out into the depths of the night.*'

Archie ran for the door with the claw in pursuit. When he crossed the threshold he turned and pointed the dagger.

'*Semper fortitudo,*' he chanted over and over again.

The wind sighed and weakened, enabling the Scout to transform itself from a claw into a fluorescent-green hand that slammed the door shut, sealing the wind inside the strongroom and leaving Archie safely on the other side.

Archie stared at the keyhole and saw it fill up with intense dark-green light; for now, at least, the Scout was preventing the wind escaping. The door began to rattle and bang and there was furious screeching coming from inside the room, but he was already running down the corridor towards the stairs. All around he could hear the wail of the storm outside, blowing in the pipes and in the air vents, and as he reached the top of the stairs a cold draught reached out and gripped his ankles.

He ran past his father's office and an icy draught swept towards him from under the closed door. He felt it nip at his face, trying to slow him down, but he kept on running, through the security door into the reception area, where he unlocked the first set of doors. When he opened the main entrance doors a gust of wind roared past him into the bank as he hurried out, pulling the door shut and locking it again.

He stood on the bank steps, shaking and breathless and very afraid.

He didn't have the watch or the rabbit foot. He didn't even know where Rufus was or where to start looking for him. What was he to do? Who could help him now?

# Chapter Thirty-six

Jeffrey and Cecille were in the Land Rover heading in the direction of the village square. Jeffrey was driving while Cecille held on to the dashboard, as if willing the vehicle to move faster. She was wearing her red jacket and furry hat with the earflaps.

'Rufus had no right telling Archie about the curse,' she said. 'That was our job.'

'But we didn't tell him, did we? Perhaps there are too many secrets in our family.'

Cecille threw him a guilty look and then changed the subject. 'Where are we going?'

Jeffrey didn't answer her question. Instead he said, 'Let's hope we're not too late.'

Cecille didn't like what she was hearing. 'Too late for what?'

They took another bend and there was the screech of tyres over the sound of the howling wind.

Jeffrey decided to delay telling Cecille about Huigor.

He didn't see any point in worrying her. Instead he told her that Rufus, and quite possibly Archie too, planned to enter the bank outside of normal business hours.

Cecille looked at him with her bottom jaw hanging open, while considering this latest twist in the Rufus mystery. The Land Rover hit a bump in the road and Cecille was tossed towards the roof, which seemed to help her regain her usual gusto.

'I *knew* Rufus was up to no good. That's why he came back, isn't it? To rob us.'

Jeffrey was shaking his head. 'Not *rob* the bank. Gain access to it. Rufus's last entry in his diary was Sunday evening. He mentions having to find a way into the bank, to check out the strongroom with the possibility of conducting a search after hours –'

'It's just as I suspected,' Cecille interrupted. 'All those cards and presents were his instruments of corruption. He's nothing more than a criminal.' Her confident voice suddenly gave way to a wail. 'Oh, Archie, Archie, where are you?'

'Sshhh,' hissed Jeffrey. 'I can't think clearly if you start all that. We need to keep calm. Think clearly.'

He was so preoccupied that he ended up taking the corner into the square too quickly and had to slam on the brakes to avoid the Christmas tree, which was now blowing around in the middle of the road. The tree was still attached to a long piece of rope that had become

266

entangled on a railing and it was taking the strength of three men to hold it down against the wind. A fourth man was trying to untangle the rope and as the car came to a standstill he turned round and blinked into the glare of the car headlights. Jeffrey lowered the window and the car was instantly filled with a cold draught. Stewart, the left-footed bank teller, walked towards them, almost tripping over the rope he was disentangling. He smiled, his bleached-blonde fringe blowing across his eyes.

'Hello, Mr Stringweed.' He gave the inside of the car a quick glance. 'Blustery night. I hear the road to Breckwall's blocked with falling trees.' Then, noting one person in particular was missing, he remarked, 'Forget to take Archie home with you?' He smiled at Jeffrey's blank expression. 'Not left him sitting in the bank, have you?'

'*What?*' said Jeffrey.

'You *saw* Archie in the bank?' said Cecille.

Stewart looked at Jeffrey carefully. 'Don't you remember? He walked through to your office just before closing time.' His voice drifted away. '. . . Didn't he?'

Jeffrey pushed the car door open, sending Stewart flying, and in the glow of the car headlights he leapt over the Christmas tree and ran across the square towards the bank, his long black coat billowing like a giant bat. His keys were already in his hands as he ran up the steps, and moments later he was inside the building with Cecille following close behind. Seconds later, the crash of the door blowing shut echoed throughout the dark building.

'Wait for me,' Cecille cried, as she followed the yellow trail of Jeffrey's torch.

Together they went through the security door into the corridor, flashing the torch into every corner and opening every door along the way. When they came to the stationery cupboard Jeffrey remembered the glow of light through the keyhole he was sure he'd seen earlier. This time he showed no hesitation in turning the handle and seemed relieved when the door opened.

The first thing he noticed were the corned-beef sandwich crusts lying on top of a box of photocopying paper.

'He's been in here,' he told Cecille.

The next door he opened was to his office and a current of cold air shot past him as he shone the torch into the four corners of the room. The holly that had decorated the wall clock was now lying on the floor surrounded by shattered glass from a broken windowpane, but there was no sign of Archie.

'Follow me,' he said, racing down the stairs to the basement.

The door to the strongroom was banging and rattling furiously, and from behind it they could hear a strange moaning and shrieking.

'He must be locked in there,' said Jeffrey. 'We're coming, Archie,' he shouted as Cecille overtook him and pushed open the door. 'But that door was locked,' Jeffrey tried to say through the huge gust of wind that came rushing out of the door and escaped along the corridor.

'Archie?' Cecille called into the empty room. 'What was he looking for in here?' Her eyes were wide and staring in the light of Jeffrey's torch. 'Why would Archie want to rob the bank? What are you hiding from me?'

But Jeffrey was otherwise occupied. He was shining his torch on to the floor at something gleaming by his foot. He bent down and picked up a piece of bright-green foil, and as he unfurled it a large frog's eye stared back up at him.

The small group that had been trying to secure the blowing Christmas tree in the square was waiting as Jeffrey and Cecille re-emerged from the bank. Stewart looked expectantly over Jeffrey's shoulder.

'Where's Archie?' he asked as the heavy door slammed shut. 'No sign of him, then?' he persisted, and then, smirking to himself, added, 'Haven't forgotten him again, have you?'

Jeffrey was trying to stop himself from shaking. Fear for Archie had certainly set in, but he felt something else too, something he'd not felt in a long time. He turned to Stewart and said, 'Get someone to come and board up my office window. Then I suggest you get home and get some rest. I want you in my office at eight thirty tomorrow morning to discuss your attitude.'

Stewart's fringe had blown flat across his eyes, but he was so surprised by Jeffrey's new and unexpected authority that instead of pushing his hair aside he found himself giving a nervous half-salute.

'Y . . . y . . . es, sir, Mr Stringweed,' he stuttered from beneath the flattened fringe. 'I'll get the window sorted straight away,' and he gave another nervous half-salute.

Cecille, meanwhile, had jumped back into the Land Rover. '*What* is going on?' she demanded as Jeffrey climbed in. 'Is Rufus with Archie?

Jeffrey shook his head. 'Stewart mentioned trees down on the road to Breckwall. Rufus must be stranded there.'

Cecille put her head into her hands and when the tears began to flow she searched her pockets for a tissue. When she couldn't find one, she opened Jeffrey's briefcase, which was lying on the floor at her feet. By now she was sniffing loudly.

'I need time to think clearly,' Jeffrey said as he

rubbed his head, trying to make sense of the thoughts flooding his brain. 'We drove down here pretty fast,' he said after a while. 'Could easily have missed Archie walking up the road.'

Cecille nodded and Jeffrey started the engine. 'I'd bet he's at home by now.' He turned to his wife. 'I mean, where else would he go?'

Jeffrey was suddenly blinded by a strobe of intense light. He blinked away the light spots and saw that Cecille was pointing her torch at him. To his disappointment, in her other hand was the rabbit foot on the gold chain. In her lap was an old drawstring pouch. He blinked again and as his vision cleared he saw her expression quite clearly. It was a look of disgust.

'I hope this is not what I think it is, Jeffrey?'

'It's exactly what you think it is,' he said, knowing she had just removed the drawstring pouch from his briefcase.

'We agreed . . .'

'No,' he retaliated. 'You asked me to get rid of it, which I did . . . I put it in the bank.'

'Well, it's not coming back into the house.' She was holding the chain as if she had a dead rat by the tail. She looked inside the pouch and found the watch. 'Is *this* what Rufus was after? Is this what they were going into the bank for?'

Jeffrey nodded.

Cecille was looking even more confused. 'But why?'

A strong gust of wind rocked the Land Rover and a flash of distant lightning forked across the sky.

'Let's go home,' said Jeffrey. 'Make sure Archie's not there on his own, waiting for us. I'll explain everything then.'

Cecille seemed to calm down at the prospect of going home and the possibility of finding Archie there.

They drove back along the winding streets. Jeffrey kept his speed down so Cecille could hang her head out of the window and shine her torch into dark alleyways, just in case Archie was still making his way back to Windy Edge. Although they caught occasional glimpses of faces at windows, trees blowing, gates swinging and one or two people battling their way through the wind on their way home, there was no sign of Archie.

'Quick, shut your window,' Jeffrey shouted as a large wave broke over the sea wall in front of them.

The windscreen wipers were struggling to clear the water when Cecille asked, 'Why didn't Archie tell us he knew about the curse?'

'I don't know for sure,' said Jeffrey, 'but I can tell you, he's not cursed yet.'

Cecille was relieved but confused too. 'But the curse always falls on the tenth birthday of the first-born son.'

'Apparently not. According to the diary, the curse falls when a tornado by the name of Huigor blows in, which can be on or soon after the tenth birthday. The tornado is due tomorrow. Archie and Rufus plan to break the curse together, but if Archie has been in the bank on his own it seems likely he is going to try and do it alone.'

'But how can Archie break the curse on his own?' Cecille wanted to know. 'He's only ten years old!'

They had driven clear of the sea wall and Jeffrey pulled the Land Rover into the side of the road, and turned to look at Cecille.

'The solution to Archie breaking the curse is in your hand.'

Cecille lifted up the torch. 'This?'

'Your other hand,' said Jeffrey solemnly.

Cecille lifted her other hand, which was empty.

'The grey drawstring pouch,' said Jeffrey. 'Archie's got all the other presents Rufus sent. I checked before we came out.'

Cecille was trying hard to conceal her irritation. 'Why didn't you send them back to Rufus?'

'They're part of my history. '

'A history of bad luck!' she retorted.

'You know, Cecille, there have been occasions recently that made me think you don't want a better future for Archie.'

Cecille sounded shocked. 'That's ridiculous! I'm his mother. I just want to overprotect him.'

'You said "overprotect" him.'

'No, I didn't.'

'Yes, you did! You said you "want to overprotect" him? Why?'

Cecille's eyes were wide and staring. It was bad enough Archie was missing, but now Jeffrey was behaving very strangely.

'Has this got something to do with the diary?' she asked him. 'If it is, I want you to tell me now.'

Jeffrey's patience was running low. 'According to Rufus's diary, each of the presents is a talisman,' he explained. 'Each talisman belonged to a Stringweed ancestor and is destined to protect Archie against the tornado. That's why I got the watch and the rabbit foot out of the bank this afternoon. After reading the diary, I realised he needed it. The tornado wasn't expected until tomorrow, but . . .'

Cecille gave a heavy sigh of relief. 'Then we have till tomorrow?'

Jeffrey shook his head. 'It's early.'

'How early?'

A gust of wind rocked the Land Rover.

'Any time now.'

Cecille looked out of the windscreen at the storm-lashed night.

'This is all Rufus's fault! If it wasn't for him we'd still be living in blissful ignorance.'

'There's nothing blissful about living in fear,' Jeffrey announced in an unexpectedly loud voice. 'I intend to do all I can to save Archie from that fate, so stop wailing and give me the pouch.'

She shook her head.

'I insist,' said Jeffrey, and he pushed his hand closer.

Cecille's bottom jaw was opening and closing again in a very confused manner. 'Archie's still a child. He can't battle a tornado . . .' Her voice trailed off as she sat staring at his outstretched hand.

'The pouch!'

She took a shaky breath. 'I can't . . . I . . . I threw it out of the window.'

# Chapter Thirty-seven

Rather than walk back along the main street and risk being seen, Archie cut through unlit narrow lanes and dark gardens wearing his see-in-the-dark goggles. He decided against using the torch in case it drew attention towards him. Fifteen minutes later he was standing at the door of the one other person who knew about Huigor. To Archie's surprise Ezekiel seemed to be expecting him.

He looked Archie up and down and then stuck his head out into the wind.

'On your own, are you?'

Archie nodded.

'Right,' said Ezekiel, 'ready when you are.'

He was wearing his crash helmet, a coat with a large fluorescent-green band across the chest, and bicycle clips around his ankles, but it was his old 50cc scooter he pushed out of the hall and down the wooden plank at the side of the doorstep. There was just enough light from the oil lamp in the living-room window to allow him to find the ignition and turn on the engine. He handed Archie a spare helmet.

'Jump on,' he shouted above the roar of the wind, the squeaking of the spinning weathervane, and from somewhere behind them, the erratic notes of a wind chime. 'And hold on tight,' he added.

Archie grabbed hold of Ezekiel's coat and jumped on. He would have preferred it if Rufus had been with them, but at least he was no longer alone, and he was relieved to find that Ezekiel seemed to know where he was going. They set off up the hill at a leisurely thirty miles an hour, with a seventy-mile-an-hour wind pushing them all the way past Archie's house. Archie kept his head low, only giving a quick glance towards his bedroom window. It was now closed, which meant his mother, and therefore his father, knew by now that he was gone, and since the Land Rover wasn't parked in front of the house he guessed they were out looking for him. The only pair of eyes to see him ride by belonged to the dog next door. It peered at them from over the top of the gate, its mouth opening and closing, barking madly into the wind.

On and on the wind blew Archie and Ezekiel towards the top of the hill, until the road came to an end and the rough track began. The ride was now much bumpier and at times Ezekiel had to stop the scooter altogether as a particularly heavy gust threatened to blow them over. Eventually the track became too over-grown to navigate and they came to a halt beside a crumbling disused cowshed. They manoeuvred the scooter into the shelter of the shed and prepared to walk the rest of the way, keeping their helmets on as protection from the icy blasts. Archie pulled his torch from his jacket pocket, switched it on and they walked out into the night.

Ahead of them lay bleak moorland, and with the wind blowing so strongly it was difficult to walk upright. They bent their heads low, pushing their way through the gusts, forcing one foot in front of the other, but their pace was slow and it didn't help that Ezekiel kept stumbling and catching his feet in rabbit burrows.

Though his torch batteries were running low Archie could make out the decaying perimeter fence of the old airfield, which was just as well because Ezekiel's exhaustion meant Archie had to more or less drag him along.

'Not far now,' he shouted, though he couldn't be sure Ezekiel could hear him, but then the old man nodded. Archie's other concern was whether the hangar would give them enough shelter. Even now, he could feel the sea spray on his face: fine particles of water blown inland from mountainous waves smashing against the cliffs. He licked his lips and tasted the cold salt water, and hoped the tidal wave that Huigor was creating was still a long way off.

They climbed over what was left of the fence and then, after negotiating the cracked concrete paving and overgrown weeds, walked inside the shell of the hangar.

Ezekiel slumped against a wall and slid to the floor. He looked very old indeed, particularly because of the way his head had dropped down to his chest, and his breathing had become rapid and irregular. Archie felt a new fear; a tornado was one thing, a dead body was another.

'Ezekiel? Do you think you can walk just a little further? Look!' And he shone the torch on to Rufus's aeroplane.

Ezekiel seemed to perk up enough to stagger over to it. Archie took the gold key out of his pocket, unlocked the passenger door and pushed Ezekiel inside. Then he unlocked the pilot's door and climbed in. He put the key in the ignition, took off his crash helmet and opened his rucksack. Ezekiel was clearly in need of sustenance, so he gave him some of the chocolate-frog fragments.

To Archie's relief Ezekiel recovered remarkably quickly and, once his breathing began to settle, Archie asked, 'What should we do now?'

'No idea,' the elderly man gasped through a mouthful of chocolate. 'Suppose we'll find out when

Rufus turns up.'

Archie could hardly bear the disappointment. 'But Rufus isn't coming. I thought *you* knew why we were here!'

They looked at one another and then looked out through the window towards the gaping hole where the hangar doors had once stood.

The aircraft gave a violent shudder as if to remind them of Huigor's imminent arrival and the helplessness of their situation.

'Why did you take us up here?' Archie asked.

Ezekiel kept staring out through the doors. 'Saw you both sneaking out late the other night. Made a little investigative trip up here on my own and found the aeroplane. When Rufus said troop reinforcements were flying out to Moss Rock, I assumed that's where we were going.'

Archie tried to remain calm. 'Rufus was talking about Icegulls! Not *real* troops!'

Ezekiel turned to look at him. 'So he isn't coming?'

Archie shook his head and they both resumed staring out through the doors to the stormy darkness beyond.

'*Semper fortitudo?*' he said hopefully.

'Latin,' Ezekiel informed him. 'It means "courage to the end".'

Archie was impressed. 'It's the Stringweed motto.' As he thought back to the family crest and the motto held aloft by two eagles a thought occurred to him. 'The Icegull told me I had friends who would help when the time was right. Well, where are they? I need them now.'

No sooner had he said the words than a heavy thump landed on the cockpit roof. Something began moving overhead towards the front of the aircraft. Archie leaned forward and at the same time a large green eye slid down the windscreen to look back at him.

Archie sat back in surprise, but the torch was still pointing straight at the window, illuminating the head of a large Icegull carrying a pouch in its beak. It began tapping at the glass. Archie opened the door and leaned out to take the pouch that was being offered to him. What lay inside made him gasp. Very carefully he pulled out the chain with the rabbit foot attached to it and hung it around his neck. Then he took out a gold watch and after examining it pinned it to his jacket.

'You know what this means, don't you, Ezekiel? I've got all my presents!'

Ezekiel had no idea what Archie was talking about, but because Archie appeared to be in control of their precarious situation he thought it quite reasonable to ask, 'What do we do now?'

Archie, however, didn't know, but he was sure the answer lay with the cards. He began flicking through them and rereading their messages. Then pulled all the gifts out of his rucksack and began identifying them with the cards.

*The ice awaits the warmth of the glow* must surely apply to the torch. He decided the card which read *Look into the eye of the storm* referred to the magnifying glass.

*Run with the speed of the wind* was the rabbit's foot.

*Do not measure time, let the hands find the path.* That must be the watch.

*Unlock the prison of fear* could only be the key.

He put the small wooden flute to his lips and blew a few random notes. Instantly three more large Icegulls landed on the plane with a thump. He considered this for a moment and blew one more cautious note. Another Icegull landed on the wing beside him.

'*Clouds gather to the music.* I call the troops with the flute! We're saved, Ezekiel.'

All he needed now were the flying goggles.

He turned and shone his own torch on to the back seat of the aeroplane. There were the goggles and he held them up in triumph as he read the final card.

'*He who has vision sees beyond the horizon.*'

'True indeed,' said Ezekiel. 'And when I get my breath back we'll sort out this tornado.'

Archie looked at Ezekiel, who was now eating a corned-beef sandwich, crusts and all. He certainly didn't look strong enough to withstand a tornado. To protect him Archie knew he would have to get as far away as possible and quickly.

He hung the flying goggles around his neck, filled his coat pockets with the magnifying glass, the torch and the flute and took a deep breath. The sensation of butterflies fluttering around in his stomach continued as he opened the aircraft door.

'Where are you going?' Ezekiel asked through another mouthful of corned-beef sandwich.

'To get my dad's Christmas present,' said Archie, and he shut the door on a very confused-looking Ezekiel.

# Chapter Thirty-eight

Westervoe was like a ghost town as Rufus cantered along the deserted unlit streets. With the prospect of trees falling, roofs being blown away and heavy seas flooding the roads, everyone was staying inside, taking shelter from a storm that had not reached its peak. Lightning lit up the sky as he rode into the square and he sighed with relief as he made out the outline of someone huddled in the bank doorway.

'Archie?' he shouted as he rode up to the bank steps and leapt from the horse.

The figure stood up and Rufus saw to his disappointment that it was a man.

'Still not found him?' the man asked. He stuck out his hand, inviting a handshake. 'Stewart Bain,' he said beneath his wind-blown fringe. 'I work at the bank.'

Rufus quickly shook his hand and introduced himself. Then he asked the question that was concerning him.

'Is Archie lost?'

Stewart explained the situation. 'Weedy . . . ah . . . Mr *and* Mrs Stringweed are out looking for him. Archie was in the bank earlier but disappeared by the time they got here. Can't imagine he's gone far in this storm. I'd bet he's sheltering somewhere dry and cosy. Wish I could say the same about myself.' He turned and pointed up at the large hole in Jeffrey's office window. 'I'm stuck here trying to sort out this lot.' He turned back to Rufus. 'Suppose you wouldn't know how to board up a window, would you?'

But Rufus had already swung back up on to the horse and was cantering across the square, like a highwayman disappearing into the night on his black steed.

The waves were running high over the sea wall. Small boats were rearing up out of the sea, straining to break loose from their anchors. Rufus whispered encouraging words into the horse's ear as it walked through the floodwater, and then they gathered speed again and headed up the hill to Windy Edge.

Jeffrey's Land Rover was gone and the house was in darkness, with not even torchlight or a candle to light the windows. Rufus knew then they were still out looking for Archie. Where could he have gone? In desperation he found himself shouting, 'Archie? Where are you?'

He was answered from an unexpected source. The dog next door had both paws resting on top of the gate and it gave a single warning bark.

'You got something to tell me?' Rufus asked and the dog barked again.

Rufus stared into its eyes and the message it gave made him reach down and open the gate. 'Find them!' he told the dog. Then he said to the horse, 'Fast as you can. Don't let your hooves touch the ground.'

The horse reared up on to its hind legs, all sign of tiredness gone, and it set off up the hill at a gallop in pursuit of the sprinting dog.

# Chapter Thirty-nine

There was no moon, or stars, or flickering green light to show the way as Archie walked out of the hangar into the night. The only glow was from his torch, and with the batteries about to run out there was barely enough light to show the ground around his feet. The wind was stronger too, blowing straight into his face as though trying to get inside him, filling his nose and mouth and lungs with ice-cold air. It filled his ears too with the screeching of what sounded like a hundred aeroplanes taxiing down the airfield runway, but above it all he heard a voice say, '*Do you concede?*'

Archie shook his head and tried turning, but the wind suddenly changed direction. It was no longer pulling the breath from his lungs, but spinning him around and pushing him forwards.

'Oh-oh-oh,' he said as he was carried along with a force that barely allowed his feet to touch the ground. He couldn't stop himself being blown towards the edge of the cliffs that were so close he could feel, hear and smell the sea water pounding against the rockface. His arms and hands were flailing around, reaching out to grab hold of anything, and in his desperation he dropped the torch.

'H-e-e-el-p!' he shouted, but his voice was lost in the deafening roar of wind and sea. He tried shouting help again, but it was too late. Suddenly there was no ground beneath his feet, just blackness as he began falling, somersaulting and tumbling through the ice-cold spray towards the jagged rocks and mountainous waves far below.

He had barely time to choke out a scream of terror when he landed heavily upon something slippery and wet. He lay perfectly still, afraid any movement would throw him off the ledge towards the sea. For the moment at least he was safe, but how was he to climb all the way back up the cliff face in the dark without help? Home seemed a long, long way away, particularly since no one knew where he was.

He was trying not to cry when a jagged flash of lightning lit up the sky and he saw everything clearly. The sea beneath him had been whipped up into white-tipped angry waves that came speeding towards the cliffs looming above him, jagged and black. But what he couldn't understand was how the cliffs came to be moving, passing him by, sailing away on the wind. How could that be? He began to wonder if he was already dead. If he was, then he didn't like being dead at all, because this wasn't anything like his idea of heaven.

Another flash of lightning confirmed it wasn't the cliffs moving – it was himself. He was lying upon a soft white cloud. He turned his head and warm feathers skimmed his cheek as he floated upwards and onwards. Beneath him he could feel the gentle rise and fall of a heartbeat. Do angels have heartbeats? he wondered. He would have preferred heaven to be brighter, sunnier and with no wind, but perhaps the angel was on its way there – yet no matter how wonderful heaven might turn out to be, he didn't want to go there without his mum and dad.

Archie sat up and looked back at what he was leaving behind, but all he could see was blackness, all he could hear was the wind and the sea. He was cold and wet, which confused him too, because he didn't think ghosts felt the cold. Another flash of lightning lit up the sky and his very-much-alive and beating heart gave a lurch as a large green eye turned and looked back at him. He didn't know where they were going, but for the time being at least he was safe, sitting on the back of a large Icegull, and to be sure he clung on tight.

On and on they flew out to sea, drawing nearer all the time to the lightning. During a particularly power-ful strike he caught a glimpse of a huge wall of water, still on the horizon and moving towards them.

The gull banked sharply to the left. Archie lay flat on his stomach and clung to the bird's neck, burying his face in its feathers. Another flash lit up the horizon and he dared to take one more look out across the waves. If he wasn't mistaken the wall of water had changed direction and was following them as they headed towards Moss Rock.

They flew in over the cliffs and headed inland. Below him Archie could see the green landing lights that had guided Rufus's plane in to land. The Icegull descended, gliding in on the wind, and the small green lights moved and flickered and changed shape before taking shelter in the heather. Above the wail of the wind he could hear the squawk of many birds calling. He looked up and a shimmering white cloud of Icegulls was dipping and diving and changing shape as more and more birds began to congregate.

One or two flew by on their way to join the flock, their bright-green eyes staring into his, their heads bowed majestically as they stretched their wings and soared upwards. A thought occurred to Archie as he watched them disappear into the shimmering white cloud. Perhaps the Icegulls were his very own angels.

# Chapter Forty

Six or seven gulls flew alongside Archie to accompany his descent towards the mouth of the cave. Inside, the walls were lined with gulls, their bright-green eyes casting a fluorescent-green glow from every ledge and every available space on the ground, but the only sound to be heard was the steady beat of wings as they flew further and further into the cavernous space. Not only was it absolutely silent, it was icy cold. On they flew, gliding over the heads of gulls nestled on the ground, and Archie was beginning to wonder just how deep the cave could be when two large green lights blinked up ahead.

The huge Icegull he'd talked to on his last visit reared up out of the dark. It stretched its wings and there was sudden movement on the ground beneath them as birds fluttered away, leaving a space for Archie and the Icegull to land. Archie slid off the gull's back and stood before the towering bird. Though its beak did not open he heard its voice deep inside his head.

'Come closer.'

Without Rufus beside him he felt afraid, but then, as the bird read his hesitant thoughts, he heard its voice again.

'Do not be afraid. You are with friends.'

Archie took a step closer, and then another, and the bird settled down on the ground in an attempt to make itself appear smaller. It tilted its head towards Archie and looked at him with plate-size eyes full of kindness.

'Huigor draws near. Are you ready?'

Archie shook his head. 'I don't know what I'm supposed to do.'

The gull nodded thoughtfully.

'Huigor feeds on water, air and fire. Above ground he is invincible. Your task is to bring him to earth, but there will be little time. His path of destruction is determined. He must be trapped by the sky and earth. Be ready. When the lightning enters Huigor's centre it must be drawn down through a human heart before it touches the earth. That heart must be yours.'

'You mean I must let Huigor swallow me up and then be struck by lightning?'

The gull nodded. 'It is the only way.'

'On my own!'

'You have everything you need. The only thing we cannot give you is courage. That you have already;

whether you choose to use it is a decision only you can make.'

'I don't think I'm strong enough.'

'Run like the wind, for you have the speed of an animal. Battle him, for within the dagger you have the strength of a hundred Huigors. The watch is your eyes, observing hidden danger, and the torch will burn walls of resistance. Most powerful of all is the magnifying glass; it will echo tenfold all it sees. Use it wisely.'

'But what about the tidal wave?'

'It is merely a distraction. The troops will attend to it.'

'Can't they attend to Huigor too?'

'Let me show you something.' The Icegull raised his head and let out a loud sigh that echoed around the cave, its breath creating a cold draught against Archie's face. Archie watched as the gull's breath froze into a sheet of ice that stood between himself and the bird.

'Do not concern yourself with the wave,' he heard the gull say. 'We shall take care of it.'

Archie looked around as a murmur of agreement went up amongst the other birds. The giant Icegull continued, 'Huigor is coming in further up the coast. He intends to wreak havoc on the village before blowing back out to sea. You must leave, and quickly. The troops will give you a safe passage, but it is the out-stretched hand of courage that will guide you to your destiny.'

Archie wished more than anything that Rufus was beside him at that moment. Rufus would know exactly what to do.

'Take the torch from your pocket,' the bird told him. 'The green button will turn it on. The red button will turn it off.'

Archie's hands were frozen from the cold, but he pulled out the old torch Rufus had sent him. The Icegull spread its wings and flew upwards in a perfect straight line, hovering about ten feet above.

'Now, shine the torch on to the ice.'

Archie switched on the torch, but there was no glow of light; instead a white flame shot out from the bulb and melted the sheet of ice separating them.

He tried giving a whistle, but as usual it didn't work. Instead the cave was filled with the squawking of many nervous birds. He switched off the torch and the Icegull floated back down.

While Archie examined the torch and the pool of water left on the ground, the gull was saying, 'You must go now before Huigor blows in. There is not much time.'

Almost simultaneously the birds let out a loud un-settled screeching.

'Someone approaches,' he heard the Icegull say.

The roar of the wind seemed to congregate outside the mouth of the cave, and for a brief moment a strong moving light crossed it and was gone again.

'An aeroplane,' said Archie excitedly.

Birds were suddenly flying out of his way, creating a clear path as he walked towards the entrance, stooping to stop himself bumping into a low-flying bird. A couple of times he felt soft wings brush against his face. When he reached the mouth of the cave he heard the unmistakable roar of an aeroplane engine above the growl of the wind, and he saw lights coming in to land, bouncing around on the ground and heading quickly towards him – far too quick, he thought, as the lights from the plane drew closer, dazzling him with their bright glow, until they came to a halt only a few feet away from where he stood. The engine died and the propeller slowed to a standstill.

Archie stared up at the bright-red paintwork. The door was pushed open and Rufus shouted above the wind, 'Glad to see you in one piece. You'd better jump in. That wave is ready to hit and I'd rather not be here when it does.'

The giant Icegull suddenly appeared behind Archie.

'The troops are ready. Go now.'

Archie boarded the aeroplane beside Rufus and fastened his seat belt. Soon they were on their way, easing away from the cave entrance until they had enough room to turn round. Then it was full throttle and they were thundering along the path of green lights with the wind against them. Just when it seemed they were running out of turf the front wheels lifted and they were airborne.

The aeroplane dipped violently. Rufus straightened it up, and out of the dark Archie saw the glowing green eyes of six Icegulls flying either side of them.

'Where have you been? How did you know where to find me?' Archie asked Rufus.

'It's a long story, but I saw you go over the cliff. Thought you were a goner.' Rufus gave Archie a sideways look. 'Then I saw the Icegull.' He turned back to check the instrument panel. 'Got Monika out. Suspected you were headed for Moss Rock. Thanks for leaving the key in the ignition.'

'But what about Ezekiel?'

'He's fine. Going home by horse, with a dog escort.'

Archie was distracted from asking questions about horses and dogs by the erratic dipping of the aircraft, which was flying dangerously close to the waves.

'Rufus? The Icegulls are climbing higher in the sky. Do you think we should follow them?'

'What's that?' he heard Rufus ask over the roar of the engine.

'The Icegulls are flying higher than us,' Archie shouted. 'I think maybe you should follow them.'

A Scout suddenly appeared directly in front of them and Archie felt himself pushed back against his seat as

Rufus tilted the aeroplane's nose up. In the aircraft's lights they could see the birds about twenty feet higher and still climbing, but that wasn't their main concern. A flash of lightning had lit up the sky, illuminating a huge cloud of gulls heading their way.

'Oh, no,' Archie moaned, and he covered his eyes with his hands.

'Always keep a steady head,' Rufus was saying as they flew towards the flock. 'Never panic.'

Archie opened his green eye and watched as the birds separated to clear a path. Thousands of other green eyes flashed by as they safely flew to the other side of the flock. He was about to give a sigh of relief when another flash of lightning lit up the sky and straight ahead was the giant tidal wave, towering above them; only it wasn't moving because it was now a solid wall of ice.

'Pull up!' Archie screamed, but even he knew there was no time to avoid a collision.

He pulled the torch from his pocket, pulled the goggles up over his eyes and opened the plane door. As the aeroplane flew towards the wall of ice he pressed the torch button and a stream of white light shot out, melting a huge hole that was big enough for them to fly through.

'Whatever you do, don't switch that thing off,' Rufus shouted as they entered the tunnel.

Archie was keeping his eyes on the torchlight, but through the walls of the tunnel he could pick out frozen strands of seaweed, crabs and lobsters staring back at him. Then a particularly huge eye loomed close, only a few inches inside the ice, and Archie could make out the hulk of a frozen whale. But he kept his concentration focused and his hand steady while the white-hot beam pushed the water ahead, until they flew straight out the other side behind a cascading waterfall.

Archie switched off the torch. Just before pulling the aeroplane door shut he looked back to see flashes of lightning fork through the sky and strike the wave, shattering it into blocks of ice that crumbled into the sea.

The Icegulls were waiting for them on the other side of the wave and they resumed their flying position ahead of the aeroplane.

'Better keep our eye on them this time,' said Rufus. 'There are bound to be a few more surprises waiting up ahead.'

Archie gripped the dagger handle in readiness.

# Chapter Forty-one

The Icegulls took them on a path back over the air-field and across the moor and then, as they flew over the hill, the darkened village was lying below. Archie spotted the yellow glow of an oil lamp at a window close to the church spire and, recognising it as Ezekiel's house, was able to get his bearings. He looked out of the window as they flew over Windy Edge, wishing he could jump out, just for a minute, to let his mum and dad know he was OK. Perhaps at that very moment they were looking up at the aeroplane. He gave a wave just in case, by some miracle, they could see him.

Unknown to him, the red tail-lights parked at the bottom of the hill, close to the sea wall, belonged to Cecille and Jeffrey's Land Rover. They had driven full circle around the village after failing to find Archie at home, stopping at George and Sid's houses and even knocking on Ezekiel's door in their search for him. At that very moment they were back dodging the waves breaking over the wall, looking for the canvas pouch Cecille had thrown out of the Land Rover window.

'Am I seeing things or did an aeroplane just pass overhead, chasing a flock of swans?' Cecille asked.

'Back in the car,' Jeffrey decided. 'We're wasting time. The pouch isn't here.' And then more specifically, 'I think I know where Archie is.'

There was much door slamming and fastening of seat belts and the splash of tyres accelerating through the flood water. Moments later they were speeding through the deserted streets and out into the open countryside, the wind so strong Jeffrey was having trouble keeping the Land Rover moving in a straight line.

'Where are we going now?' Cecille asked this new Jeffrey she barely recognised.

'Following the aeroplane lights,' he said.

Cecille was leaning forward, gripping the dashboard. 'I thought we were supposed to be looking for Archie.' Her voice was slightly more anxious, slightly louder.

'We are,' he replied in a matter-of-fact tone. 'And if my suspicions are right, Archie's on board that aeroplane.'

Cecille, however, was less restrained. 'Archie flying in an aeroplane? But he's scared of heights. He gets car sick ... and ... oh, no ... what if he gets hit by lightning?'

'I think we have to stay positive, Cecille,' Jeffrey

replied with exaggerated calmness. His eyes were fixed on the sky, but his anxiety showed in the shake of his hands.

'Whose aeroplane is it?' Cecille asked, but even as she asked the question she knew the answer. 'Oh, no. Not Rufus? That's how he got here on Saturday night, isn't it!'

Jeffrey put his foot down hard on the accelerator. 'Hold on.'

They raced away from the outskirts of the darkened village and sped into the black night along deserted country roads, flanked on either side by the black hulks of towering mountains. Occasionally they displayed their size through increasingly frequent flashes of lightning.

A startled rabbit began running along the road in front of them, weaving from side to side, forcing Jeffrey to slow down while the tiny aeroplane lights faded into the distance.

'When did Rufus learn to fly an aeroplane?' Cecille was saying. She could hardly contain her confusion. 'He can't even pour a bowl of cornflakes without spilling them.'

Jeffrey flicked the car lights off and on, and the disorientated rabbit disappeared back into the night. He pressed his foot down hard on the accelerator again and they set off at breakneck speed, narrowly missing broken tree branches lying at the side of the road. All the time he kept watch on the aircraft lights.

'Looks like they're turning.' Jeffrey braked heavily and took a sharp left turn on to a mountain track. The Land Rover swayed as they scaled the track and he gripped the wheel tightly as he looked up into the sky. 'I hope Rufus knows what he's doing.'

As the weather grew stormier, Cecille was becoming more and more frantic, because as far as she was concerned they were in the middle of nowhere with no real proof that Archie was even on board the aircraft. She kept telling herself he could just as easily be back home by now and that they should turn round and head back to Westervoe.

'Who asked Rufus to come and break our curse, anyway?' she suddenly announced.

'It's not a case of being asked,' Jeffrey told her. 'Huigor is not just Archie's curse. Unfortunately there are others who will be affected by his presence.'

'Who?'

'You, for one. If Huigor isn't broken tonight you will find yourself cursed too. Then you'll discover how pouring a bowl of cornflakes without spilling any becomes the most exciting part of your day.'

Cecille stared at him. 'Me? Cursed? But that's impossible?'

'Why? Do you know something?'

'No!'

'If Archie doesn't succeed then all three of us face the same future. But he needs all the presents Rufus sent. Unfortunately he is now two short, thanks to you throwing the pouch out of the window.'

Cecille seemed to regain her senses. 'I didn't mean to . . . it's as if something was telling me what to do . . . I'm sorry . . .'

But Jeffrey wasn't listening; he was otherwise preoccupied, because the aeroplane lights had reappeared low in the sky and were heading straight towards them.

# Chapter Forty-two

The lightning strikes were becoming more and more frequent, and closer too, and the wind was throwing the aeroplane around like an Icegull feather. It kept dipping and then rising again and lurching from side to side. Archie wished they would land soon, but in the meantime he and Rufus sat in silence, each of them keeping their eyes on the gulls they were following, readying themselves in preparation for any more nasty surprises up ahead. All the time Archie kept hold of the dagger. He was trying not to think about the ache in his stomach that stretched all the way up to his throat. Or the way he couldn't quite catch his breath or stop his hands from shaking. He felt sick too. And his eyes kept pricking with unwanted tears as he imagined being sucked up inside a tornado and thrown out into the night.

He kept telling himself there was still time to change his mind. He didn't have to accept the challenge. He could go home any time he liked. He was suddenly jolt-ed out of these thoughts by the aeroplane banking to the left and Rufus saying, 'What's going on?'

The gulls were turning and Rufus struggled to swing the aircraft round and follow the birds' new path.

'Wind has changed,' he said. 'Never known a wind to change so quickly. Then again, we're not dealing with any old wind, are we?'

Archie watched the gulls swoop out of sight.

'Hold on,' said Rufus. 'We're looping around, and if I'm not mistaken we're going to land on the top of Ork Hill.'

Another flash of lightning lit up Rufus's face. Archie decided it was an expression of extreme concentration and had nothing to do with fear.

'Just keep focusing on the horizon,' Rufus was saying to himself. 'Don't look left or right. Keep an eye on the target.'

They sat in silence, listening to the wind, listening to the aeroplane engine, listening to the rapid and loud beat of their own hearts.

'Not sure if I can land in this wind,' Rufus suddenly announced, and he pulled the nose up and they were rising again. 'Sorry, old chap. Let's give it one more go.'

'This is serious, isn't it, Rufus?'

Rufus nodded and the aeroplane shuddered.

Archie pulled the flute from his pocket. 'I'm going to

call the Icegulls.'

'We don't have time to wait for them.' This time Archie definitely heard fear in Rufus's voice. 'Wind's getting too strong to fly Monika. I don't think I can keep her up much longer.'

Archie didn't hesitate and he blew the flute over and over again.

Rufus swung the aircraft round and headed once more towards the landing path. 'Hang on,' he said as a particularly strong gust rocked the aeroplane.

A flash of lightning lit up the ground around them and Archie sat open-mouthed as hundreds of Icegulls rose up out of the heather and grass, creating a wall either side of them to form a protective shield against the buffeting wind. Two regular lines of fluorescent-green lights remained on the ground, creating landing lights.

'Perfect timing!' said Rufus as lightning flashes lit up the landing path as if it was daylight.

Archie gripped the dagger handle and they began their final descent. As the lights picked out the war memorial at the top of the hill, he saw quite clearly what he was expected to do – if only Rufus could land them safely.

# Chapter Forty-three

Jeffrey's Land Rover was struggling to reach the top of Ork Hill. Sometimes it barely moved as it lurched and revved over potholes, large stones and generally uneven ground. Cecille was tempted to jump out and walk, but the lightning strikes showed up how desolate and dark the hillside was. By remaining inside the car she was at least safe from the thunderous and biting cold wind, although a headache was forming at the base of her skull. As she began to rub away the pain she saw Jeffrey's face in the glow from the dashboard lights. He didn't seem like his usual mild-mannered self, quite the opposite in fact, and as she searched for a word that would best describe his new demeanour, she surprised herself by coming up with 'determined'.

'Let's not panic,' he was saying as he searched the sky for aeroplane lights. Soon after the Land Rover came to a halt as the headlights picked out a giant boulder blocking their path. 'Don't forget your torch,' Jeffrey said before turning off the engine and headlights.

Cecille was still searching for her torch, even as Jeffrey jumped out, with the ferocity of the wind almost pulling the door from his grip.

'If you're coming, come now. There's no time to lose.' He slammed the door shut.

A flash of lightning showed the torch to be wedged down the side of her seat. Cecille grabbed it, got out of the car and ran through the darkness, shouting to Jeffrey to wait. But her voice got no further than the next gust of wind. Another flash of lightning showed Jeffrey as a dark figure at the top of the track and the light from his torch disappeared as he walked over the summit.

Cecille opened her mouth to shout to him, but a particularly strong gust pushed her backwards over a huge rock and she rolled down the track, coming to a sudden halt inside a very large pothole. Somewhere along the way she had lost her hat. She sat up.

The hillside had become very still indeed. She listened to the new, unexpected silence, wondering what strange freak of nature was occurring, when a thunderous roar made her heart skip and she covered her head with her arms.

The aeroplane flew overhead so low in the sky she could almost have touched it. She looked up just in time to see the tail-lights skim the top of the war memorial and then disappear over the summit.

'Archie?' she whispered, waiting for the sound of the crash. When it didn't come she scrambled back up on to her feet, trying to ignore the throbbing pain in one of her knees, and ran the last few metres towards the summit.

She caught up with Jeffrey as he stood looking out across the hilltop. A small dip in the summit concealed a flat plain of grass lit by green light. On either side was a huge wall of white birds. At the end of this makeshift runway was a light aircraft, its propellers coming to a halt.

'What is happening?' she whispered in breathless terror.

'Don't you think it strange how the wind has dropped?' said Jeffrey. He was searching the sky during the increasingly frequent flashes of lightning.

'Nothing can surprise me any more,' said Cecille. 'I'm all surprised out. All I want is Archie back. I just want him safe.'

'We'll get him back,' said Jeffrey. 'But he won't be the same.'

'What do you mean, not the same?'

'Quiet!' he hissed. 'Switch off your torch. Listen.'

She listened. 'What?'

A breath of wind brushed her face and ruffled her hair.

'There,' said Jeffrey. 'Did you hear that?'

'No, I didn't –' she began, when a deep growl-like laugh sounded close to her ear. She swung round and looked into the darkness.

'You heard it, didn't you?' Jeffrey was asking.

Cecille nodded slowly, uncertainly, then the laugh came again, whirling around them, and this time an accompanying voice hissed, '*He's coming.*'

She gripped Jeffrey's hand. 'Who is it?'

'It's the wind. Archie hears it too.'

'What does it want?'

'Archie. You.'

A flash of lightning revealed a mass of black cloud rising up over the other side of the mountain, and as the cloud rose higher they saw the ominous outline of a funnel shape.

Jeffrey grabbed Cecille by the arm and pushed her under some overhanging rocks into a small cave. 'It's Huigor! Take cover.'

'Archie!' she screamed as another fork of lightning flashed across the sky, so brightly she closed her eyes. Thunder cracked overhead, and then the wind returned as the black cloud closed in on them. Somewhere amid the chaos Cecille heard the screech of birds. She opened her eyes just as Jeffrey's hands were pulled from hers and in the next instant his face disappeared behind a wall of white feathers rising up between them, sealing her inside the cave.

It was completely dark but for the green glow from the birds' eyes, all staring at her, all silent, all waiting. She took a nervous step forward to retrieve her torch, lying in a corner near the sealed entrance. A row of beaks opened menacingly and one or two gulls gave a warning squawk. She took a step backwards.

'Archie needs me.'

The birds continued to stare at her.

'What do you want?' she asked.

The answer came in a strange whispering voice from inside the walls of the cave. 'We await the truth.'

'Who's there? What truth?' she asked.

The birds continued to stare at her, with patient, unblinking eyes, for what seemed like an eternity. Eventually she could bear it no longer.

'What difference would it make to tell the truth?'

Cecille waited for an answer that didn't come. Time was passing. From outside the cave and beyond the wall of birds she could hear Huigor roar. She moved towards the entrance and the gulls opened their menacing beaks again.

'You don't understand,' she wailed. 'I must protect Archie.'

The whispering voice rippled along the cave walls. 'You can protect him by revealing the truth. Do you have the courage?'

'Courage! I need courage every day! The Stringweed curse is my curse too. I have watched it eat into Jeffrey's heart and now it wants Archie's. Ten years I've waited for this day, knowing that when the time came I could do nothing to save Archie from his fate.'

'We await the truth.'

Cecille shivered. Archie and Jeffrey were at that very moment at the mercy of Huigor, and her only chance of helping them was to escape this prison. She took a deep breath, and when she had composed herself enough she asked, 'What if they won't forgive me?'

'From truth comes forgiveness.'

The roar of the wind outside the cave sounded in Cecille's head; she felt its power as the earth trembled beneath her feet. She began to feel dizzy as though caught up in a vortex that was sucking the life out of her, and her eyes began to close. She suddenly felt so very tired. If only she could lie down and sleep until Huigor was gone, but the whispering voice inside the cave would not let her rest.

'Already you weaken. Soon the curse will run through your blood too.' The voice was beginning to sound very distant. 'There is not much time. Renounce the past, before it is too late. Find the strength . . .'

Cecille listened to the voice, trying to remember what it was she had to do. If only she could concentrate, if only she could stay awake.

'He cannot succeed without you. Do not fail Archie now.'

She opened her eyes. 'Archie?'

The cave was filled with an ice-cold sigh.

'Will you speak the truth?'

She looked at the wall of birds and into the many eyes staring back expectantly, but it was Archie's eyes she saw reflected in the fluorescent-green light and she felt stronger.

'Yes,' she whispered. 'I will speak the truth.'

# Chapter Forty-four

Archie had imagined Huigor to be big, but nothing in his wildest imagination could have prepared him for the black shape sweeping across the sky: a giant upright snake, with gaping jaws ready to swallow up everything in its wake.

He and Rufus were staring wide-eyed out of the aeroplane window, rooted to their seats, watching the formidable shape draw closer with each flash of lightning.

'That's Huigor, all right,' said Rufus. 'Just the way Ezekiel described him rising up out of the sea near Moss Rock.' Rufus turned to Archie. 'Are you ready?'

Archie was trying hard not to feel absolutely terrified at the prospect of coming face to face with Huigor outside the relative safety of the aeroplane, but the time was now upon him to make his decision. He suddenly felt very cold. Rufus took his hand, prised open his tightly clenched fingers and placed the gold key in his palm.

'Unlock the prison of fear,' he said. 'Courage to the end.'

As Archie clutched the key a warmth passed through him and he began to feel calm enough to ask, 'Will I die?'

'Being cursed is a living death.'

Archie nodded. He had made his decision. His voice held a nervous wobble as he said, 'I have to get up to the war memorial.'

Rufus nodded. 'You know I can't go with you. This is between you and him. But remember, let the artefacts guide you.'

Archie handed the key back to Rufus. 'I don't need this now. Keep it to protect yourself from Huigor.' Then he pushed the flying goggles up on to his brow and opened the aeroplane door. Immediately the cold wind pulled him outside. The walls of Icegulls were already breaking up and the Scouts were pulling themselves into small pinpoints of light. He was on his own.

He gave one last backward glance to the black funnel twisting towards him.

'*Let the artefacts guide you*,' Rufus had said, and Archie reached up and squeezed the rabbit foot hanging around his neck. The effect was immediate. He felt his legs strengthen and he began to run, propelled forwards in long powerful strides that skimmed the ground. He felt a surge of exhilaration and excitement and an overwhelming energy that told him he could do anything. But as he continued to run, the darkness began to disorientate him and he struggled to find his direction. He gripped the watch pinned to his jacket and pressed the gold button. Instantly the earth glowed lava red and through it a twisting thread of luminous orange appeared, showing him the route to take.

The path ensured his footsteps avoided boulders and hidden holes, and he found himself running so fast he could barely feel the earth beneath his feet; he could have been running on air. But he knew without taking a backward glance that Huigor was closing in. He could feel his power feeding on the air above and he heard his laugh, like the growl of a thousand lions moving in for the kill, which only made him run faster. He kept his eyes fixed on the war memorial and, as it loomed closer, took the dagger from his pocket. Squeezing the rabbit foot again he leapt upwards, soaring into the air to land lightly on to the memorial base.

Immediately the colour drained from the earth and the orange path faded too. He was back in the darkness of night with just enough light to outline the bronze figure of an airman towering above him, his hand raised triumphantly towards the sky. The hand of courage, the Icegull had said.

If he had any chance of succeeding at the challenge, Archie knew he would have to climb up on to the airman's shoulders. That way the lightning would strike the highest object, the dagger, but from where he stood it seemed an almost impossible task; the statue had to be at least five metres high. Then he remembered the magnifying glass inside his coat pocket.

It was small and circular and set in a gold surround. The Icegull had said it would strengthen tenfold all that it saw, but there was nothing at all to suggest how it would help him climb the statue.

Huigor gave another roar and the crack of thunder from a nearby lightning strike reminded Archie how little time he had, but he wasn't about to give up yet. He put the magnifying glass between his teeth and, with the dagger still in his hand, he began to scale the statue, but his feet persisted in slipping against the smooth surface and his fingers failed to find a grip.

Another flash of lightning lit up the hilltop and he saw the black shape of Huigor, snaking towards him, only seconds away. He watched it pick up the aeroplane as though it were made of paper and then toss it aside.

Archie lay down on the base of the memorial and slipped the dagger beneath his stomach, covering it with the weight of his body. Then with both hands free he clung to the airman's bronze boot. Nearby he heard the screech of birds, but their cry was lost as he was finally engulfed beneath the swirling, howling tornado and Huigor roared in triumph.

He couldn't breathe, couldn't see, and as his fingers began slipping from their hold he looked up in terror.

Huigor was sinking steadily closer towards him.

'Help!' he shouted and the glass fell from his mouth. 'Help me, somebody!' he screamed at his own reflection in the glass, but the darkness was already closing in.

Firstly his legs began to rise, pulled upwards by the force of the wind, and then he felt his body lifted until only his hands were gripping the statue. His arms ached as he clung on, but he was no match for Huigor's power. His fingers were wrenched from the bronze boot and he felt himself lifted skyward. He reached out blindly for the dagger but all he could grasp was the air, filled with choking acrid dust. His arms waved wildly as he felt himself sucked upwards by his feet into Huigor's vortex.

Icegulls loomed out of the darkness, their green staring eyes challenging him as they flew past, their wings beating helplessly against the spiralling wind. Discarded feathers fell against his face, and as he screamed for help they filled his mouth. Archie fought against Huigor's might with all the strength he could find, but he knew there was nothing more he could do. He was no match against a tornado's power, but still he thrashed out with his arms, searching for something that hope could cling to. And then, out of the spinning darkness that was Huigor's heart, he saw it: a huge outstretched hand looming out of the dust. Archie grabbed hold of it and clung to the cold metallic fingers of the statue.

'I won't let go, I won't let go,' he told himself as Huigor gave an angry roar. He closed his eyes and saw the knight Rufus had told him about, standing high up on a Romanian castle tower, his body turned away, to gaze far into the distance. Archie began to imagine himself as that knight. He imagined himself in red and silver armour, the dagger in his hand, and he imagined the feeling of strength it gave him. He imagined himself winning this battle.

Was it his imagination, then, that his wrists were being gripped tightly and his body pulled back down and anchored on to the airman's shoulders? Archie opened his eyes, and he felt the dagger thrust back into his hand, its familiar strength flowing through him, more powerfully than he had ever felt its power before. He felt stronger than ten knights, he felt taller than ten statues and he felt ten times more determined to cast off Huigor's curse. He grasped the dagger tight in readiness as the lightning clouds swirled across Huigor's gaping mouth.

The sky exploded. White blinding light poured through the funnel and forked towards him, and he raised the dagger high. The first surge of lightning hit the blade. It shot through his hand into his arm, hitting his heart as if it had been pierced with a block of ice, so heavy and cold he couldn't stop himself shuddering as it filled his lungs, and then so hot it began melting his bones. The funnel turned from black to white and long black arms of jagged lighting stretched towards him like tentacles, wrapping themselves around his body, squeezing the breath from his lungs. He dropped his head in search of air. Through the mist of hazy white light he found himself looking into a pair of eyes, one green, one blue, their clarity so strong and bright that within them he saw a vision of an Icegull staring back at him. Then he heard the voice, deep inside his head.

'Huigor twists with rage, but his power weakens. He fears your strength, your resolve. Hold fast. The sky draws its bow. Soon the bonds of time will be released. Open your eyes. Clarity is truth. Acceptance is power.'

The vision of the gull faded, leaving Archie staring back into the one green and one blue eye. He knew then he was looking at his own magnified reflection. The black tentacles released their suffocating grip of his chest and air returned to his lungs. He raised his head and looked skyward and as he did so the flying goggles slipped down from his forehead and covered his eyes. He was plunged into a new darkness. Slowly he began to focus. Huigor's spinning walls still rotated around him, but as his vision cleared he saw dark shadows begin to take form within these walls. As he continued to watch he saw them move. Huigor roared and twisted like a trapped wild animal.

An explosive crack of thunder echoed outside of the funnel. Archie looked up to see a fork of lightning ten times larger, faster and burning more brightly than any he had yet seen speeding through the very centre of Huigor, and it was heading straight towards him.

'This is the one,' he said, closing his eyes. He thrust the dagger upwards, stretching the muscles in his arm until they ached. 'I challenge you in the name of all first-born Stringweed sons,' he shouted as the first bolt of lightning hit the tip of the dagger.

This time he felt nothing other than a strong rippling current of warmth. He could hear the wind somewhere outside of where he was, but at that very moment all was calm. He kept his eyes shut against the blinding white flash. For a moment he didn't exist; he was nothing more than ice and heat and light. He was metal too as he melted into the bronze of the statue.

The strength began to drain from his body – he wanted to sleep, to keep his eyes closed, but a persistent drumbeat wouldn't let him rest. The beat grew steadily louder and stronger and he felt it vibrate in his chest, keeping him awake. Then another heart began beating to the same rhythm, and another and another until there were so many beating hearts he thought his head would explode, but just as suddenly they stopped. He raised his head, opened his eyes and looked into the dark silence. The weight of his exhaustion made his arm drop by his side and he heard a metallic clatter as the dagger hit the bronze statue. There was no other sound; no wind, no roar, no thunder, and he felt his eyes begin to close against the dark.

Then a huge snakelike face made of dust and shadows reared up in front of him. It opened its jaws wide and roared and a cold wind blew across Archie's face.

*'Fear has a cold touch,'* it said. *'Colder still when it grips your heart. Ask your father,'* and it laughed cruelly. The face was now so close he could feel its icy breath. *'Your heart is strong. You have fought well. The earth threatens to destroy me. I feel its pull. But the battle is over. Your courage is mine. It will release me from this earthly confine.'*

Archie tried raising the dagger but he had no strength left. The choking dust burned his throat, and though he could barely speak he whispered, 'I am not afraid of you.'

The grotesque face laughed menacingly. *'So much courage . . . I shall feast well.'*

The gaping jaws opened wider, but deep within their blackness a faraway voice could be heard. The statue began to shake. The dagger fell from Archie's hand. The snakelike face began to twist and contort.

It threw its head back and tried to roar but the voice inside its mouth was growing stronger and more persistent. It was a voice Archie recognised. He listened as Cecille began renouncing the curse in the name of her ancestors and calling for the release of all souls trapped by Huigor.

The face began to dissolve. Dust filled its mouth,

distorting its words.

'*Tread carefully*,' it moaned. Its one remaining eye stared threateningly at him. '*Where the night and shadows meet, there shall I lie.*'

Out of what was left of the mouth, Cecille was calling to him. 'Courage to the end,' he heard her say.

'*Semper fortitudo*,' he whispered back.

A piercing shriek reverberated inside the tornado and a hundred rogue gusts came speeding down Huigor's walls, helpless against the force of the earth's pull.

The snakelike face crumbled and fell to the ground in a spinning cloud of thick grey dust. The wailing stopped and there was a calm silence. Archie waited, and as the choking dust began to clear he raised his head and looked up through the funnel towering above him. The moon was directly overhead, pouring silver light into the darkness and illuminating the moving shadows. They began to take shape and emerge from out of the funnel walls and look down on him from the ledges. Pale, translucent people, old and young, men and women, children too, began climbing down the slow rotating layers and dispersing in all directions. He watched one figure in particular stride purposefully towards the statue and disappear behind the base with a much older shadow, following in its footsteps. When all the shadows had walked free Huigor shuddered, then the stillness at its centre was violently broken by the eruption of a huge explosion of light.

Spinning rings of rainbow colours – purple, orange, red, yellow, green and blue – rippled out and spread across the hilltop, creating a multi-coloured crater, so brightly fluorescent that Archie had to blink against the glare. Then all the colours merged together, creating one pale-blue fluorescent light, and from out of it flew the giant Icegull. It stretched its wings and glided towards Archie.

'Let me see your eyes.'

Archie pulled the goggles from his face. The gull's eyes were so near he could see himself reflected in their green glow.

'You have met the challenge, Archie. Huigor is destroyed. All captive souls are liberated. Your father's courage is restored. Your grandfather's too. Even now, energy and strength flow through their bodies, bringing renewal.'

Archie closed his eyes and, like a dream, he saw the knight again, high upon the castle turret, only this time he turned around and bowed. When he raised his head Archie saw his father's face smiling back at him.

The vision faded, and though his eyes were still closed he was aware of the beating of wings and the sensation of feathers against his cheek. He was also aware of being carried in someone's arms, and of being lowered so gently to the ground that he was reminded of flying on the back of an Icegull. When he opened his eyes he saw a man smiling at him, looking so dishevelled and exhausted that Archie hardly recognised him.

'Dad?' he whispered in a small exhausted voice.

'Yes, it's me,' Jeffrey replied wearily. He set Archie down on the memorial base and then leaned himself against the statue for support before sliding down to sit beside him. In his hand was the magnifying glass, which he slipped into his coat pocket. Then he picked up the dagger lying next to him on the plinth.

'It was you, Dad,' said Archie. 'You held up the magnifying glass and you gave me the dagger. *You* were the hand of courage!'

A small pinprick of green light appeared from behind the statue and expanded into a soft glow, illuminating Jeffrey's face.

'You know, there were a couple of times today when I felt sure I was holding the dagger in my hand. Like a knight, ready to do battle.' He handed the dagger to Archie. 'This is yours, I believe.'

'Your courage is back, Dad. I saw it walk out of Huigor. I saw it walk around the base of the statue looking for you. Grandpa's too, walking tall and strong. Now he'll be able to come home from hospital. Did you see it, Dad? Did you see your courage?'

But there was no need of an answer to his question. Archie already knew as he looked into the eyes of the man smiling back at him that he had given his dad the best Christmas present ever. Just as he had said he would.

# Chapter Forty-five

A woman's concerned voice could be heard calling, 'Archie? Jeffrey? Where are you? Can you hear me?'

'Over here,' said Jeffrey.

The moving glow from a torch appeared through the darkness and Cecille's face hovered above it, looking scared.

'Tell me you're both safe?'

'One battle-weary but triumphant knight,' said Jeffrey and he lowered Archie down from the monument base into her arms.

'Two battle-weary knights, by the look of it,' she said through tears of relief. She went to kiss Archie's cheek, but he wriggled free.

'I'm OK, Mum.' When his feet finally touched the ground he added, 'Don't fuss.'

'Don't fuss?' She shook her head incredulously. 'You could have been killed.' But her concern quickly turned to horror. 'Archie! Is that a *dagger* you're holding in your hand?'

'Yes!' He held it up so she could see it more closely. But it was the steady, determined look in his eyes that she was really examining. A look that said, 'Don't treat me like a baby'. So, Jeffrey had been right. She'd got Archie back, and he wasn't the same.

'It's a very handsome-looking dagger,' she conceded.

'You mean I can keep it?'

'I'm sure you will be very responsible with it,' said Jeffrey, lowering himself down from the memorial. He stood looking at Cecille. 'How are you? I trust the Icegulls looked after you?'

She nodded uncertainly. 'There's something I must tell you. It's about the man from Exeter . . .'

'Oh, you mean Professor Neville Himes.'

Cecille was now confused. 'You know?'

Jeffrey began brushing tornado dust from his coat. 'He phoned me this morning at the bank. Said he'd phoned the house and didn't get a very warm reception. The police were mentioned, I believe.'

Cecille looked embarrassed. 'Well, naturally I wouldn't really have called the police.'

Jeffrey swiped one more patch of dust from his coat. 'Professor Himes explained the situation very clearly.' Cecille detected a note of disappointment in his voice as he added, 'Though I would have much preferred to hear it from you. Bravery takes many forms,' he reminded her.

Cecille noted there was something different in the way Jeffrey talked and the way he stood, taller and straighter, but what was particularly different about him was the assured look in his eyes.

Archie was looking from his mother to his father and then to his mother again. He found himself back in the grown-up world where nobody talked any sense at all.

'Why don't you just say what you have to say, Mum? It can't be any scarier than battling a tornado. Courage to the end, remember?'

The look in Archie's eyes told her that what she had to say would not come as a surprise to him.

'I heard your voice calling to me inside Huigor,' he told her.

Cecille took a deep breath and turned to Jeffrey. 'I am a descendant of the man who put a curse on the Stringweed family. Originally our name was Khan, not Caine. When I found out I was too ashamed to admit it. I felt I was to blame in some way. When Professor Himes telephoned me today he said I was helping the curse by being so protective of you both. It was the Khan blood, you see, using me to try and stop you breaking the curse. I didn't realise that's what I was doing. I'm sorry.'

'How long have you known?' Jeffrey asked.

'A week or so. I contacted Professor Himes back in November, through a company that can trace your family tree.'

Jeffrey stared at her in confused silence as she continued her explanation.

'I thought a family tree printed on a tea towel would make a nice Christmas present for you . . . but then Professor Himes started phoning me. Going on about International Curse Exterminators. That our family name was originally Khan and did I know anything about a curse . . . and that the unlikely combination of a Khan marrying a Strongwood made Archie stronger. That the mixture of our blood flowing through Archie's veins weakened the curse . . . and as the last remaining descendant I had to renounce the curse, which I did . . . in the cave . . . to the Icegulls.' She looked apologetically at Jeffrey. 'All those phone calls, the wrong numbers, well, they were from Professor Himes . . . Jeffrey? Say something. Please.'

But Jeffrey couldn't speak. He continued to stare at her as he searched for words and then they came out in an incredulous rush. *'You thought a family tree on a tea towel would make a nice Christmas present?'*

At this point a rather stunned-looking Icegull, with a serious lack of feathers, swooped low over Cecille's head and landed on the wing of Rufus's aeroplane, which had been blown close to the monument.

Rufus was climbing out of the cockpit. 'Is everybody safe and accounted for?'

'All Khans and Strongwoods present and correct,' said Jeffrey. 'Any collateral damage?

'Monika's got a few scratches on her paintwork, but nothing serious.'

Rufus looked up admiringly at her dusty paintwork as the Icegull began rearranging its windblown feathers. The gull looked as confused as Archie, who was trying to work out why Rufus wasn't interested in his battle with Huigor.

'I broke the curse, Rufus.'

'What curse would that be?' Rufus replied, though he appeared far more interested in pulling a large clump of heather away from a wheel.

'Huigor,' said Archie, who was beginning to feel very disappointed in his uncle. 'Don't you remember . . . ?'

'Ah!' Rufus suddenly spun round with a huge smile on his face. '*That* curse,' and Archie knew he'd been teasing. Rufus walked purposefully up to him and took the dagger from his hand. 'Kneel!'

Archie knelt down and Rufus gently touched each of his shoulders with the blade.

'For great bravery and fortitude in the face of unimaginable fear, I proclaim that you, Archie Stringweed, have proven yourself a worthy knight. Restoring honour to our family and releasing imprisoned souls from a despicable curse. You have proved yourself to be a worthy member of I.C.E.: International Curse Exterminators.'

Archie's tired eyes blinked wide. 'International Curse Exterminators?'

Rufus pulled a small box from his jacket pocket and opened it. Inside was a gold chain attached to a gold hoop.

'By the power bestowed upon me, I present you with the Medal of the First Order.' He placed the chain over Archie's head. 'Arise, Archie Stringweed. You are now a member of I.C.E.'

Archie stood up.

'Do you have the coins?' Rufus asked.

Archie unzipped his trouser pocket and gave the coins to Rufus, who proceeded to press them into place either side of the hoop.

'The medal that came by post on your birthday was sent by Professor Himes,' he explained. 'Our Honorary President. He decided to send the other medal by Icegull, as a gentle introduction to their charms.'

Archie admired the medal and chain, which he could see clearly in the glow from Cecille's torch.

'Are you a member of I.C.E.?' he asked.

'Indeed I am, Archie. All members are curse exterminators.'

Cecille gave a worried gasp, which she quickly

suppressed, and the ceremony continued.

'Being a curse exterminator brings many responsibilities,' Rufus announced. 'One of which is a vow of silence regarding our activities. I'm afraid you will not be able to tell your friends about I.C.E. Top secret, you see.'

Archie's eyes were very wide indeed. 'So, am I a kind of knight?'

'You are indeed,' said Rufus.

Archie was about to give a whistle, but decided against embarrassing himself, particularly since a curse exterminator would be expected to whistle.

'A job well done,' said Rufus. 'May I shake your hand? Man to man?'

Archie pulled his shoulders back and stood as straight as he could on rather shaky legs, while Rufus shook his hand and gave an airman's salute. Archie saluted him back.

'Stand easy,' said Rufus, and Archie dropped his hand.

Cecille and Jeffrey broke into a round of applause and began congratulating Archie on his bravery. Jeffrey then shook Rufus's hand and Cecille quite unexpectedly planted a kiss on his cheek.

'I want to thank you, Rufus, for everything you have done for Archie. For the Stringweed family,' she told him.

When he had got over the sudden kiss Rufus said, 'You played an important part too, Cecille. Well done.'

'Hear, hear,' said Jeffrey, squeezing her hand. 'From now on the Stringweeds look to the future.' He turned to Archie. 'Isn't that right, champ? How are you feeling?'

'A bit tingly. Like I'm full of electricity.'

'Look, Archie!' said Cecille, who was pointing in the direction of an orange glow, far in the distance. 'You must have put the power back on at Westervoe.'

'All aboard,' Rufus decided. 'Monika's got just enough fuel to get us back as the Icegull flies.'

'Come on, Cecille,' said Jeffrey. 'Let's fly home. We can pick up the Land Rover in the morning.'

'Who wants to sit in the front?' Rufus asked. 'No arguing, now.'

'Dad does!' said Archie. 'Don't you, Dad?'

'Yes,' said Jeffrey. 'I believe I do.'

They all climbed aboard and Cecille looked out of the window at the two rows of Scouts flickering either side of the landing strip, as if it was the most natural thing in the world. She smiled when Jeffrey gave a small cheer as the plane began to move.

Archie reached for her hand.

'It's a wishing star,' he told her as he placed a small glass object in her palm. 'Now you can wish any time you want.'

The plane was gathering speed and the sound of the revving engine drowned out Cecille's words, but Archie knew she had said, 'Thank you.' Cecille leaned closer so he could hear her say, 'There's a rather nice pair of roller boots in the hardware shop window. Why don't we go and have a look at them tomorrow? If you feel up to it.'

Archie shook his head. 'I've changed my mind about Rollerblades.'

'You have?'

'Yes,' he said as they sailed up into the starry sky. 'Now I'm a knight, I really think I should learn to sword fight.'

'Oh,' Cecille gasped, before quickly composing herself. 'Well, if that's what you really want . . .'

'Count me in too,' Jeffrey was saying. 'And a few abseiling lessons might come in handy for our mountain hike in the spring, and . . . and . . . and . . .' His voice had trailed away but his mouth remained open as he stared out of the window in silent wonder.

They were now fully airborne and flying through a pale moonlit sky filled by millions of stars of differing brilliance and size. Below them lay a white shimmering cloud that appeared to change shape as it floated upwards.

'An honorary fly-past,' Rufus announced as the cloud engulfed them and they were surrounded by hundreds of Icegulls flying alongside in steady formation, the moonlight upon their outstretched wings and their green eyes shining through the dark. Archie pressed his face against the window, trying to pick out which bird had appeared at his window with the medal, which one had carried him home after his first trip to Moss Rock and which one had saved him as he fell from the cliff. But he knew they were all his friends. He gave a wave and they suddenly soared higher into the sky and swung away to the left in the direction of Moss Rock, their bodies turning to silhouettes as they crossed the moon. Two balls of green light that flew with them threw out a farewell strobe of light.

'Look, a shooting star,' said Cecille excitedly. 'And there's another.' She closed her eyes and, clutching the glass star in her hand, said, 'Quick, make a wish before they disappear.'

Much as he tried, Archie couldn't think of one single wish to make. At that moment he had everything he could ever want.

He looked down at the medal that hung around his neck. It was too dark to see it properly but he traced with his finger the engraving of the bird and its outstretched wings. As he did so he was surrounded by a soft green light and he looked up to discover the giant Icegull's eye filling the window beside him. He lifted the medal to proudly show it off to the bird.

'Valour such as yours releases great power,' he heard it say. 'Keep it safe, for there will come a time when such bravery will be called upon again.'

As suddenly as it had appeared, the bird was gone. Archie put his face to the window, searching the sky, but the only movement to be seen was the white shimmering cloud drifting towards Moss Rock.

He looked at his medal and this time his fingers traced the words inscribed around the gold hoop that held it in place.

*Archie Stringweed. Curse Exterminator.*

Pride filled his lungs until he could hardly breathe. He felt his mouth curl up into a smile and sheer happiness rushed up through his throat so fast he couldn't hold it in. He took a deep breath and the aeroplane was filled with the clear notes of a perfectly formed whistle.